I
NEVER
KNEW
YOU

OLIVIA RYTWINSKI

ISBN: 9798742695400

PublishNation
www.publishnation.co.uk

For Mike, Aleks & Lily

Acknowledgements

Thank you to my friends, family, and editor, A J Humpage for their wonderful advice, feedback and support during the writing of this novel. I couldn't have completed the journey without them.

'I love you without knowing how, or when, or from where. I love you simply, without problems or pride: I love you in this way because I do not know any other way of loving but this, in which there is no I or you, so intimate that your hand upon my chest is my hand, so intimate that when I fall asleep your eyes close.'

— Pablo Neruda

Prologue

When we fall in love we lose ourselves for a while. It's as if our emotions and feelings are sucked up into a whirlwind and become too volatile for us to control and make sense of. But in time the winds begin to calm and we find ourselves once more - altered forever by the experience, whether our love continues or not.

However, I feel a greater consideration is this; in any relationship, and even after years of loving and living with the same person, can we ever truly know them?

For it seems to me that however much we think we share who we are with the one we love, we hold a part of ourselves separate - a part that belongs to us alone and which we have no choice but to keep locked securely inside. Whether these fragments of ourselves are treasure or something darker, only we can know. That is, unless we are prepared to share them.

~ Anya Kubik

Chapter 1

Memory is a curious and bewildering mistress.

Each one of us are players in our own life drama and only partly in control of what happens to us and in turn the memories that we must carry throughout our lives. But once these memories take up residence in our minds, we live at the mercy of their influence.

Exactly one week after celebrating my thirteenth birthday, my childhood came to an abrupt and unexpected end. I was neither ready nor prepared.

A glance at my watch told me I had enough time to run home, pick up my dance kit and still get back to school for the start of afternoon class. Dance was my favourite lesson of the week, and Mrs Snoggin was insistent that we could only take part if we wore the correct attire.

I paused at the gateway to our home in Marble Avenue, and I rested my hands on my hips to catch my breath and to ease the stitch in my side. Home, since I came into the world, was a flat-roofed, art deco house, painted white every five years and dated back to when houses had been built to last, or so Dad liked to remind us.

I flung my house keys and school bag on the hall floor and noticed a small parcel and the post piled neatly upon the sideboard. The postman hadn't delivered when I'd left for school, which had been after my parents had set off to their respective places of work.

As I unhooked my dance kit from the coat stand, the sound of voices and movement from upstairs broke through the silence.

I paused and called from the foot of the staircase. 'Mum?'

No reply came.

3

I sprinted up the stairs, stopped on the landing and listened. I heard voices; muffled and alien, which drifted from the spare bedroom. I trod softly across the floorboards, turned the handle and popped my head through the doorway.

I will never forget what I saw – the memory remains imprinted like a black blot in my mind. Disturbing and unyielding.

I spun around, fled blindly down the stairs and onwards through the open doorway. My heart thundered in my chest and blood rushed through my head sending my vision into a spin. Tears spilled across my cheeks. At the bottom of the street, I looked both ways. School lay to the right. But instead I turned left and sprinted; my feet ground against the footpath. If I ran fast enough the images of what I saw might shatter and my mind would return to some sort of order. I raced through the gated entrance to Rowntree Park and as I continued running across the grass to the bandstand my sweat and tears became indistinguishable. The air tore through my lungs and throat while all around me autumn fell from the branches and dead leaves scattered beneath my feet.

I ripped off my blazer and hurled it to the floor, then dropped, wheezing and breathless onto the bench. Everything around me blurred and I closed my eyes. I took long, deep breaths. Slowly in for seven, then out for seven, as the school nurse had recommended. I repeated this until I could no longer feel my heart bursting to escape my chest.

I opened my eyes and I tried to distract my mind as I often did when my thoughts deafened. Still breathless, I tipped my head back and gazed up into the branches at the yellowing leaves that dipped in the air currents. Gradually, the madness that whirled in my mind receded and calmed.

By now Mrs Snoggin would have marked me absent, and my friends would have accused me of skiving. The school would no doubt call Mum and Dad this afternoon. Those things didn't bother me. Mum would know the reason why.

When the sound of a child's laughter roused me from my thoughts, I turned to see a mum swinging her little girl round and round in dizzying circles. Their faces were filled with joy and wonder.

I wiped furiously at my eyes. What I'd seen and heard at home returned and darted through my head like bluebottles. A sickness lay in the pit of my stomach and my throat ached. I knew all about sex; that adults 'did it'. Mum and Dad must have at some point, although I couldn't ever recall seeing or hearing any evidence of it between them. They never kissed or held hands, and on the rare occasions when Dad put his arm around Mum, she'd shrug him off with a, 'Not now, darling', or 'Stop, Daniel. That tickles'.

But what I'd seen minutes ago was raw and bestial. It reminded me of the time I watched a stallion mating with a mare at the riding stables. Mum had been kneeling on the bed, her mouth wide and panting, and her face flushed with sweat. Her long curly hair hung loose and messy and her breasts swung like pendulums. And the man, a stranger, all black body hair and muscle, on his knees behind her, one thick hand that clutched her hip, the other hand groped at her breast as he thrust himself at her. They grunted and moaned, at least until Mum saw me. But this wasn't Mum; usually so smartly dressed in her suits with hair coiffed to perfection. Not until a spark of recognition that turned to horror when she saw me in the doorway. I didn't hang around for a chat or an introduction to her friend.

So, that was sex. Not the romantic, loving act hinted at in some of the movies I'd seen. Mum had seemed like a crazed animal. I couldn't rid the image of them from my mind and I thought I might puke. How would Mum explain it when I went home and what possible reason could she give for what that man had been doing with her - doing to her?

And it was at that moment, I realised that was what we were only dressed up to give us the appearance of something superior and smarter. My tummy heaved and churned the more I considered this. We were animals with clothes who also went to school or work, read books, ate with cutlery, drove cars and even rode other animals in our bid to appear civilised. Why hadn't I worked this out before? We'd had talks in science and life skills but they hadn't shown us what sex really looked like. Humans weren't special like the Bible told us we were. To my surprise, it felt weirdly reassuring. For a long time I stared out across the park, not seeing or hearing anyone or anything as I tried to come to terms with what I'd seen.

Chapter 2

Ebony's hooves sounded familiar and comforting against the cobblestones as I led him alongside the mounting block. And when he lowered his head and nuzzled my pocket in search of a treat, I ruffled his forelock and planted a kiss on his velvety muzzle. He stood patiently as I drew the reins over his head and climbed the four stone steps. Taking care, I slipped my foot into the stirrup and swung my leg over his back then settled my seat into the saddle. For a moment I remained still and breathed - everything felt good. After I'd adjusted his girth, I gathered up the reins, then turned him towards the archway that led from the stableyard.

The sun crested above Redhill Woods and burned the sky pink and orange. Golden rays arched across the meadow and I felt a warmth cloak my skin and soften my thoughts. Overhead, only a liquescent jet trail broke the endless and cloudless sky. I leaned over and stroked Ebony's strong black neck and inhaled his scent. It felt heavenly to be back in the saddle again after an enforced break. As we continued, the creak of leather and the gentle thud of Ebony's hooves through the summer grass was accompanied by the trills of birdsong. I breathed the air - scented with morning dew. At the brow of the hill Ebony's pace quickened and he chomped at the bit, eager to stretch his legs. I gazed out at the grass and wildflowers as they swayed in the breeze; their speckles and hues like a finely embroidered quilt, and I longed to relax the reins despite my doctor's warnings.

Ebony came to a sudden halt and dug his hooves into the ground. His ears pricked forwards and he whickered. Up ahead I saw a deer and her fawn emerge from the trees and begin to nibble at the sweet summer grass.

I bent forward and whispered, 'Good boy.'

If we remained still and quiet we might not disturb them.

Roe deer were a common sight in Wensleydale, but there was something magical about an up-close encounter. And being on horseback often allowed us to bridge the fear barrier between us and these shy and beautiful creatures.

Ebony remained still but snorted the air.

I'd left our daughters, Stevie, eighteen, and Rose, sixteen, asleep at home, despite Stevie insisting she would be up to accompany me. I wasn't surprised when I'd gone in to wake her and she'd shrugged my hand away and shrunk back beneath the bed covers. It had been well past midnight when I'd heard her return home the previous night.

Although I loved a companion to ride out with, it felt special this morning to be alone with my horse and my thoughts. I ran a livery yard which was demanding and stressful but it had been doubly difficult since my operation as I'd been limited to what I could do. Most of our clients were a delight to have around and happy with the care and the facilities, but there were one or two for whom nothing was ever quite up to par. Thankfully, I joint managed the yard with my sister-in-law and best friend, Gemma, who had gone all out to keep things running smoothly.

This morning, I wasn't going to dwell on our awkward clients. I felt fit again and with only the occasional twinge to remind me to take it easy.

The two deer continued to graze.

I rode Ebony wide and hoped not to disturb them, but as we drew nearer, a horn blast sliced the silence. Startled, Ebony shied, and I lost my stirrups, slipped and almost fell. I wriggled back into the saddle, but when I looked up, the deer had already fled.

The horn had sounded like a lorry which was unusual here due to the narrow lanes and with it being only a minor route to the Yorkshire Dales. I slipped my feet back into the stirrups, squeezed my calves and Ebony broke into a canter. I raised my seat off the saddle and leaned across his neck. The familiar feeling of power and strength beneath me and the wind against my skin felt glorious, and I urged Ebony faster up the hill. We galloped adjacent to the woods and stopped at the stone folly on the crest of the hill. The woodland, mainly oaks and elms, were richly green with summer foliage. A network of trails ran through the woods and we often took advantage of fallen branches to make easy jumps for the horses. The grey gritstone blocks used to build the gothic style folly were spotted with moss and lichen and an engraved plaque at the entrance to the folly displayed the year it had been built – 1910, designed and built by principal builder, Gerald Kubik, my husband, Toby's, great grandfather.

The folly was a well-known landmark in the area and had been one of the reasons Toby had followed in his great grandfather's footsteps to become an engineer, rather than follow his father into farming. Toby often talked about how he would build another, grander folly further along the ridge and at the far end of the woods, just as soon as he had the cash to fund it. Two years ago, he'd spent entire evenings working on his designs and drawings, which he'd then framed and hung above his desk. And although a part of me thought it was an unaffordable pipe dream, it was an exciting idea I hoped he'd one day be able to realise.

I looped Ebony's reins through the tethering ring on the folly wall and gazed up at the castle tower. The turrets reached the upper branches of the trees that encircled it and every year or two we'd call in tree surgeons to cut them right back. Today, the trees carved out a pocket of sky - blue and white. I jogged up the spiral staircase to reach the open turrets and leaned against the wall to regain my breath and orientation. I felt lightheaded. Six weeks ago, I'd had surgery to remove a large ovarian cyst. For months prior to its discovery, my abdomen had swollen but I'd put it down to hormones and bloating. I'd grown increasingly self-conscious and my sexual appetite had petered out almost entirely. This had created tension between me and Toby, and only now, with the clarity of hindsight, could I see how foolish I'd been not to get myself checked out sooner.

I closed my eyes and leaned back to feel the sun, warm and soothing on my skin. Today would be another scorcher and I pulled my jumper over my head and tied it around my waist. I looked over the turrets and along the valley towards the village of Holgarth in the distance, miniature and nestled like a gemstone between Balcaster Top and Gray Fox Moor. All along the valley, the fields and hillsides were speckled here and there with sheep and cows, grazing on the pastures. Elsewhere within view, grey stone cottages and farm buildings were scattered here and there.

I looked down the grassy hillside at a herd of cows that plodded en mass along the lane - their bellows and grunts drifted upwards. Amongst the commotion, I heard raised and angry voices as an articulated lorry came to a stop. The cows clambered onto the verges and jostled against the lorry to squeeze past. Maria Walker, the owner of neighbouring, Shadow Blithe Farm, brought up the rear with her sheepdogs. I imagined the driver had taken a wrong turn and couldn't turn around. Maria's shouts and hand gestures left me in no doubt as to her views on the obstruction.

Down below, Ebony snorted and stamped his feet.

I leaned over. 'Ebony...' I called.

I hurried back down the steps and as I re-emerged into the daylight, Ebony reared up against his tether and his forelegs thrashed the air. His ears were pinned back and his nostrils flared pink. As I reached for his reins he bounded forwards and knocked me to the ground.

A dull ache spread across my abdomen and cautiously, I stood back up.

The whites of Ebony's eyes flashed.

'What is it, boy?' I stroked his face.

I heard a rustling amongst the undergrowth and I spun around.

'Morning.' A bearded, middle-aged man in a high-vis jacket and theodolite propped over his shoulder marched straight up to me.

'Will you please stand back?' I said. 'You're frightening my horse.'

He raised his hands in surrender, and his eyes widened as they lowered and lingered on my chest. I glanced down and saw the buttons of my blouse had come undone, which left my bra and cleavage exposed. I turned around and cursed inwardly as I buttoned them up.

I untethered Ebony and threw his reins over his head. 'These are private woods. You'll have seen the notice on the gate.'

'Let's try again shall we?' He held out his hand and gave a close-lipped smile. 'Good morning. I'm David Atkinson.'

'And the reason you're here?' I asked, reluctantly taking his hand.

9

'The landowner's granted permission for me to conduct a ground survey.' His tone had lost any hint of pretence at friendliness. 'And who are you, precisely?'

'I'm the landowner,' I said.

'But you don't sound like a gentleman.' He propped his theodolite on the ground and leaned upon it in a casual manner. 'The gentleman that I spoke to.'

'I'm also the land manager,' I continued. 'And so permission is through me.'

He waved his hand at me, dismissively. 'I informed Mr Kubik when I'd be visiting. I'll call him if you need proof.'

'Please do that,' I said. 'And while you're at it, can you pass him on to me?'

He pulled his phone from his pocket and proceeded to make the call. He gave me a fake smile as he waited and then left a message. 'You'll simply have to take my word for it.'

'What exactly are you surveying?'

'I'm not at liberty to say,' he replied. 'Besides, how do I know you're a joint landowner? You don't look like one.'

'Don't be ridiculous. I don't need to prove anything to you.' I'd had my fill of his arrogance. 'Leave, and either I or my husband will call you later.'

He lifted the theodolite back onto his shoulder. 'You're the one who should leave, dear lady. Jump back on your pony and I'll say no more.'

My anger flared and I lifted my foot into the stirrup and mounted. I swung Ebony round to face him. 'I'm asking you politely to leave, right now.'

'I've no intention of going anywhere.' He cocked his head to one side. 'Unless you're prepared to take a walk in the woods with me first.' He sniggered at his pitiful attempt at humour.

I urged Ebony closer. 'Then I'll call the police to escort you off.'

He waved his arms, and Ebony flinched back. His laughter mocked and he turned and walked calmly back amongst the trees.

My face burned with fury and I watched him until he'd disappeared from view then I turned Ebony towards home and urged him into a gallop back down the hill. I only reined him in as his hooves clattered beneath the archway and into the stableyard.

Chapter 3

That evening after eating dinner with the girls, Toby returned home, even later than usual. I'd phoned him several times without getting through and then missed his return call. I decided against ringing the police because if Toby had given Mr Atkinson permission, I'd have looked like a fool and have wasted police time. All day I'd seethed inside and rehearsed what I'd say to Toby.

'Hey, Dad,' both girls chimed as Toby walked into the kitchen.

He hung his jacket on the back of a dining chair. 'Evening, my lovelies.'

He avoided catching my eye and didn't kiss me, as was his usual way. Which, given my current mood was probably just as well. My messages must have left him in no doubt as to my thoughts on our intruder.

He scanned the worktops. Opened the oven door and peered in. 'What's for dinner?'

'Soup,' I said. 'There's a carton in the fridge.'

'Oh, OK,' he said, sounding suitably unimpressed.

'I've been busy,' I said.

'Aren't we all,' he replied, stiffly. 'I haven't stopped all day and I could eat a scabby donkey.'

'Yuk!' shrieked Rose.

Stevie flicked her eyes upwards. 'Not heard that one before, Dad.'

I didn't mention that there was all manner of things he could eat. He could work that out for himself.

Toby bustled about, banged cupboards and clanked crockery. He'd never been good-humored when hungry and tired.

Only last week, Stevie and Rose had finished their respective exams, which left them with almost three months free before Stevie headed off to University and Rose commenced her A-Level studies. They both deserved some downtime after all the pressure of the past year, but I also saw it as an opportunity for them to take on some responsibilities in the yard. However, Stevie was also making her mark as a three-day eventer and would be spending some weekends away, competing in events

Rose, sensitive and intuitive, soon picked up on the tension between Toby and me. She pushed back her chair. 'I'm riding out with Jake so I'll go saddle up Pepper.'

Stevie's eyes shot up from her phone. 'Mind if I tag along, sis?'

Rose gave a long and heartfelt sigh and I guessed she had a soft spot for Jake and this was her opportunity to spend some time with him. Most of the girls liked Jake. He was nineteen and in his first year at Hull University studying Politics. It was clear why the girls were drawn to him. Aside from his fair curly hair and handsome face, he was an engaging conversationalist. His glamorous mum, Julie, also kept her horse at Willows End.

'If you want to,' Rose replied with a reluctance Stevie seemed oblivious to.

Stevie pushed back her chair and jumped up. 'Let me go get changed.' She swept her thick locks from her shoulders. 'Jake promised he'd race me on Ginger. He doesn't realise he hasn't a chance against me and Jody.'

I tried to catch Stevie's eye, but diplomacy had never been one of her strengths. With her long coiled hair, vivacious personality and voluptuous figure, Stevie could probably charm any man into loving her. I sensed she was aware of her feminine prowess. Rose's charm lay in her gentle ways, her pale complexion and tall dainty figure. She was still growing into her looks and seemed quieter in her demeanor and altogether more subtle in her ways.

Once Toby and I were alone, I sat in the armchair and looked out of the French windows and onto the garden. I sipped my tea and contained my anger.

Toby set his bowl on the table and looked my way. 'I did try to call you back, you know?'

'Yes,' I replied. 'You did…once.'

'Let me explain.' He paused, thinking. 'Firstly, I forgot to tell you about the arrangement with Mr Atkinson, which is my mistake.' He raised his hands in a placatory manner. 'In my defence I'm charging round like a lunatic because I've got too much on. And I don't mean my dinner plate, unfortunately.'

'And why was he surveying our woods?'

'To look for underwater supplies needed for a local excavation project. There's the stream, too.'

'What about the river?'

'They said they needed to survey for less obvious sources.' Toby's phone pinged and he reached into his pocket.

'How much water do they need? And what sort of project is it?'

Toby appeared not to have heard me and instead stared at his phone.

'Toby?'

'Sorry?'

'What's the project?'

'A well, I believe. A mile or so away.'

'And would they pay us for any water they used?'

'Of course. That's why I gave them access.'

I was tempted to remind him I was the land manager, but it seemed petty.

'When they contact you again, please can you copy me in on any emails? And let me know if you take any more calls.'

'Of course. Will you forgive me?' He looked across at me with an expression I knew all too well and my mood softened.

He mopped his soup bowl with a hunk of bread.

'Fine,' I said. 'But only this once.'

He slotted his bowl into the dishwasher and poured a glass of wine. 'I need this.' He took a sip and walked over. 'Want some?'

I took the glass and raised it to my lips.

Toby worked crazy hours and I realised that forgetting to tell me about the surveyor had been a genuine mistake.

'How was your day?' I asked.

He perched on the footstool in front of me. 'I wish people were more competent at their jobs. Crown Construction have put James Temple in charge, and you know our history. How he got the position of Regional Director is beyond me. Must have bribed his way in. His rottweiler PA wouldn't even let me speak to him.' Toby rubbed his fingers back and forth across his forehead. 'Said he'd call back but I know he's avoiding me.'

'Poor you.' I leaned forward and kissed him on the lips.

'How are you feeling after your ride? I hope you were careful?' His eyes, wide and dark, danced playfully.

'I was uber cautious until I came across that surveyor. He wound me up good and proper and without thinking I galloped back.'

Toby glanced at the doorway, took the glass from me and set it on the floor, then taking hold of my wrists he moved my hands to my sides. Slowly, he lifted my shirt and ran his hands over my ribs and over the curve of my breasts. His fingers caressed and I felt a rise of desire.

I heard footsteps in the hallway.

Smartly, Toby rearranged my top. 'I'll check you thoroughly later. But at least your nipples seem to be in fine fettle.'

I chuckled. 'You know it wasn't my breasts they operated on?'

'No need to. They're perfection.'

The tension between us melted and I sat on his lap and snuggled close. He wrapped his arms around me and kissed me, his lips gentle and sweet.

I felt his phone vibrate in his pocket and he shifted his weight. 'Sorry. I must see if it's James.'

'Let him wait,' I said, pulling him closer.

He kissed the tip of my nose. 'Wish I could, but I can't.'

Toby lifted me up and pulled the phone from his pocket.

'James. Thanks for calling back.' Toby threw a thin smile my way and headed out of the kitchen

I eavesdropped as Toby's words grew increasingly agitated between pauses. For the past year or so he hadn't stopped working; sending emails first thing in the morning and late into the evening. There were times when I'd woken past midnight and found he still hadn't come to bed. Of course, I was always on call to our clients and catering to their various demands, but Gemma, Toby's younger sister, who didn't have a husband or children, probably put in more hours than I did.

Gemma had ridden and worked with horses all her life and was also my best friend. I'd have discussed the whole Mr Atkinson episode with her, but she was away visiting their aunt in Keswick and not due back until tomorrow. I imagined how

Gemma would have reacted to Mr Atkinson's arrogance – she was sharp-witted, strong and feisty. She'd have kept a cool head and seen him off the property.

I walked into the hallway as Toby stormed out of the office. His face was flushed and his eyes narrowed as he passed me.

'What an effing tosser,' he said.

He booted Freda's toy bone like a football and it ricocheted off the wall and crashed into the photo frame on the sideboard.

The picture slid over the edge and shattered against the stone floor.

'What's happened?'

Without replying, Toby marched out of the front door and slammed it behind him. The door frame shuddered.

My heart pounded as I bent down to pick up the pieces. Toby rarely lost his temper, and so when he did it was always unnerving to witness.

I shook the fragments of glass from the photograph. We'd had it for years. In the picture, Stevie, Rose and I wore traditional Swiss dresses, with our hair plaited and ribboned. Toby too was traditionally dressed in shorts, long socks and colourful braces.

My mother had bought us the outfits during a business trip to Switzerland, but with no fancy dress occasion to wear them, we'd dressed up for a photograph. The afternoon stuck in my mind - the girls skipping and laughing beneath the willow trees, and Toby, moaning and forcing a smile. He'd always loathed the picture and at one point had even tried to hide it. Said he looked a 'right twat'. His words. But everyone else adored it - especially the girls. Well, he'd finally got his revenge. I wiped the photograph against my shirt and felt relieved it was undamaged, although, on closer inspection, I noticed a scratch across it. I heard the skid of tyres on the gravel.

Toby's reaction seemed way over the top. I knew James' company owed some consultancy fees from months ago, but it was less than a grand which wasn't huge on the scale of things. Maybe there was more to it.

I wanted the day over with and I longed for nothing more to relax in a deep bubble bath, read my novel and zone out. Then I remembered I still had the horses to bring down from the upper pasture.

I grabbed the lead reins from the tack room and as I walked up the track I heard the distant clatter of hooves and voices. I turned around and saw Rose, Stevie, and Jake trotting the horses down the drive. They rode abreast with Jake's Welsh Cob, Ginger, nestled in the middle. We'd only broken Pepper, Rose's chestnut gelding, eight months previously, and although he'd been a fast learner, he appeared way too frisky and in need of some intensive schooling. I could see from his arched neck and his high tail carriage that he made it hard work for Rose. With ears pricked and feet that pranced, he looked desperate to get ahead of the others.

Rose loved his spirit. 'He'll be a magnificent eventer once he's reached his potential,' she assured me several times, and, 'I've never ridden a more responsive horse.'

The sky had grown thick with clouds but the air remained warm and sweet with the heady scent of wildflowers. Buttercups, poppies and pink cuckoo flower grew tall along the sides of the track and when I heard the distant rumble of thunder I hoped the pastures might be blessed with rain.

As the track steepened I wondered if I'd overreacted with the surveyor, and even Toby's failure to forewarn me about it. Perhaps I should be more supportive given the pressure he was under.

I leaned on the gate and rested my chin on my arms. Max and Grecian stood head to one another's rump and their tails swished the flies from one another's heads. And as I watched them, their tails keeping rhythm with one another, I felt a sense of calm wash over me.

I gazed back down the hillside to our home and the stables huddled amongst the trees, gardens, and paddocks. And on down the long stretch of the lawn to the line of willow trees with tendrils that brushed the riverbank and dipped into the flowing water. A light mist had drifted in from the river and swirled over the grass and towards the Oak tree at the centre of the turning area. With our home, Willows End behind, it was an extraordinarily beautiful view and one that altered every day with the changes in the seasons and sunlight.

I unlatched the gate, clicked my tongue and rattled the bag of pony nuts. Alerted, the horses pricked up their ears, turned their heads and trotted over. They clamoured for a morsel as I clipped on their lead reins.

I turned the horses towards the yard. Summer leaves, still green but scorched dry of moisture, flittered across the track before me and crunched beneath my feet as I walked. Poppies grew tall amongst the yellowing grasses like splashes of blood. The red sun had sunk so low over our home that I could gaze directly at it and a cooling breeze brushed against my skin. Beside me, the horses shook their manes and tails and I was reminded to order more fly fringes to see them through the long hot days. I couldn't recall a summer as dry and persistent.

When I returned inside, the house felt unusually silent, other than for Freda who scampered at my heels. I opened a tin of dog food and mashed some into her kibble. She wolfed it down as if she hadn't eaten in days, then curled up, content, in her basket by the back door. I took out a bottle of sauvignon blanc from the fridge and sloshed it into a glass. Then I headed upstairs to run my bath.

As 'Gabriel's Oboe' began to play I lit a scented candle and sank into the warmth and bubbles. It felt like luxury after the heat and arguments of the day.

With my head submerged I ran my fingers through the tangles in my hair. The sound of watery music filled my ears and my mind drifted into clearer waters.

Chapter 4

I heard muffled words. Startled, I opened my eyes and sat up as the water streamed from my face and hair.

Stevie stood over me - breathless, her words incoherent and her face streaked with tears. 'Rose...she's...'

I stood up as my heart began to batter against my ribcage. 'What's happened?'

Stevie's uncontrolled cries rent the air.

I stepped out of the bath and grabbed my towel. 'Please, Stevie. What is it?'

'Rose fell and Pepper dragged her. She won't wake up.'

'Where is she?'

Stevie's body shook with sobs and breaths before she managed to splutter. 'Dad's taking her to Richmond General.'

I took hold of her hand. 'Try to take slower breaths.'

Stevie sat on the edge of the bed. 'Her face is bleeding. She won't wake up.'

Still soaked with bathwater, I hurried into jeans and a T-shirt. 'Was she breathing?'

'Yes, but... what if she dies?'

We hurried down the stairs but in the hallway I couldn't find my car keys which I normally kept on the sideboard. I remembered the broken photo frame. I knelt down and peered beneath the gap. My hand couldn't reach beneath.

I jumped back up. 'Help me move this, Stevie.'

Between us, we dragged the sideboard away from the wall. My keys were laid amongst the dust and detritus beneath.

As we set off to Richmond my hands shook on the steering wheel, my legs felt jittery against the pedals and my thoughts were in a whirl of broken scenarios and questions.

'Did Rose's helmet stay on?' I asked.

'Yes, but it was badly cracked.'

'So Dad was there?' I said, trying to sequence everything together.

'It was Dad's car that spooked Pepper.'

'But Pepper's OK in traffic,' I said.

'It was on Swallow bend. Rose was trotting ahead. Dad slammed his brakes.'

'Was he speeding?' I could picture Toby driving with his usual steely determination. He'd always driven too quickly and he was furious when he'd left, which would have fuelled his speed.

'No, Mum. Pepper was in the middle of the road. Rose wasn't in control.'

I turned right onto the lane, pressed my foot to the floor and sounded the horn at every bend.

Stevie shrieked when a pheasant ran into the road in front of us. 'Slow down, Mum.'

I swerved, and the pheasant took off with squawk and a flurry of wings. I adjusted my speed despite my desperation to reach Rose.

We caught up with a tractor trundling along and with no room to pass, I blasted the horn again. The tractor juddered to a stop and I watched Maria Walker climb down from the cab. She walked towards us, her eyes fixed on mine.

'Damn,' I cursed. 'It would be her.'

I opened the door and shouted, 'Maria, please. I need to get past. Rose has been dragged by Pepper.'

Without a word, Maria nodded, turned and headed back to the tractor as quickly as her aging legs could carry her. She clambered back in and steered the tractor up the bank. I edged past and even when I felt the car scrape the tractor wheel, I kept going. As we drove on I pictured Rose hanging from the stirrup, with terror-filled eyes and her lightly clothed body scraping along the tarmac.

Stevie sobbed beside me.

At the hospital, I quickly gave up searching for a space and pulled into a disabled bay.

'I'm scared, Mummy,' said Stevie.

'She's going to be OK. She has to be.'

I took Stevie's hand and we dashed through the double doors and into Accident and Emergency. I hurried straight past the queue of people at the front desk.

19

I sobbed over the counter. 'Rose Kubik's been brought in. She was dragged by her horse and unconscious.'

The nurse looked up. 'You're Mum?'

I nodded.

'Please take a seat and I'll find out where they've taken her.'

'I have to see her,' I pleaded. 'She needs me with her.'

The nurse apologised to the woman at my side and turned back to me. 'I'm sorry but we have other emergencies. Your daughter is in good hands, so please take a seat while I'll find out what I can.'

With reluctance Stevie and I walked into the waiting area, full of people of all ages who looked either miserable or in varying degrees of pain and discomfort. I scanned the room for free seats. Nearby, a young boy clutched his hand and wept into his father's shoulder.

The father looked up at me and his brows pinched together. 'Look at this place.' He flicked his eyes around the waiting room. 'We've been here over an hour and no one's even been to assess his injury.'

'But he's in terrible pain,' I said. 'This is all wrong.' I turned to Stevie. 'I'm not waiting.' I marched back to the desk and stood watching the nurse I'd already spoken with. She was talking quietly on the phone and I tried to catch her words. For a moment she caught my eye and my insides shuddered as I continued to watch and wait for her to finish. At one point she gave an almost indiscernible shake of the head, and my mind reeled with possibilities. Finally, she replaced the receiver.

'Please tell me where my daughter's being treated,' I begged.

Her eyes softened and she pushed back her chair. 'Follow me.'

She led us down a long corridor with closed doors on either side. As we walked I heard a persistent wailing coming from somewhere.

We turned into another corridor and continued in silence until the nurse paused in front of a door - Family Waiting Room 2. She knocked and popped her head round before leading us in. When I looked down at the soft, low chairs and boxes of tissues, my legs weakened and the walls seemed to close in.

She indicated for us to take a seat. 'The doctor will come and speak to you.'

Stevie still gripped my hand.

'Why can't I see her?' I said.

'She's being treated nearby. That's all I can tell you.' She turned away and clicked the door softly behind her.

As I wrapped my arms around Stevie and held her close, I could only envisage the worst. If Rose was dead, the nurse wouldn't have told us. That's why we were waiting for the doctor.

I heard the door and Toby walked in. But this wasn't the same Toby I saw each day. His face paled before me as he rubbed a trembling hand through his hair.

He took a breath and appeared to brace himself. 'Rose is still unconscious. Her femur is broken and she has bruises and lacerations. They're taking her for a CT scan.'

'No wonder she screamed.' I had so many questions. 'Is she breathing all right?'

Toby nodded. 'And her vital statistics are stable, I think. She's on oxygen, strong painkillers, and a drip. She might need surgery on her leg but they'll know more after the scan and X-Rays.'

'What happened?' I accused.

'Did you explain?' He looked at Stevie.

Stevie nodded.

'OK.' His eyes flickered as he spoke. 'I turned the corner at Swallow bend and Pepper was in the middle of the road. The moment I saw them I slammed the brakes,' Toby's voice wavered. 'I see it still, so clearly. Pepper reared up with a dreadful cry. Rose screamed and fell but her foot got hooked in the stirrup. Pepper was terrified and headed back towards home.'

'It was horrible,' Stevie interrupted. 'I tried to grab the reins as he passed us but he was going too fast. I caught Rose's eye...' Stevie's sobs grew louder.

'Come here my darling. She's going to be OK.' I held Stevie close, but inside I knew that nothing was OK.

Toby continued. 'I jumped out of the car and ran to try and catch Pepper. Then thank God, Rose's foot came loose.'

But I knew there was more to it. 'How quickly were you driving?'

'Jesus, Anya!' He fired back. 'I was not speeding and if you're trying to blame me...' His voice broke. 'My little girl... I'll never forgive myself.'

'When I think of the times I've pleaded for you to slow down,' I said. 'Every journey I saw the potential for this. And you were fuming after that call with James.'

Toby sank slowly into a chair and looked down at the floor.

'This would be a joke,' I said, 'if it wasn't so horrible.' The pain in the back of my throat intensified.

'But Mum.' Stevie went over and took her dad's hand, protective. 'It could have been any driver. Dad was unlucky. Rose was unluckier still,' she said through her tears.

Toby looked up at me and his eyes grew intense. 'I know I was angry,' he said. 'And with good reason. But I swear to you, I was driving safely. I was coming home to you.'

I slumped into the chair.

And despite the sickness and fear that clawed at my insides, I recognised his sincerity.

'I'm sorry. I needed to know,' I said, and loathed myself for trying to blame Toby, who loved Rose as much as I did.

It seemed forever that we sat and waited for news. We barely spoke as we each drew in on ourselves.

Stevie's phone buzzed. 'Jake wants to know what's happening. He's fed Pepper and checked him over. No scratches on him. Nothing.'

'That's good of Jake,' I said, but only wished that Pepper's and Rose's injuries could have been in reverse.

Twice, I went out into the corridor to see if there was anyone around who could tell us something. What was taking so long?

I sat down again and stared at the clock as the seconds ticked agonisingly by.

Finally, there came a knock at the door and a young female doctor walked in - tall and slim with her auburn hair in a high ponytail.

The sympathy in her eyes made me fear the worst.

I stood up.

'Dr. Nowak.' She shook my hand. 'Rose has regained consciousness.' She paused. 'But hasn't yet spoken. She doesn't appear to be in pain but she is on strong medication. We can't find any evidence of brain trauma for which we can thank her helmet. And similarly, there's no signs of internal bleeding.'

Relief flooded through me with such force that I felt the blood rush to my head and I went lightheaded.

I clasped the doctor's hand. 'Thank you!'

'However,' she continued, 'we're concerned there may be some bruising to Rose's spine. The spinal cord is intact, as appears on the CT scan, but we'll take her down for a more detailed scan. I'm concerned she hasn't shown movement in her uninjured leg. But it may well be the swelling or the heavy sedation.'

I felt a wave of nausea. 'Please, can I see her?' I said.

The doctor turned to us before she opened the door to the treatment room. She had a gentle face. 'As I explained, Rose is sedated so she's drowsy. Hold her hand but please only one of you speak at a time.'

By her bedside I looked down at Rose, so still, and her features delicate and pale as mist against the pillow other than for a deep and bloody scratch on one cheek. I took a step closer. Her eyes remained shut. She seemed so small and fragile - bruised and silent amidst all the machinery that surrounded her. A drip fed into her arm and a vital signs monitor beeped and flashed close by.

I stifled a sob. Toby put his arm around my shoulder as I took Rose's hand in mine. I squeezed lightly just as my heart was being squeezed.

'Rose. It's Mummy and Daddy,' I said. 'Stevie, too.'

I felt the faintest squeeze in return.

'You're going to be all right, Rose,' I said.

Her eyelids flickered, then opened. 'Mummy.' Her voice was barely above a whisper.

My heart swelled. 'I'm here, sweetheart.'

'I feel so strange.'

'You've been given medicine for the pain.' I glanced across at the doctor. 'You've broken your leg, darling.'

She blinked and confusion fell like a shadow upon her as her eyes searched mine. 'Why don't I feel any pain...or my legs?'

And in that instant, all of my hope was snuffed out and my fear magnified a thousandfold.

23

Chapter 5

For three fear-filled weeks I remained at Rose's beside. I listened to her worries, tried my hardest to reassure her and felt frightened for her future, whatever it might hold, until finally, the doctors told us she could come home. That night I went home and spent the evening setting up her new bedroom in the spare lounge. It used to be the girls' playroom when they were small but when they reached their teens we'd converted it to a space where they could sit and hang out with their friends.

Throughout Rose's stay in hospital, I washed her, cared for her, encouraged her to eat, and struggled to sleep as she slept beside me. Each night Toby visited and he stayed over at weekends to give me a little respite. But at home, I slept even less. I was terrified that if I wasn't with her something would happen to take her away from us. The shock of her accident and what could have been became ingrained in my mind's eye.

When I'd learned to ride as a child, a friend of mine had died after she'd fallen and been dragged by her pony. Each day I felt thankful that Rose was alive. But it was the unknown extent of her spinal injury that scared me beyond anything I'd ever experienced. And if I felt that way, how must Rose feel?

For the first time in my life a crippling sense of dread floored me. I lost all motivation for the yard, least of all keeping on top of the finances, which was my area of responsibility. The house was a tip - heaps of dirty laundry, waste bins overflowing, scummy sinks, the fridge and cupboards bare of essentials. But I no longer cared about these things. They seemed trivial in comparison. Gemma was doing all she could to help, but she was worried about Rose too, as well as having to manage the yard almost single handedly. Gemma didn't complain though and I felt wracked with guilt.

At the very least, I had to get my head together to be able to support Rose when she came home.

I felt hopeful that being surrounded by her family would improve her wellbeing and may even help her begin to put the accident behind her. Or at least to come to terms with it.

The night before we were to bring Rose home, I climbed into bed and reached for my Kindle. The words on the screen swam before me.

Toby slipped his hand under the duvet and stroked my thigh. 'Leave your story and let's hold one another.'

I twitched my leg. 'Sorry. I want to read.'

'I don't want sex. Though I had hoped we'd be more intimate after your operation, not less.'

'Please, Toby,' I said. 'Before Rose's accident we were good again. I've barely been home and I'm too anxious.'

'But it's been weeks.'

'I know and she still has no feeling in her legs.' I turned to him and saw his confused expression. 'Oh, you mean since we made love?'

'We'll sleep better if we love one another more.'

'Maybe you can switch off, but I can't.' I returned to my Kindle.

'I don't switch off either,' he said. 'I never will from what I saw. For my part in it. But I still need you.'

'I'm sorry, Toby, but it's impossible right now.' I avoided his eye and stared at the screen in front of me.

He tutted and turned over.

An hour later, Toby snuffled in his sleep and I'd even managed to finish my book. The final chapters had been an emotional ride but for a short while the story had drawn me in enough to take my mind off everything else.

As I placed the Kindle on the bedside table, I heard shuffling footsteps out on the landing. They grew louder and erratic and there came a thud. I leapt out of bed.

Stevie sat slumped on the floorboards with her back against the bannister. Her eyes stared wildly and her fingers clawed at her scalp.

I crouched beside her. 'Sweetheart. Whatever's the matter?'

She gripped my arm. 'Rose is dead. Pepper's trampled her.'

'No, my darling.' I took her hand. 'Rose is OK and coming home.'

Stevie's eyes searched mine. 'She's bleeding. Her eyes...'

'It's a bad dream. Rose is getting better.' I cradled Stevie's head but her eyes darted nervously and she seemed lost in delirium. 'Let's go downstairs and I'll make us a warm drink.'

As I led her down the staircase Stevie stopped and clutched onto the bannister rail. 'Help her.'

I tried to calm her and after I'd turned on the kitchen light and we sat down at the table I watched her confusion fade.

'My leg's throbbing,' she said.

'Can you show me where?' I asked.

She placed her palm on her thigh and winced. 'It started before I went to bed. I took some Ibuprofen but they haven't worked.'

'Mind if I look?' I asked.

She nodded. I lifted her nightshirt and touched her skin. She recoiled.

'Sorry, sweetheart.' I rearranged her nightshirt. Her leg felt cool and there were no signs of bruises or marks.

I realised it was the same leg and site as Rose's broken femur.

'I think you're having sympathy pains for Rose.'

She looked at me and her eyes swam with tears. 'You mean I can feel her broken leg?'

'Yes, and it's because she's coming home and everything's still so uncertain.' I went to the medicine drawer, popped two paracetamol from the foil packet and ran some water into a glass.

Stevie's brows knitted together as she swallowed her tablets. 'If I was Rose I'd never ever ride a horse again.'

The following morning Stevie came down for breakfast dressed in jodhpurs and her thick auburn hair neatly plaited to one side.

I felt relieved to see her relaxed and smiling. 'How are you?'

She picked up a glass from the draining board. 'I'm OK. I'm sorry I woke you.'

'You didn't. I was only reading.' I passed over the carton of apple juice. 'Do you remember what you dreamt?'

'It felt so real,' she said, sitting down and pouring some juice into a glass. 'Why do the worst dreams go on for so long?'

'They just feel longer. Plus, you were half awake.' I reminded her. 'And how about your leg?'

'It feels fine,' she said.

'I've been thinking. This has been a shock for all of us, but you and Dad watched it unfold. I can't imagine how it's impacted on you.'

She nodded. 'I think about what might've been.'

I reached across the table and took her hand. 'I do, too, however hard I try not to,' I said. 'Come with us today to bring her home.'

Stevie thought for a moment. 'I'd like to, but Gemma's offered to coach me and Jody over some jumps.'

'That's good,' I said. 'It'll take your mind off things.'

Toby drove us home from the hospital with Rose's new wheelchair folded up in the boot. Throughout the journey, Rose barely spoke but stared out of the window.

'I could take you round to see Pepper when we get home,' I said.

Beside me, Rose made no response. I caught Toby's eye in the rearview mirror.

'Perhaps you'd prefer to settle in at home first?' he said.

Rose nodded.

'Of course,' I said, realising I'd been insensitive. 'There's no rush to do anything at all.'

The previous day when Toby and I had spoken to Rose's consultant, he'd said, 'Don't expect too much from Rose. Her physiotherapist will continue the exercises with her. Encourage her, gently.'

'What can exercises do if she has no sensation?' asked Toby.

'They'll keep the blood flowing, reduce the compression and facilitate the return of feeling.'

I felt encouraged by his words but as there were no secure assurances I was left in a state of anxiety.

'I'm ninety percent certain. We've seen this happen a couple of times previously and Rose is an otherwise strong young woman.'

The remaining ten percent left too much scope for uncertainty. But I knew I must mask any negative thoughts for

27

fear of passing them on to Rose. We must be optimistic in the face of any doubts she might have.

We'd added Rose's furniture and pictures to her new bedroom to make it feel welcoming and familiar. We'd filled her dressing table full of her accessories and make-up but since she'd arrived home, she'd shown no interest in them. Her mood remained low and I could only sympathise.

Either myself, Gemma or Toby cared for Rose, and Toby would spend entire evenings sitting and chatting with her or watching films together. He was trying hard to make amends.

Rose had always been her Daddy's girl. They were both outdoorsy and often hiked and cycled together. Toby called them their 'expeditions'. They also shared a love of all things technological. Both were clever with computers and used them in innovative ways. They were active on social media too. Many times I'd voiced my concern to Toby at the amount of time Rose spent online, but he insisted he was 'friends' with her and she always handled herself maturely. I was a reluctant user of Facebook which I used purely to keep our clients up to date about plans for the yard and Gemma was keener on managing that aspect of the business. This suited me well.

Chapter 6

I popped my head round Rose's bedroom door. 'You've got a visitor.'

Without looking up she shook her head and continued typing on her laptop. 'I'm not ready to see anyone.'

'It's Jake,' I said.

She lifted her eyes. 'Oh?'

'You know he's been asking to see you.'

She gazed despairingly down at her legs. 'But look at me.'

'Trust me, broken leg or not, you grow more beautiful every day,' I said.

And she did look beautiful. Her freshly washed hair coiled in gossamer curls around her elfin features. The cut on her face had healed and the colour had at last returned to her cheeks.

'All right,' she said. 'I suppose it'll be nice to see him.'

'He comes bearing gifts.'

I called Jake in from the hallway and Rose blushed when he greeted her with a huge smile and perched on the end of her bed.

I resolved to contact her closest friends to ask them to drop by. Their absence only confirmed that Rose had asked them not to visit. She needed face to face contact with people.

I made a fresh cup of coffee and settled into the armchair beside by the Range. Freda did her usual trick and jumped onto my lap unannounced making me spill my hot drink.

'Anya?' Gemma's voice echoed from the hallway and I heard the front door as it clicked shut. Freda leapt off my lap and ran out to greet her.

'In the kitchen,' I called.

Gemma strolled in with Freda under her arm who wriggled to get down.

'Oh, go on then if you won't give me a cuddle.' Gemma let Freda down who scampered around her feet.

'I'll make you a coffee and we'll write a list of what needs doing,' I said.

'Have you got any of those salted caramel capsules? I need caffeine and sugar.'

'Think so, if Stevie hasn't guzzled them.'

'I've already written a list,' said Gemma. 'You can add to it.' She unfolded a piece of paper and read it through.

I turned on the coffee machine. 'Jake's here. He's in with Rose.'

'I keep thinking about how tough it must've been for Jake and Stevie to see it happen,' said Gemma. 'Toby, too.'

'Stevie had a nightmare the other night. She was delirious, and upset about Rose.'

'Yet on the surface Stevie appears OK,' said Gemma. 'Trauma can be delayed so we'll keep an eye on her.'

I set her cup on the table. 'Strange how the mind blocks things but they keep bubbling back up.'

Gemma took a sip. 'Shall I talk to her?'

'Please. Say if you think she needs counselling. I'm looking into some for Rose.'

Gemma handed me the to do list.

'You're a good mum, Anya.' Gemma's eyes watered. 'They're lucky girls.'

I sighed. 'Not so lucky right now, but I'm trying my best. I've neglected Stevie.'

'Well, you're back now. And I've been taking care of Stevie.'

'I know and I'm grateful. Stevie loves you.'

I knew Gemma well and I recognised her regret at not having children of her own. Despite her upbeat demeanour, she'd faced real sadness more than once. She and her late husband, Euan, had tried for several years to have children. But tragically, Euan had died when Gemma was thirty-four. I recalled it vividly still. His sudden death and the fallout had been traumatic for all of us, and to make it worse, the circumstances that surrounded his death had never been fully established. The inquest concluded that after drinking excessively at a garden party we'd held here, Euan had fallen into the river. During the party he'd gone missing and it wasn't until three days later that he'd been found washed up on the muddy bank of the river which flowed through Willows End. It was devastating, and ever since, Gemma had battled not to let his death destroy her.

I felt and shared her loss every single day. However, I had my reasons for preferring not to bring Euan up in conversation unless Gemma did first.

I turned to the list in front of me. 'I'll prioritise schooling for Pepper. When Rose is better I want him a hundred percent bombproof. And if he isn't I'll buy her a plodder. Which she'll no doubt complain about,' I said.

'He's a decent ride, but honestly, I find him difficult to handle,' said Gemma. She pulled a pen from her shirt pocket. 'You might find Rose isn't keen to get back on him in a hurry.'

Gemma was the finest horsewoman I knew, so I knew her words to be a genuine warning. And anyway, what further warning did I need, having almost cost Rose her life?

I hadn't had a chance to ride Pepper since the accident and I resolved to rectify that.

Gemma set the pen on the table then looked up at me. 'I was thinking about Euan this morning.'

'I know he's never far from your thoughts,' I said.

She pulled out a chair, sat down and began to pick at her thumbnail. 'This might sound dramatic, but I'm beginning to feel that Willows End is cursed. I know it was years ago, but Mum dying was completely out of the blue. The way that she died still haunts me. Then Euan. And I know he drank too much and not only at the BBQ. Then after Euan, Dad's heart gave way. Now our precious Rose. Only thank God she's alive and recovering. Her accident has churned everything back up.' She paused a moment. 'What if it's more than a coincidence - a chain reaction?'

I saw her concern was genuine and I didn't want to dismiss her words too quickly.

'Euan's death was an horrific accident. As was Rose's.' I reached for Gemma's hand. 'And your wonderful Mum...' I hesitated. 'Life... and death is unpredictable. That's the harsh truth. Not curses.'

'But usually life is predictable. We fall in love, plan our babies. Couples grow old together, get ill and eventually we or our loved ones die.'

31

'But look at the people you know and you'll see they've experienced sadness and death, too,' I said. 'It more often comes down to luck and circumstances.'

Gemma often brought up the death of her Mum and Euan together. She'd also lost her dad soon after Euan. Three of the most important people in her life had left her. And as her words sank in I found her suggestion unsettling.

If only she could move on from Euan's death. It would save her and all of us so much heartache.

She gathered up her strawberry blonde hair and secured it into a ponytail. Gemma was as strikingly beautiful as her brother was handsome and three inches taller than my five foot six. And although she and Toby shared similar features, her beauty was unsurpassed by anyone I knew. Since Euan's death she'd had many admirers, but despite taking them as lovers she refused to commit to any of them. She'd cool off the moment they revealed they genuinely cared for her or if they showed the slightest hint of jealousy or possessiveness. She'd had many lovers, and she never hid them away, even when they were married.

'I'm not the one cheating.' She'd argued when I'd suggested she could be more discreet. It seemed the married ones held more appeal. No doubt because she knew they'd never want to make their relationship permanent.

Not one of them lived up to Euan. That was the problem. And she was trying her hardest to fill a void that was not ready to be filled.

Occasionally, when I thought about it, I almost envied her freedom. I could barely admit that to myself, let alone to Gemma.

'Jake's been in with Rose a long time,' said Gemma, and the subject turned away from Euan. 'Shall I pop my head in?'

'I'm not sure she'd appreciate that,' I said, and got up to open the door for Freda who scratched to go out.

'Interesting though...' she said.

I looked at her and waited for her to elaborate.

'What is?' I finally asked.

'I wonder if Jake will mention he and Stevie are an item.'

'Since when?' I asked.

'Since Rose's accident, as far as I'm aware. It must have thrown them into one another's arms, literally.'

'That's the last thing Rose wants to hear. Why didn't I know?'
Gemma gave a small smile. 'You've been distracted of late.'
'I know. But how did you find out? Did Stevie tell you?' I felt
an unwelcome stab of envy at Gemma's closeness to my girls.
She hesitated.
'How, Gemma?' I insisted.
She grimaced. 'I saw them in the woods together.'
'And what precisely were they doing in the woods?'
'Only kissing. Fully clothed. Although I didn't hang around
to find out what happened next.'
'In that case, pop your head in and say hello. Right now,' I
said.
'Yes Ma'am.' Gemma jumped up. 'Got a bicky I can take as
an offering?'
'Hold on.' I opened the biscuit barrel, picked out a handful of
chocolate digestives and placed them on a plate.
We walked into the hall and I hovered as she knocked on
Rose's door and went in. Freda clung to Gemma's heels, eager
for a crumb. I stood in front of the framed Chagall print. There
was something about the painting that always made an
impression on me. The vivid colours, the lovers, the shades of
light and dark and the oddly placed images that never failed to
steal my thoughts into the realms of fanciful preoccupation. It
drew me in until I became her and he became my lover. All of
Chagall's paintings suggested to me a world that revolved
entirely around love - that love and desire were the purest and
strongest motivating forces for all living creatures. And that was
why we were driven to seek out and find the most powerful love
open to us.
'Freda!' I heard Gemma chide.
Moments later I heard laughter. I turned away and left them
to it.
So, Stevie was with Jake. My mind had been elsewhere, but I
wasn't usually oblivious to things going on around me. Not that
I'd interfere. Stevie was a woman who knew her own mind and
we'd discussed relationships and contraception.
'I generally waited for at least a month before I slept with a
new boyfriend,' I told Stevie, and emphasised there'd been only
a handful prior to meeting her dad. That had been a slight fib,

because I'd leapt into bed with Toby on the third date, without either of us giving thought to protection. However, my eighteen-year-old daughter didn't need to know that. I might have been only nineteen when I met Toby but I'd already had two serious boyfriends plus a couple of other intimate relationships.

I jogged upstairs to change our bedsheets, and as I did, my thoughts lingered on Gemma and her preoccupation with Euan. It concerned me that she still questioned how he'd died, which, given Euan's drinking habits, seemed unfounded.

Chapter 7

I met Toby under unconventional circumstances. After eight months at Leeds University, I decided to quit. My reasons were complex, but suffice to say, it was a huge relief to put it behind me. From the outset, I loathed the course. The professors and students were nice enough and I'd enjoyed the social side of University life. However, I'd chosen the wrong subject which had ruined the experience from the outset. One of the main reasons I stuck it out for as long as I did was because I knew Mum would be disappointed. She was the partner of an accountancy firm, loved her job and was a workaholic. However, after eight months of prizing my eyes open during lectures and lacking the motivation to complete assignments, I finally gave up trying.

'I get a brand new car and I'm on a graduate starting salary,' I said to Mum and Dad who were sat at either end of the cream leather sofa.

Dad tapped his foot nervously and peered across at Mum who looked at me with a poker face and arms folded.

'Who will you be selling to?' Mum asked, followed by a sharp intake of breath.

'Farmers, equestrian centres, livery yards,' I said. 'So it's a fantastic career move. I spent a day in the field with the Sales Director and he thinks I'm a natural salesperson. I'm excited and it feels right.'

As I spoke I felt strong and confident. If nothing else, living away from home had fostered an independent spirit in me. I was happy with my decision and I no longer cared what Mum thought. I'd be financially secure and wouldn't need to ask them for more handouts.

'I don't know what I'll tell my friends,' Mum said, her lips twitching somewhere between horror and exasperation. 'I had such high hopes for you.'

'Just tell them I was headhunted,' I said.

'Ahh!' She nodded. 'Good idea.' She unfolded her arms. 'Do you think they'll believe me?'

'I was joking, Mum.' I laughed. 'Who gives a damn what they think.'

On the first day out on my own I had four farms to visit, all existing Homer Feeds customers and all within a relatively short driving distance. My first call had been to a Mr Kubik who I'd spoken to on the phone. I had no problem reading a map, but many clients lived in the back of beyond in the Yorkshire Moors and Dales. I followed a dizzying maze of narrow lanes to reach Willows End Farm. When I realised I'd taken a wrong turn, I stopped to consult my map again. I could see where I'd missed the junction and manoeuvred to do a three point turn. I hadn't realised it was too tight and I misjudged the length of the car. The last thing I recall had been a sensation of falling backwards as the car hurtled down the bank at an alarming speed. After that, blackness overcame me.

I felt warm air on my face and heard a voice.

'Can you hear me?'

A touch on my cheek. A light pressure against my neck. I opened my eyes. A blurred figure. I blinked. Gradually, my eyes refocused and I became aware of wide lips and deep brown eyes beneath heavy brows.

'How many fingers am I holding up?' The man said, his tone deep and serious.

I blinked again. 'Two?'

'Excellent,' he said, and considered me closely.

'Who are you?' I said.

'I'm Toby. What's your name?'

'I'm Anya. Anya McGregor.'

Miraculously, I hadn't been hurt, but was shaken and in shock. He lifted me out of the car and held onto my arms as I stood on unsteady legs.

He glanced down at my feet. 'You've lost a shoe.'

He propped me up against the bonnet and reached into the footwell. He examined my shoe for a moment. 'Not the most practical footwear for a muddy field,' he said and hunched down and slipped it onto my stockinged foot.

My heels sank into the soil and I forced a smile. 'I wasn't planning on making any excursions into fields.'

'Mind if I?' He placed an arm around my waist. 'I don't trust you won't fall.'

'I don't either,' I said, and went a little lightheaded. I took a few steps forward and stumbled.

He gripped me tighter. 'Steady.'

He steered me up the bank to his car and as he lowered me into the passenger seat I felt a surge of conscience and turned to him. 'I hope you weren't in a rush to get anywhere.' I noticed he had kind eyes.

'Nothing I can't easily rearrange,' he said.

I stretched my legs into the footwell.

When he reached over and fastened my seatbelt I inhaled the scent of him - subtle and musky.

'Is my car a write off?' I asked, remembering this was the first day of the only real job I'd had.

'There's a big dent where you hit the gate but it may recover.'

'It's not my car,' I said, and groaned. 'I've quit Uni and this is my escape route.'

'But YOU seem OK and I'd say that's more important. Wouldn't you?'

'Not really. My life depends on me not messing this up.'

'Stop worrying,' he said, and touched my knee lightly. 'I'll get it towed to ours and checked over. I can take you anywhere you want.' He paused for a moment and scrutinized my face. 'I should take you to your home or the hospital. You might have a concussion.' His brow furrowed. 'You're pale.'

'I haven't been driving long. I was careless.'

He took my wrist and felt for my pulse. 'You won't make the same mistake again. Does your head hurt?'

'That's my hand,' I said.

'Umm,' he said, and his eyes narrowed. 'Perhaps a touch of concussion.'

'I'm fine, really,' I said, although I knew I wasn't and because he'd been so kind, I was about to cry.

He kept hold of my hand. 'So, where were you heading?'

I swallowed the lump in my throat. 'Willows End Farm. To see Alan Kubik.'

His eyes glinted. 'Then I should introduce myself.' He shook my hand. 'I'm Toby Kubik, son of Alan.'

'Really?'

'Really!' he replied. 'Do you know my father?'

'We've only spoken over the phone.'

'I couldn't drive on by when I saw you disappear over the bank.' He straightened up and brushed the curls off his face. Your car bounced like a rubber ball down the bank.'

'Then I'm extremely grateful,' I said.

As we set off he gave a wave to a horse and rider that approached from the opposite direction.

'Why did you quit your course?' he asked.

'It didn't suit me. Accounting. Dull as ditchwater.'

'Some of us are more creative. It doesn't suit us to be constrained by facts and figures.'

'I wanted to be a dancer. But foolishly, I listened to Mum who said accounting was exciting and it offered more security.'

'A shame,' he paused. 'I'd like to see you dance.'

'I love all styles - modern, ballet, salsa. I'm no Darcy Bussell but I put my heart and soul into it.'

'I can imagine that. I like dancing, too, after a few pints.'

'You're funny,' I said.

'Anya's a pretty and unusual name.'

'My mum's from Sweden. But she's lived here since she was tiny. We visit Gramps and Nanna sometimes.'

He looked over at me. 'You do have the look of a Swede.'

'Not the root vegetable, I hope.'

He tipped his head back and guffawed. 'You're funny, too.'

I sniggered. 'And I'm normally such a good driver.'

He laughed even more.

'No one ever admits to being a bad driver, or lacking a sense of humour.'

'True,' I said.

'And I expect you've seen a few accidents but only through your rearview mirror?' He glanced my way and his nose crinkled.

'Stop,' I said, and tried not to laugh and cry at the same time. He seemed an incorrigible flirt, but I found him delightful.

He dressed well, too. Not the usual farming attire of overalls, with flat cap and wellies.

'Do you enjoy farming?' I asked.

He grimaced. 'I don't work on the farm, not since University. I've always helped Dad in the holidays. No choice there.'

I noticed that when he laughed his thick hair bounced in a most appealing way.

'So,' he continued. 'I imagine quitting Uni must have been a big decision?'

I'd hated my course but I didn't want to explain the other reason that I'd left. It felt too raw to share, least of all with someone I'd only just met.

'It seemed the natural decision, in the end,' I said, without elaborating.

'Is your career living up to expectations?'

He was mighty curious, I thought.

'Can you believe this is my first day?'

'Oh,' he said. 'Well, you mustn't worry. Dad's softer than Pooh Bear and he's been with Homer Feeds forever.'

He spoke with a subtle northern accent. His voice reminded me of one of my lecturers.

Alan Kubik, a slighter version of his son and with sun-brown weathered skin, insisted that I borrow his car to complete my sales calls that day and before I left, he plied me with mugs of sweet tea and a bowl of lamb casserole with dumplings.

'You're a wonderful cook, Mr Kubik,' I said.

'Not much choice. My wife, Kim, died when the children were young. I've never met anyone who could live up to her - cooking or otherwise.' He spoke flatly, as though he'd long come to terms with her death. And yet I suspected this was a well-rehearsed act.

'I'm sorry,' I said, and glanced at Toby, who appeared engrossed in his meal.

When I returned their car later that evening, Toby insisted that he take me to dinner. I could hardly refuse his kind offer.

Chapter 8

A month after Rose's accident I felt confident enough to leave her for an hour or two and I took a ride out with Gemma across the moors to Malham Cove. Stevie offered to keep her sister company. It felt wonderful to breathe in the open air at last but my mind was never far from home.

After our ride we turned the horses out in the upper pasture and as we set off back down the hill, I watched Toby steer his Maserati onto the drive. I looked at my watch. It was unusually early for him to be home.

From here on the hillside, Willows End looked glorious in the afternoon sun, with the river water shimmering beneath the willows on its journey east, and Walnut Cottage, chocolate box pretty, to the far end of the paddock. The Yorkshire stone of Willows End House appeared almost white with the sun reflecting on it and the decking area we'd built to take advantage of the views to the woods and folly beyond looked inviting for a glass of chilled wine.

Our home, built in 1785, stood a stately three stories high. The attic rooms were largely unused as the bedrooms on the first floor were more than enough for us even when we had guests to stay. Walnut Cottage, Gemma's home, was built two years after Willows End and had originally been allocated to the housekeeper and her family - a perk that by all accounts ensured the housekeepers never wanted to seek employment elsewhere. Toby's dad, Alan, had been the first of the Kubiks to insist there would be no more live-in servants and when Gemma had married Euan, Alan handed over full ownership of Walnut Cottage to them.

As we walked I turned to Gemma. 'Will you have dinner with us?'

She picked at a loose string in the lead rope and for a moment she seemed absorbed in the task.

'It's tuna rice and salad. I'll even throw in a hard boiled egg and a chilled glass of sauvignon blanc.'

She looked up and seemed to register my words. 'That would be lovely, thank you. But no wine. I'm on the wagon.'

Gemma wasn't a big drinker but she was never on the wagon. 'Why?'

She hesitated for a moment. 'No particular reason.'

'I'll join you on the wagon.'

She gave a heavy sigh. 'Actually, there is a reason.'

'Oh?'

'Rob was over Saturday night. He thinks he's quite the connoisseur and brought over a few bottles of mega expensive wine. I drank more than I should.'

'Did you wake up with a sore head?'

'Worse than that. I don't even remember going to bed,' she said, quietly.

I stopped. 'What do you mean?'

Gemma's head was half bent to watch her feet and she twisted the toe of her riding boot into the soil. 'When I woke up Rob had gone.' She lifted her eyes. 'That was a bonus, as the night before I'd told him it was over.'

'I thought you really liked him.'

'I thought so too, until he started suggesting we try weird stuff.'

'What sort of weird stuff?'

She hesitated a moment. 'Wanting to tie me to the bed posts and shave me. And I don't mean my legs. And wanting me to do the same to him.'

'Some people do like to try unusual things. But it should only ever be mutual.'

'I know Brazillian is a trend, but I like myself neat and au naturel. Plus, there's no way I'd fancy a man who shaved his privates.'

I gasped. 'Christ Almighty. Me neither.'

'Apparently, it's cleaner,' she said, with a sniff of disbelief. 'I just don't get my kicks that way.'

'Nor me, Gemma,' I replied.

'My guess is he's either into the prepubescent look,' she continued. 'Which is vile in itself, or he doesn't like getting them stuck in his teeth.' Gemma exploded into laughter and then sputtered, 'I don't think his wife would appreciate it either.'

Her laughter sounded manic and I wondered where this was heading. 'Harder to explain than a piece of spinach,' I said.

'And I don't expect his wife's a strawberry blonde either,' she added. She turned away and continued walking downhill.

I jogged to catch up. 'There's no way I'd let a man go anywhere near my lady garden with a razor blade,' I said. 'Not even a qualified gynaecologist.'

I turned to face her and her eyes brimmed with tears.

'Gemma. What is it?'

'That's why I drank so much,' she said. 'I was working up the courage to dump him.'

I didn't like where this was going. 'What happened?'

'Rob had sex with me, despite my being comatose.'

'You mean he raped you?'

She nodded once and lowered her eyes.

I held her close and felt a trembling go all through her as she began to cry

Eventually, I said quietly. 'Did he hurt you, physically?'

We drew apart and as she wiped her eyes she shook her head. 'Physically, I think I'm OK. I do feel sore. But I can hardly complain to him about his technique.'

'You need to see a doctor, Gemma.'

'We were in a relationship.' She turned away. 'I've no intention of doing anything but wallow in my own idiocy.'

I swallowed to keep my own tears at bay.

'I'll be fine,' she said.

'You need to talk it through. See a counsellor at the very least.'

'I will talk it through. With his wife.'

'You don't mean that,' I said.

'Why not? She deserves to know, doesn't she?'

'Forget about her. Think about yourself. And his wife can find out for herself what a cheating ratbag he is.'

'She probably already knows.'

'Then will you talk to me? Don't suffer with this on your own.'

'You're the only one I can talk to,' she said.

'At least we two have each other.' I pulled a clean tissue from my pocket and gave it to her.

She blew her nose. 'You have Toby, too.'

'But some things are easier to talk about with a girlfriend.' I didn't want to mention mine and Toby's problems. Gemma had enough to think about.

'I knew from the start Rob was an arrogant rat. I should have kept well clear.'

'I'm worried about you, Gem. This is serious. He should be challenged and prosecuted.'

'Of course he should. But you know nothing will come of it. We were in a relationship. An illicit one at that. I've sent texts and photos. How do you think that would make me look if it all came out?'

She was right. All it would do would be to cause further upset for her.

'OK. But talk to me. At anytime. The middle of the night, if you need to.'

Back at the stables and still tearful, Gemma walked across the paddock to ours while I went to lock up the tack room. There were empty crisp and sweet packets, grooming brushes and various items of clothing strewn around. I made a mental note to remind the children of some basic tack room etiquette.

When I entered the kitchen, Stevie was chopping vegetables and humming along to a song on the radio, while Gemma rinsed vegetables at the sink.

'Where's your Dad?'

'Upstairs,' Stevie replied cheerfully.

'I'll nip and see Rose,' I said. Then I turned around and added. 'The tuna's marinating in the fridge.'

'We've already found it,' said Gemma.

When I went through to Rose's room, she looked up from her laptop.

'Did you have a nice ride?' Her voice sounded full of regret but she forced a smile.

'Pretty at Malham as always. But on the hot side of hot and tiring too. Pepper was well behaved.'

I sat on the edge of her bed and tucked my legs up. She flipped the lid down on her laptop.

'Don't mind me,' I said.

'It was only YouTube.'

'Gemma's staying for dinner. Will you come through?'

'Sure,' Rose replied.

'I'll ask Dad to help you.'

I stood up to leave. 'I don't suppose you've had any twinges or movement?' I asked, hopefully.

'Actually, I did wonder if my toe twitched earlier.'

'Really?'

'I think I imagined it,' she said. 'Wishful thinking and all.'

'I'm sure it must be real. Let me know if you feel more movements.'

'Course,' she reopened her laptop and in seconds was lost to her screen.

Toby stepped out of the en-suite; a towel draped loosely around his hips.

I tugged playfully at his towel. 'Hot, isn't it?'

His towel fell to the floor.

'Too hot for sitting in meetings with no aircon,' he said.

'Boring, too, I imagine.'

'Sure is,' he said, without smiling. 'Still, one of us has to work.'

'Hey you.' It wasn't like him to be snarky.

He kicked at his towel. 'I'm tired, that's all.'

'Will you help Rose through to the kitchen?'

He didn't appear to hear me and opened the wardrobe.

'Oh, and guess what?' I said.

'Huh?'

'Rose felt a twitch in her toes. At least she thinks so.'

He swung round. 'Thank God!' He zipped up his shorts. 'I'll go see her now.'

'She's going to be OK,' I said. 'I feel certain.'

'If she isn't,' he said. 'I'll not forgive myself.'

I knew he meant it. I also knew that if I'd been the one driving that day I'd have been consumed with guilt. I felt bad enough that I hadn't been there to protect her.

I touched his cheek. 'It wasn't you. It could easily have been another car, another driver.'

'I have nightmares where I see the scene unfolding all over again. I see other things, too. But mostly, Rose in her wheelchair, sobbing and watching the rest of the world go by. A spectator. A bystander to life.

'Rose doesn't blame you. Nobody does.'

'You did at first. And the more I think about it, the more I know you were right.'

'That was unfair of me.'

'I'd have probably done the same thing,' he said.

'No you wouldn't.' I placed my hand upon his chest. 'That's the difference between you and me.'

I felt his heartbeat pound beneath my palm. 'Are you feeling OK?'

'I will be.' Gently, he lifted my hand away. 'When Rose is better.'

I linked my hand with his as we walked down the stairs together and a delicious aroma of grilled tuna drifted our way.

In the kitchen, Gemma caught my eye and grimaced.

I mouthed, 'What?' but she didn't respond.

Stevie turned round. 'Mum?'

'Yes, sweetheart.'

'Can Jake come for dinner?'

'Jake Parsons?'

She frowned. 'Is there another Jake?'

'Yes, of course he can. Any particular reason why?'

She chewed her bottom lip. 'And, would it be OK if he stayed over tonight?'

Gemma appeared engrossed with the bowl of salad, as she tossed the leaves furiously.

I tilted my head to the side. 'You mean, stay over with you?'

Her eyes grew wide as she ran her fingers through her hair. 'I love him.' She gasped.

'Oh,' I said. 'That's wonderful.'

She hugged herself. 'And he loves me.'

Joy sprang from her every pore.

'Of course he does.' I held her face and kissed her. 'How long have you been seeing one another?'

Her mouth curved into a smile. 'Since Rose's accident. It sort of threw us together.'

'Then yes, he can stay over. Have you mentioned any of this to Rose?'

'Not yet, but she'll be cool. She likes Jake.'

The irony of her words seemed lost on her.

'But does she only like him as a friend? That's what I'm trying to say,' I said.

'She doesn't like him that way,' said Stevie, aghast. 'She's only just sixteen and Jake's nearly twenty.'

'It's fine,' I said. 'I'll talk to her.'

I heard a rap at the back door and Jake poked his head through.

Stevie skipped over, pulled him inside and planted a kiss on his mouth. I glanced at Gemma who raised her eyebrows.

'Hi, Jake,' I said.

'Hi, Anya, Gemma.' Jake grinned and slung an arm around Stevie's shoulder.

'I hope you like tuna,' I said.

'My favourite,' he said, and he drew Stevie close.

Hell, I thought.

And right on cue, Rose wheeled herself through the doorway, followed by Toby.

When Rose saw Stevie and Jake together her mouth fell open. She turned away from them, blinking, and her eyes glistened.

'Hey, Rose.' Stevie let go of Jake, went over and kissed her on the cheek. 'Jake and I are an item.' She waited for Rose to respond to her big announcement.

Rose stared up at Stevie without smiling or speaking.

'What's up, Rosie?'

Eventually, Rose spoke. 'That's...nice for you both.' Her voice trembled. And without another word she turned her wheelchair around. 'Sorry, Mum. I'm not hungry.'

In the doorway her wheel knocked against the doorframe and Rose scraped her hand. She yelped and Toby and I stepped in to assist.

'Please. I'm not an invalid,' she snapped, and headed into the hallway.

'I'll go after her,' I turned and said to the others.

'I should leave her,' replied Gemma. And she whispered, 'She probably needs a good cry.'

46

'What's up with Rose?' Stevie asked, but she cast her eyes downwards.

'Don't worry, love. It's not your fault.'

'I thought she'd be pleased about me and Jake.'

'Maybe you should have told her before?' suggested Gemma, her voice gentle.

Stevie didn't reply and turned to Jake.

'It's difficult for her,' I said. 'Imagine how you'd feel if you were cooped up all day, unable to walk, ride or do anything much.'

Jake took Stevie's hand. 'I think she needs to get used to the idea. We've all been friends for a long time.'

'You're right, Jake. Thank you,' I said.

After dinner, I carried a tray of food to Rose. She sat in her chair and stared out of the window. She didn't turn around as I set her dinner on the coffee table.

'I'm sick of this, Mum.' She waved a hand at her legs and burst into tears.

I hunched down beside her. 'I know, my love. But your body is healing. It'll just take time.'

'I feel like I'm going crazy. I don't sleep well, my head is constantly whirring with stuff. And look at Stevie, smiling and laughing, eventing this weekend... in love with Jake.' Rose's sobs intensified.

'Let me share a story with you.' I cupped her palm in mine. 'It'll come as no surprise for you to know that at your age I had an all-consuming crush on a boy. He had no idea how I felt and I was too shy to tell him. Then my best friend asked him out. And the cruel thing was, she knew how much I liked him.'

Rose wiped her eyes. 'Not much of a best friend.'

'A lot of the girls fancied him. He had that thing; confidence, could talk to girls without blushing. He made everyone he spoke to feel special. Your sister, because she's older, has a lot of confidence. You, my darling girl, are just as pretty, and in time your confidence will grow and you'll have boys desperate for your attention.'

'It'll be horrible seeing them together. What if she marries him and I'm forever wishing he'd fallen for me?'

'Sweetheart.' I repressed a smile. 'I don't think they'll marry. They're both so young. And Stevie's off to Uni where she'll meet many new boys. Whatever you do, don't repeat that,' I added.

Rose's lips curled into a smile.

'Trust me,' I said. 'I might not know it all, but I'm pretty sure I know Stevie. And going away to University can change the strongest of relationships.'

Rose stuck out her chin. 'Well, I wouldn't want her cast offs. So as far as I'm concerned, Jake's history.'

'That's my girl. Fighting talk. He's a good friend to you and sometimes that's better. And one day, in time, you'll fall in love with an interesting and intelligent boy who'll want nothing more than to love you unconditionally.'

'Thanks, Mum.'

And I thought, how quickly we often were to move on from regrets and life's let downs. As a girl I became good at colouring in those disappointing blank spots that life frequently dropped in my path.

When I returned to the kitchen, Toby whistled as he filled the dishwasher and Gemma chopped leftovers for Freda who yapped and spun in circles.

'That dog will do every damn trick she knows to get some food,' said Toby with a glance over his shoulder.

'And she has quite the repertoire,' replied Gemma, as Freda rolled over and over. 'I wonder if she gets dizzy doing that.'

'I'm meeting a client at The Black Horse,' said Toby, as he rammed the dishwasher shut.

'Ask them here if you like,' I said.

'He asked if there was a decent local. And as he's the client...'

'Hopefully he won't expect you to ply him with drinks all night.'

Toby tutted. 'Hardly. It's important business not a social tête-à-tête.'

After Toby had gone, Gemma and I settled in the living room to drink our tea.

'So,' she said. 'What's up with Toby?'

I turned to her. 'What do you mean?'

Her brows knitted together, 'Come on, Anya. I know Toby as well as you.'

'We're both worried about Rose. That's all,' I said.

She lifted her cup and took a drink. 'Something's not quite right.'

'He was fine at dinner,' I said. 'It's Rose. Plus it's no picnic being a one man consulting band. Anyway, you and he got on well tonight.'

'When you went to see Rose, he was muttering to himself. I couldn't understand a word he was saying and when I asked him, he blanked me.'

'He does do that sometimes. More frequently recently.' I gave a nervous laugh. 'First sign of madness.'

'I'd keep an eye on that. Have a talk with him when he gets back,' she suggested.

It wasn't like Gemma to interfere or offer advice on our marriage. I found it patronising and when I finished my tea I made an excuse that I needed to catch up with some admin.

'No problem. See you tomorrow.' She smiled, kissed me on the cheek and closed the door behind her.

The moment she'd gone, I felt a rush of guilt. She probably felt messed up after she'd been drug raped. Something like that would have deep and lasting repercussions.

I went to collect Rose's dinner plate and tried to persuade her to come and watch a film with me.

'I'm reading some research,' she said, looking at her laptop. 'You choose a film and I'll come through soon.'

'What's the research?' I asked.

'How to stay positive in the face of tragedy. I'm finding it helpful.'

'Tragedy?' I said, alarmed. 'Can I have a look?' I peered round.

She tilted the screen down. 'It's a self-help site. And I'd rather keep it private.'

Which made it quite clear that she didn't want me to see her reading material. I left, with my concern piqued.

I selected a romantic comedy but half an hour later I was still sitting alone and had almost nodded off to sleep. It wasn't anywhere near as funny as the ratings suggested. I turned it off and popped my head around Rose's door.

Rose had fallen asleep. Her laptop was balanced precariously on the edge of the bed and I picked it up. The screen sprang to life with a website I wasn't familiar with - 'We will help YOU'.

It appeared to be a chatroom for users of wheelchairs. I noticed a login button at the top and went to sit in the armchair. I recalled an old password Rose had used for an online kids club; Pinto6, her first pony. Worth a go. But invalid. I tried a few more combinations and as I was about to give up, the chat tab opened.

'Welcome back, Rose.'

Perhaps it was a positive that she was talking to others in a similar predicament. Although it seemed pessimistic given her longer term prognosis. I felt a pang of conscience and placed her laptop on the bedside table.

I took several slow breaths and head to the wine rack, tonight's wagon abandoned. Tomorrow, I'd mention to her that I'd seen the site on her laptop and hoped that might encourage her to talk to me about her concerns.

With glass in hand I headed to the office. I'd take the opportunity to catch up with some admin and if nothing else, it would make me sleepy. I took a sip of wine and set the glass on the desk.

Other than our bedroom, the study was my favourite room in the house. When we set up the livery yard, we converted what was then a sitting room into a comfortable study. It had the original oak panel walls, tall mullion windows and views across the garden and on down to a bend in the river. I loved spending time here which made wading through tedious admin more palatable.

When the girls were young, I'd designed and planted a varied rose garden at the back of the house with a large gazebo at its centre and with seating and cobblestone paving. Behind the gazebo ran a mini maze of paths between the flower beds and often when I had an hour spare I'd trim back or deadhead the roses and pull up the weeds. The variety of insects and butterflies the flowers attracted always dazzled and surprised me.

My desk was positioned in front of the window so I could look out at the garden through all weather and seasons. Tonight, the summer light had sunk low and the shadows from the lilac trees muted the colour of the roses which cascaded over the trellised arches.

Toby's antique desk with ergonomic leather chair, sat beside the stone fireplace, with its carved mantle, inglenook and a stack of logs to one side. Unlike myself, Toby kept his desk neat and organised, with a silver-plated Newton's cradle positioned beside a leather-bound notepad and a set of parker pens. Throughout the colder months Toby made it his first job of the day to clean out and light the log burning stove which would keep the study cosy and warm all day and through the evening. Even when we had no office work, we'd often sit here and read a book, drink and talk and listen to music.

Exposed timbers ran the length of the ceiling, and an oak coffee table was set between the two sofas, which made it an ideal room for meetings or relaxing. An earthenware bowl at the centre of the table, was filled with bright lilac heather I'd recently picked while riding on Orben Moor. Shelves laden with books we'd collected over the years filled one wall, most of which we'd read and with others still awaiting their turn. I refused to get rid of any of them. The children's books, those which dated back to picture books and horse-riding adventure stories, filled an entire shelf. Toby had suggested I box them up or give them away to make way for new books but I insisted we must keep them on display and for when the girls had their own children. Every now and then I'd pick one out and re-read it which always brought back fond memories of sitting and reading with the girls when they were small.

Since we launched the livery yard seven years ago we'd remained in profit. It seemed surprisingly straightforward. The land and two dozen stalls and stables were already in place, Gemma and I were the managers and labour, which meant maintenance costs remained relatively low.

We never struggled for clients because our fertile pastures attracted new horse owners, and as we were located at the foot of Orben Moor there was easy access to wild landscapes criss-crossed with miles of bridleways and green lanes. There were also stunning views across hills and moorland, which made it attractive riding country. Richmond, pretty and full of old buildings, was our nearest town, only eight miles away. As

Gemma had grown up at Willows End Farm, she'd known all the essential local contacts before the livery got started. Vets and a farrier, joiners, fencers and so on. I'd brought my limited equestrian knowledge and my sales and accounting experience. Gemma and I made a good team - we enjoyed one another's company, but above all, we were passionate about horses and unafraid of hard work.

Euan came to mind, as he often did during quieter moments, and I turned around and pictured him here in the study, smoking a cigarette, talking and selecting a favourite Leonard Cohen or classical track. Occasionally I'd hear his voice inside my head, although it grew fainter with the passing years.

Prior to his death Euan had been Alan's right hand man. Toby should have worked the farm; at least, in Alan's mind. Not long after we met, Toby confided that ever since he was a young boy, he'd seen how farming had exhausted and played havoc with his Dad's physical and mental health and long decided he wouldn't follow in his footsteps. This was despite knowing that managing Willows End Farm was the path he was born for and expected to take.

I remembered the times when Alan had thrown something into the conversation that made clear his disappointment with Toby for shunning this role. After all, the farm would be Toby's inheritance and therefore should have been his joint responsibility.

Fortunately for Toby, his consultancy business had grown steadily and he gained decent sized corporate clients. In truth, I felt the money Toby made should have compensated for him not working the farm and Toby even invested his own earnings to maintain and modernise their listed family home, something Alan had never openly appreciated.

Instead, Alan would sling an arm around Euan's shoulder and say something along the lines of, 'Come on, son. Let's collect those bales from top acre.'

'It's a beautiful evening for it.' Toby would interject, in a manner that suggested he delighted in their camaraderie. 'I'm meeting a client at The Spice Box for dinner.' Heavy sigh. 'I hear there's a new a la carte menu.'

Neither of them were terribly subtle and their bitterness continued to simmer beneath the surface and reemerge at regular intervals.

In private, I knew Toby and his father's conversations had been nothing like the facade they projected in the company of others. Willows End might have been large, but voices echoed through the walls and corridors like whispered secrets.

Whenever Euan was caught in the middle of their clashes he tried to appease them both. Alan had loved Euan, not only because he filled a void in the farm where Toby should have been, but because he'd been a thoughtful, mature and kind person.

Chapter 9

I suspended my hands above the keyboard, certain I'd heard a car engine. For a minute I listened, but there was only silence, save for the wind that hissed softly down the chimney breast. I continued writing my email when a thud rattled the window frame. This was followed by a much louder bang from somewhere upstairs. I flipped my laptop shut, jogged into the hallway and up the staircase. I paused outside Stevie's bedroom, but all was quiet. I checked the family bathroom, then went through to our bedroom. A strip of light shone beneath the crack of the ensuite door.

'Toby?'

I heard running water and turned the door handle. He'd locked it which was unusual.

'Toby?'

'What?' he called.

'You OK?'

'Yeah, yeah. All good.'

'Meeting go well?'

'Yep. Fine.'

I undressed and tossed my clothes into the wash basket. I passed the full length mirror and turned to face my reflection. The weeks of endless sun had turned my skin brown, despite applying copious amounts of sunscreen. I examined my new, slimmer shape and ran my hands across my abdomen and the new red scar to the right of the silvered cesarean scar I'd been left with during Rose's difficult birth. I cupped my breasts, which were still full and shapely, then I interlaced my fingers behind my head. Granted, they'd lost some plumpness, but I had breastfed both my girls.

After my recent operation I'd thrown out all of my tired underwear and bought some pretty lingerie. It felt indulgent, but as a rule, I'd always been a careful spender, a behaviour inherited from my parents. Toby had been thrilled with my purchases and couldn't leave me alone. I felt glamorous and sexy again and I loved his ardour and attention. Our sex life had been reinvigorated and almost as thrilling as it had been pre-babies. At least, that was until Rose's accident, which killed my desire in an instant.

One morning, prior to Rose's fall, I'd tried on a new underwear set to show him. Toby stopped what he was doing, turned me around and playfully bent me over, all the while singing his own version of, 'Spice up your life', substituted with 'wife'. Toby had a wicked sense of humour. Borderline sexist, but I loved him for it.

Last year, for our nineteenth anniversary, I'd booked a table at a restaurant in York followed by a night in a luxury hotel. When I'd surprised Toby with my plans his imagination had fired up and in bed that same night as we'd held one another, he'd shared his plans.

'I know what we'll do. You will wear nothing. Absolutely nothing, but high heeled sandals. And you'll put on a coat and we'll go out on the street like that. Only you and I will know that you're naked. And then I can take you anywhere, anywhere I want, anytime. We'll go to a restaurant and you won't take your coat off but you will be there for me. I can just grab you. I can stretch my hand and stretch my arm and touch you right there in the restaurant. And then I'll say, show me what you've got in there. And you'll do it. And then on the way back we can lean on a car or in an alley, a black alley. And I'll fuck you. Fuck you hard.'

And as he'd spoken beside me in the dark, I'd grown wet and weak with desire. It was why I was so drawn to him when we first met. Why I'd always love him. His sense of fun and drama that never failed to thrill me.

Of course, in reality, after dining out, we hadn't done any such thing in a dark alley but instead had kissed one another and held hands on our way back to the hotel, where we'd made love - sensual and leisurely, late into the night. Our lovemaking was no less exciting for this, and as always, rekindled an intimacy that kept us bound together.

The shower was still running as I pulled back the bed covers, switched off the bedside lamp and lay my head on the pillow.

The full moon cast a silvery glow through the open blinds and filled the room. Shadows from the trees outside danced upon the ceiling and I closed my eyes and drifted off to the sound of running water.

Sometime later, a warm and lightness of hand upon my breast roused me.

Toby whispered. 'Angel?'

I turned over.

In the darkness Toby spoke with his lips close to mine. 'I need you.'

I could taste his words - deep and velvet soft, and far too sleepy to resist, he pushed me onto my back. Slowly, he kissed my cheek, my eyes, my chin, down the length of my neck and chest and lingered lovingly upon my breasts. I arched my back and pressed myself into him as he licked and kissed me, his lips and tongue hot and sensual. When he eased his hand between my thighs, I felt my insides melt at the tenderness of his touch.

'So eager, my love.' He kissed my mouth and parted my lips with his tongue.

I traced my fingers over him as the freshness and nearness of his skin filled my senses. 'You smell divine,' I whispered.

'And you taste delectable,' he said, and planted kisses on my scar and continued further down.

I gave a blissful sigh.

Toby may have had his faults, but even after all our years together, his powers to seduce and make love to me were perfection. After some time, we fell asleep holding one another, tired and content.

A while later, I couldn't tell how long, a noise awoke me. Thuds and knocks from close by.

'Toby?' I reached out and touched the empty sheet. The bedroom door was ajar and the light spilled in from the landing. I pulled on my robe, walked onto the landing and leaned over the bannister rail. I peered into the darkened hallway. Toby sat naked at the foot of the stairs with his head and shoulders hunched.

I hurried down and knelt in front of him, but he didn't seem to see me.

I lifted his chin. 'Toby?'

He looked straight through me.

'Did you fall?'

He was shivering, and slowly, he raised a hand to his head.

I lifted his hand from his head and when I found a bump he jerked away.

'I'll fetch some ice.' I took off my robe and draped it over his shoulders. 'Don't move.'

I returned with a bag of frozen peas and he lifted his gaze. But there was something in the darkness of his eyes - a chilling and unrecognisable distance, that frightened me.

I placed the peas gently on the lump. 'What happened?'

He shook his head. 'I only remember I couldn't sleep.'

'Can you stand?' I took his hand to help him up but he pushed it away.

'I'm not a fucking invalid,' he snapped.

I stood back. 'Hey. We'll wake the girls, and Jake.'

'Jake?'

'You knew he was staying over,' I said, hushed.

'Cheeky little shit.'

'Stevie's a woman, Toby, and this is her home.'

Toby moved to stand up.

I held out my hand again. 'Let me help you.'

As he stood up, he ripped the robe off his back and cast it across the hall floor. He leaned against the handrail and rubbed both temples.

'Does your head hurt?'

He flicked his eyes upwards to meet mine, but didn't reply.

'I'll fetch you a whisky.' I ran back to the kitchen and as I poured a shot, I realised he must be exhausted if he hadn't slept. That could explain his fall and irritability.

When I returned to the hall, he'd gone. I hurried up the stairs and found him back in the bedroom and under the duvet with peas in-situ. I set the tumbler of whisky on his bedside cabinet. 'This'll help you sleep.'

He reached for the glass, raised it to his lips and knocked it back in one. 'Perhaps if you'll leave me alone and try not to snore,' he said.

'I'm sorry,' I said. 'You should have nudged me.'

He'd never told me I snored, although his snoring had kept me awake countless times. He burrowed beneath the duvet and within a minute or two, his breaths came and went with a gentle wheeze. I turned over to face him, eased closer and adjusted the peas so they rested on his crown. I looked at his profile, still strangely unreadable even after all these years, and felt a well of tenderness.

It wasn't so much his looks that had attracted me to Toby, though he was undeniably handsome, and maybe even more so than when we'd first met. No, it had been more to do with the way he made me feel about myself as a woman. He was assured and confident in how he spoke to me and touched me, and he knew instinctively how to please me, not only in bed, but my mind, too. It was his way of foreplay and his way of exciting me with his words so that when we went to bed, sex was often an inevitable result of earlier wordplay. He knew that I viewed lovemaking in the same earthy way he did. Never vulgar in his approach, but confident in how he described what he wanted to do to me, and me to do to him. All in luscious and sensual detail. Although I was no innocent when we met, he opened my eyes to what lovemaking could really be like. Sometimes, I'd wonder how he got to be that way. It was hard to imagine it was ever his dad's influence.

The following morning, Toby had a vicious bruise and a headache, but otherwise, he seemed his normal easy-going self. He rose early, made a pot of tea and scrambled eggs for breakfast.

As we cleared away the plates he turned to me. 'Sorry I was an idiot last night.'

'Don't worry. You were shocked by your fall.' I felt the bump on his head. 'Is it terribly sore?'

'Yeah, and I've got a huge bruise down my thigh.'

'Will you stay home today?' I asked. 'So I can keep an eye on you.'

'Luckily, I don't have any meetings, so I'll work in the office.' He kissed me on the lips. 'Just for you.'

Chapter 10

Eight Years Earlier

When Euan died it had been unexpected and traumatic, not only for Gemma but for all of us. Euan had been a part of our lives for so long and we all lived closely together. Everyone who knew Euan loved him. Tall and strong, his dark olive skin came courtesy of his Carribean grandfather. He had Irish born parents and his humour shone through like an emerald. He was witty and charismatic, but more importantly, he'd been sensitive to his own and others' feelings.

After his three day old bloated and bruised corpse had been retrieved from the swollen river, two miles downstream of Willows End, Gemma reacted violently, convinced that his death had been more than an accident.

'No way was Euan so drunk that he happened to stumble into the river. I don't believe it and I never will.'

Toby tried to reason with her - his words slurring. 'He was legless at the party. You saw the state he was in.'

'You mean like you are now? Are you going to take a stroll and fall into the river and drown?'

'I'm not drunk. Not like Euan was,' Toby hurled back at her.

'No. You're just pissed as a fart and can't talk or walk straight.' Gemma spat her reply.

'We need coffee,' I said, and went to fill the kettle.

And yet, Gemma had a point. It did seem odd. Why did Euan end up by the river? I remembered talking to Euan during the party and he hadn't seemed all that drunk. But my memory of the afternoon blurred and staggered beneath a haze of wine and hot sun. Had I said something to upset him that day? I could only recall the vaguest snippets of our conversation.

It was past midnight when the last of the funeral guests had gone home, but Gemma was still hyped up and overwrought. She'd refused all my offers of a medicinal whisky and had barely eaten since the accident, despite my trying to coax her with her favourite foods. Her cheeks were hollow from lack of sleep and her eyes looked bloodshot and rimmed with exhaustion from days and nights filled with crying.

She tiger-paced the length of the kitchen. Endlessly back and forth, muttering occasionally to herself.

My heart contracted in pity. 'Please, Gemma.' I took hold of her hand and she paused but refused to look at me. 'The autopsy doesn't say conclusive if there's even the slightest room for error.'

She gripped my hand and turned quickly to me. 'Stop it, Anya. Don't try to tell me his three day dead and battered body is going to reveal anything accurate in an autopsy.'

'That's what they're trained for,' I said, as calmly as I could, though I was beginning to think she might be right. Fourteen long days after the shock of his death, my mind was still a mess. 'It was conclusive.' I repeated, as much to convince myself as her.

'Believe me,' said Toby. 'If you continue to torture yourself, you're going to make your life miserable.'

She pushed my hand away, spun around to face Toby and let fly. 'My life is fucking miserable and ruined anyway.'

Yep, I thought. Tactful as ever, Toby. I glared at him.

'I don't mean now,' he said. 'You're in shock. We all are. I mean in the future. It'll stop you getting on with your life if you think that way.'

'Jesus effing Christ.' Gemma's voice rose. 'I watched my husband lowered into a dark, cold and lonely grave at the age of thirty-six. I loved him.' Then she said, softer. 'God, how I loved him.'

'We all loved him,' said Toby.

'It isn't the same,' I said to him.

'Did you sleep with him, share you days with him?' she fired at Toby. She swiped her arm across the tabletop and sent plates and glasses spinning onto the floor. 'Did you hold his hand as you slept because you longed for his touch, even then?'

We looked back at her, stunned into silence. Gemma watched me as though defying me to contradict her. Toby's face darkened. The atmosphere in the room felt fraught with emotion and sorrow.

'Don't you tell me how I should handle this.' Her eyes bore into Toby's. 'You two will be fine. Married, happy, healthy, two beautiful daughters. If I'd only had his child...' she stuttered and gasped. 'I'd at least have him or her to cling to.' Her face softened. 'To see Euan's face in theirs.'

'Oh, Gemma.' I wanted to hold her. To ease her grief. But she turned her back on me.

Alan, who had remained seated in the armchair with a pint glass in hand, said. 'Toby, be quiet.' He sounded depleted and drained.

But Toby persisted. 'I'm just saying we should only look forward, not back at the past - '

'Leave - her - be!' Alan said, firm and loud. He stood up, slammed his glass onto the dresser and marched from the kitchen.

Toby turned to me, uncertain, and I shook my head in warning. 'Not now.'

He turned to Gemma, and his shoulders slumped in defeat. 'I'm sorry. You're entitled to grieve.'

Gemma didn't respond, but continued to stare ahead and blink away her tears. Her hands remained clenched at her sides.

'It's been a long and terrible day,' I said. 'We should leave this mess and try and rest.'

Gemma, who had slept in our spare room since Euan went missing, announced quietly, 'I'm going home.'

'Let me walk you back,' said Toby.

'I want to be on my own.' Gemma grabbed her jacket, flung it over her shoulder and left through the back door without a backward glance. I went to the window and watched her walk through the side gate and she soon disappeared into the darkness. Toby stood at my side and after a minute, a light appeared on in Walnut Cottage.

'She'll be OK,' I said. 'It's time she tried to get back to some sense of normality. Or at least have time to grieve alone.'

Toby put his arm around me. 'Come here, my love.'

'Nothing will be the same,' I said, and began to cry into his shoulder.

Toby's voice faltered. 'My best friend and my sister's husband. Life deals some crap.'

That's an understatement, I thought.

With the house quiet finally, we headed upstairs. Too exhausted to wash, I threw off my clothes and fell into bed.

Toby climbed into bed beside me. He lay on his back and stared up at the ceiling. He sighed. 'I know Gemma's devastated but I'm scared her doubts are going to eat away at her memories.'

'Try to remember how you felt when your Mum died.'

'Euan's death isn't the same as Mum dying.'

'How's it different? It's all grief for those left behind.'

'Because I was only eleven,' he lifted my hand and stroked the back of it with his fingers. 'When you're young, you don't fully understand death and so you accept it more readily. Of course, I questioned it to myself, but more in how it affected me. Mum's death was medical. She couldn't have prevented it. None of us could. But Gemma doesn't understand what happened to Euan so her imagination is on high alert. As far as she's concerned, we weren't there so there's no proof.'

'How can she ever know for certain though?' I said.

'She never will. So she's going to torment herself. She'll torment all of us.'

I felt a wave of nausea. Toby was right.

He eased his arm beneath me and pulled me close. I wept and after a few moments he too began to cry in a way that only a grown man can. His torso heaved and his cries broke my heart as he shed the tears he'd contained since Euan's body was found.

'Alan?' I said, and pushed the door open.

The curtains were part drawn allowing a shaft of sunlight through that slashed the room in two.

'Cup of tea for you.' I set his mug on the bedside table and opened the curtains to a pale yellow sun and watercolour grey sky.

But even before I saw Alan's face, there was something unnatural about the shape of his body beneath the covers. With caution, I drew back the duvet. Alan had curled into a ball, his hands clutched at the collar of his pyjamas and his silver hair straggled across his face. Through the strands I saw his eyes fixed and staring. His skin was the colour of pale rain cloud.

Chapter 12

Riseham, our nearest village, was only three miles away. It lay between Bowland Top and Orben Moor and with Cradle Vale stretching out to the South. Occasionally, when weather and time permitted, I'd ride Ebony over Orben Moor, along the lanes and tether him at the village green while I ran my errands. Today, because I didn't want to leave Rose for long, I drove.

In the summer months, Riseham attracted visitors from far and wide, and because of its charming old houses, cobbled streets and stunning location, it had featured in several period dramas and more recently a Sherlock film - Scandal in Riseham. It had been a huge hit, both in the UK and internationally.

A stream flowed by the roadside, and footbridges crossed over to the tied cottages on the other side. As Riseham was surrounded by moorland, the sheep wandered freely and nibbled the verges on their way through. For this reason many of the houses had garden fences to protect their vegetables and flowers.

Despite the village's sleepy atmosphere there were over four hundred residents and a vibrant social side that gave it a real sense of community. We enjoyed the dinner-dances, wine tasting, live music and even touring theatre groups. We'd attend an event at least once a month and they were rarely dull or pedestrian, but they gave us an opportunity to mingle and have some fun. After twenty years, I knew pretty much everyone who lived in the village or close by.

I parked behind the village hall and walked up the road to the grocery store which sat between The Ivy Bistro with a reputation that drew diners from all across the region, and Riseham's much loved second hand book store - Peepers Books. I'd spent many a happy hour rifling through the bookshelves in the three-storey shop. The shop was owned by Cynthia Cowell, a kindly retired English professor. Invariably, she'd have read any book that I picked up and she would share her opinion of it, invited or otherwise. I loved the way she'd talk about the story and characters without giving away any spoilers, and such was her enthusiasm that I'd invariably make my purchase and read the first few pages before leaving the car park.

I went into the grocery store where, Polly, a friend of Stevie's from school worked behind the till.

'Hello, Polly,' I called over as I made my way to the fridge.

She set her phone down on the counter. 'Hi, Mrs Kubik. How's Stevie?'

I picked up two punnets of fresh strawberries and a carton of double cream.

'She's away in Nottingham this weekend. Three-day event.'

I pulled my card from my purse.

'We've gone contactless at last,' she said, and positioned the card reader on the counter. 'That's a long way to go for a show.'

'I'd like to have watched her,' I said. 'But at least she's gone with her new boyfriend, Jake.'

'Horsey Jake?' Polly's eyes sparkled. 'Blimey, she's a fast mover.'

'Yes, well it seems pretty serious.'

Polly's smile slipped. 'And how's Rose?'

'Keeping positive. And we're feeling hopeful that she's improving.'

When I slipped my card back into my purse, the front page of the Richmond News caught my eye.

'FRACKING IN WENSLEYDALE.'

I picked up a copy. 'This too, please.' I pulled some coins from my purse and scanned the article.

'We're all shocked,' said Polly.

'I had no idea this was happening,' I said, and continued to read.

'No one did. That new Mr Vermaak was going bananas about it earlier.'

I lifted my eyes. 'Mr Vermaak?'

'The new owner at Hollow Grange. He's got two teenage sons,' she added, and her eyes twinkled.

I recalled a recent conversation with Marianne, the landlady of The Black Horse. 'I heard the new owners at Hollow Grange were going organic.'

'I don't know, but judging by his reaction, you could be right,' Polly said, and grew animated. 'Mrs Barnes came through to see what all the palaver was about.'

'I can understand. Fracking is the last thing we need here.'

'I've heard it's bad for the environment.'

'If it goes ahead, it'll be a disaster,' I said.

'You should speak to Mr Vermaak. He's organising a protest group.'

'Really? Then I will, Polly. Thank you.'

Outside on the street, I looked up. Clouds had drifted in from the moors, the sky had darkened and a breeze whipped my hair across my face. I buttoned up my jacket, crossed the road and sat on the bench. I gazed out across the wide green of Cradle Vale. This particular bench had once had a plaque lovingly donated by Alan and dedicated to Kim, Toby's mum. After Alan had died, Gemma had a new plaque engraved with both her parents' names to replace the old one. It was a lovely way to remember them both and we'd often sit here and admire the view.

I unfolded the newspaper and held it down against the breeze. The more I read, the angrier I grew. The article implied that planning had already been agreed between Richmond County Council and the shale gas company, Quadrillum. The agreement was for an exploratory investigation on Orben Moor. My hands shook as I noted a councillor's email address for anyone who had questions. Questions? I felt incensed, scared even, and I knew the entire Wensleydale population would be, too. Not only Mr Organic Vermaak. Wensleydale was primarily farmland and moorland grazing and people depended upon it for their livelihoods. Furthermore, the natural beauty of the landscapes proved a huge attraction for hikers and tourists. And most importantly of all, I knew enough about fracking to understand the impact it would have on our water supplies, and in turn, the health of the local population, livestock and wildlife.

I'd recently watched a TV documentary that revealed how it affected those living near fracking sites in Australia and North America; severe health side effects and increased risk of miscarriage and birth defects had been highlighted as a real risk. There was no way we could sit back and allow it to happen.

And then something occurred to me. I remembered the engineer I'd encountered who'd surveyed our land for fresh water supplies. Why hadn't I considered fracking as a possibility? Endless supplies of water. Toby had given them permission. Therefore, we had assisted them, unwittingly, in pursuing their intention to drill for gas. They wanted access to our water supplies. Of course, that had been the same day as Rose's accident and I hadn't given much thought to anything other than her since then.

My heart raced as I tucked the newspaper back into my shopping bag.

'Darling, Anya.'

I looked up to see Marianne, a close friend and landlady of the village Inn, The Black Horse. I stood up, and hugged her.

'It's so good to see your friendly face,' I said.

'How are you doing?' she said. 'I've missed you.' She opened a packet of cigarettes took one out and lit it.

'I won't pretend we're fine,' I said. 'Life's pretty shitty right now.'

She offered me the packet. 'Need one?'

'I'm tempted,' I said.

We sat down together and she took my hand.

'Come over one night,' she said. 'We'll sit in the snug and leave the men manning the bar.'

'I'd like that. You've seen Toby though. He'll have kept you up to date with Rose.'

'He popped in last night, but we didn't talk. He met up with some chap and left.'

'What time?'

Marianne drew on her cigarette. 'Eightish.'

'What did he look like?'

Marianne's brows wrinkled in thought. 'Suited, blonde. Handsome enough for me to look properly as he came in.' She winked. 'At least Toby wasn't meeting an attractive woman.'

'So now I feel perfectly reassured that my husband told me he'd had an excellent client meeting in your pub, but left to go somewhere else.'

I sensed there was something going on with Toby - something secretive that he didn't want to share with me. My nerves began to fire like needles, and nipped at my insides.

'Whatever's the matter?' Marianne's eyes searched mine.

My eyes watered and I reached into my pocket for a tissue. 'Everything. I'm sick with worry over Rose. Stevie's away eventing with her boyfriend and I should be there. Toby, he's obviously lying about something.' I blew my nose and pulled today's paper from my bag. I gestured to the headline. 'And if that wasn't enough, they're going to frack in our backyard.'

Marianne took the paper and held it at arms length. 'This is the first I've heard of it.'

'Me too. They've obviously hushed it up so they can get their plans in place without any local objections. Well, they can bloody well think again.'

'What will you do?' said Marianne.

'Apparently, Mr Vermaak at Hollow Grange is up in arms.'

Marianne's eyes lit up. 'Saul Vermaak?'

'You've met him?' I asked.

'Recently widowed. Two boys,' she said.

'Life's been tough for them too, then,' I said. 'I might call him. See if we can join forces.'

'You might have to fight your way through a throng of ladies,' she said.

'Oh?'

'He's cute.' Her brows lifted. 'I mean, super cute.'

'I can talk to a handsome man without blushing or wanting to tear his clothes off.'

'Don't fib,' she said. 'You always blush.' She fanned herself with the newspaper. 'Did you see the remake of, Far from the Madding Crowd?'

'No. Only the old one with Alan Bates.'

Marianne tapped her cigarette. 'Google Matthias Schoenaerts, the new Gabriel Oak. Mr Vermaak has that rugged outdoorsy look about him. But he's black.'

'You're funny.' I chuckled. 'Thanks for making me smile.'

'My pleasure.' She kissed me on the cheek and stood up to leave. 'Don't forget to call in for that drink.' And she placed the newspaper on my lap.

When I arrived home, I checked on Rose, who was smiling and chatting on the phone. Then I headed to the office. I googled Far from the Madding Crowd with Matthias Schoenaerts. Marianne was right. A real dish. If, of course, Mr Vermaak lived up to his sheep rearing doppelganger. I googled Saul Vermaak, an unusual enough name, which I found listed on LinkedIn, of which I too was a member. He was certainly handsome. With my curiosity sparked I sent him a connection request along with a short message about how we were neighbours, then I checked out his work history on his profile page. Agriculture, farming in South Africa and organic farming since 2010. Plenty of experience then, and no doubt, plenty of concern about contaminated water supplies. I searched his connections and found a Tara Vermaak. An attractive and professional looking brunette with an active account, although she hadn't posted in several months. I imagined paying Mr Vermaak a visit. I'd be businesslike and not mention his bereavement. My computer pinged. Saul Vermaak had already accepted my connection. Seconds later, a message arrived.

'Hi Anya. Good to meet you, virtual neighbour. Look forward to meeting you. Best, Saul.'

Should I wait to reply? No. I'd approached him and I saw he was still online.

'Hi Saul, Thank you. I realise you're busy, but would it be possible for me to drop over? There's something I need to discuss.' I hit send.

I googled, 'Fracking in North Yorkshire'. Nothing came up, only other districts that were going through public appeals. I retrieved the newspaper. A Nicola Marsden had written the article. I found the telephone number for Richmond News.

After being put on hold, a man eventually came on the line. 'Nicola's out of the office today.'

'Could I have her mobile number, please?'

'Afraid not. But I'll ask her to call you.'

'It's urgent. And I'm certain she'd want to speak to me.'

'What's it regarding?'

I hesitated. 'Fracking, locally. I'm opposed and I live close to a proposed site.'

71

He paused a moment. 'OK. Here's her number. Tell her Victor gave it to you so she'll know who to blame.'

'Thank you. I'm grateful.' I must have sounded genuine or desperate.

I hung up and dialled her number.

She picked up. 'Hello.'

'Is that Nicola Marsden?'

'Who is this?' Her tone sounded clipped.

'Sorry to bother you, but my name's Anya Kubik. I've read your fracking article in the Richmond News and I live a mile or so from where they carried out initial surveys. No one knew this was even in the planning stages.'

'I see. I'm in the area tomorrow to meet with Mr Vermaak,' she said. 'Do you know him?'

'Not yet,' I said. 'But I'd like to. I can meet you there?'

After we hung up, I checked to see if Saul had replied, but he hadn't.

'Mum.'

I turned around. 'Rosie, love.'

She weaved her wheelchair behind the sofa, smiling broadly. Dappled sunlight spilled through the window onto her skin and hair. She wore a crop top and tiny white shorts that showed off her gazelle like legs, even with her plaster cast.

'Guess what?' she said.

'Tell me, darling.'

She peered down at her toes and my gaze followed hers. I watched and waited until her big toe made the smallest of wriggles.

'Oh, Rosie!' I jumped up and hugged her. 'Do you feel your feet, your legs?' My voice heaved with emotion.

'They feel sort of tingly.'

'Which means your nerves are starting to repair. How wonderful. We must celebrate. I'll find out when Dad's coming home and in the meantime, we'll bake.' I clapped my hands with excitement.

Rose's face lit up and her eyes glistened. 'I didn't ever believe...'

I left the newspaper with headline prominently displayed on the kitchen worktop for Toby to notice when he came in. I wanted to mention the Atkinson's water survey he'd authorised, but I needed to watch his reaction first.

Over the next two hours, Rosie and I baked a three layered carrot cake. We filled and topped it with creamy butter icing. Once we'd plated the cake, we scraped off the leftover butter icing from the bowl.

I licked my spoon. 'How wonderfully indulgent.'

'It's a good job we don't bake too often.' Rose let out a contented sigh. 'I'm going to make marzipan carrots, too.'

'And a rabbit?'

'Of course,' she said.

'And I'll make us a cup of tea to take away the sweetness.'

That evening, after Toby, Rose and I sat down to prawn and vegetable stir fry followed by a large slice of carrot cake each, my mobile rang.

It was Stevie and she sounded excited. 'I need to speak to Rose. She isn't answering her phone.'

'All OK?' I said. 'How did you get on today?'

'Yeah, yeah. I'm thirty-third. Please, put Rose on, if she's there.'

'Hold on.' I handed the phone to Rose and listened in.

Toby glanced over at me, puzzled. I shrugged my shoulders.

Rose's face lit up. 'Are you serious?'

'Let me tell Mum and Dad and I'll call you back.' Rose began to laugh and cry at the same time. 'This is mad.'

'What is?' said Toby, when she'd hung up.

'All the time Stevie was riding the tracks, her feet were tingling. She's never experienced anything like it and she guessed what it meant.'

I was reminded of Stevie's bad dream and painful leg prior to Rose's return from the hospital.

'You two girls are so close,' I said, and I looked into Rose's wide grey eyes.

Toby sat down beside her and shook his head.

'She even said her toes started twitching and it tickled. It gave her a fit of the giggles. And when she told Jake, he said she should see a doctor.'

'Well, he won't now she knows it's sympathy pains.'

'Did she say anything else?' I asked.

'She was crying too much.' Rose grinned. 'You know, I was upset with Stevie about Jake. And I was jealous - riding her horse, seeing Jake, doing all the things she wanted. But this proves we're closer than I thought. For her to feel what I'm feeling and from so far away. She always acts like nothing bothers her. She's even annoying sometimes. But she isn't like that deep down.'

'Ever since you were tiny, you've shared a special bond,' I said. 'You can't ever break a connection like that.'

'True.' Toby looked at me, as though to confide. 'Do you remember when they'd tell us we weren't allowed to join in their games?'

'I do.' I smiled. 'You're lucky to have one another.'

I felt an enormous sense of relief. Rose was going to be well again. That was all that mattered.

Chapter 13

I watched as Toby spotted the newspaper headline and reached into his shirt pocket for his glasses. His fringe flopped over his face and I couldn't see his expression as he read. I pottered about, putting things away in drawers and wiping down the Range. But when he calmly folded the paper and placed it back down without saying anything, I felt exasperated and speechless.

He poured himself a glass of wine, sat back down at the table and put his feet up on a chair. I waited, expecting him to say something. As he sipped from his glass, he gave me a cursory glance but otherwise acted as though nothing at all were untoward.

I poured myself a drink and returned the bottle to the fridge.

'Anything in the newspaper?' I asked.

'Not really read it yet,' he replied, dismissively.

Inside, I fumed. I marched out of the kitchen. He can't have failed to notice the article or my irritation. In the living room, I turned on the Ipod and scrolled through to find something soothing. I selected Fur Elise and as I drank my wine and leaned back into the sofa, the lilting sounds softened the rifts that raked through my mind. Toby didn't come to find me, and I already suspected that guilt played a part. After I heard him go upstairs I went up to the spare bedroom. I was neither in the mood for a confrontation, or to pretend everything was fine. Maybe I should have talked to him about the fracking. Either way, I hoped my absence sent a clear message.

At breakfast the next morning, he asked, 'So, why the spare room?' He put his arm around my waist and squeezed lightly.

I wriggled from his grasp.

'I was annoyed, Toby.'

'Why?'

'Can we talk later, in private?'

'Course,' he replied, with a shrug.

'Anyway, why the suit - it's Saturday?'

'Ahh. A client meeting. Forgot to mention it.'

Rose wheeled herself in. She wore a pretty summer dress and whistled as she reached into the cupboard for a bowl.

'I'll get off.' Toby gave Rose a hug. 'Did you sleep well, sweetheart?'

She beamed up at him. 'I really did, Dad.'

'Excellent. Me, too,' Toby said, and winked at me.

Affection and cuddles one minute, a patronising wink the next. I realised there were times when I had no idea how Toby's mind worked or how he felt about me. He could be such a contradiction. I thought men were supposed to be the easier sex to read. But that had never been so with Toby. And regardless of the number of years we'd been together, the older he got the more complex he seemed to become. Despite his easygoing external demeanour, I knew he was selective about what he chose to reveal or conceal, which often left me feeling confused or wondering how to make things right again.

Or perhaps in this instance I was the one in the wrong.

Mid-morning I drove over to Hollow Grange to meet with Saul Vermaak and Nicola Marsden.

Weeks with barely any rainfall had left the track leading to the farm, earth dry, and when I glanced in the Edit mirror, I saw a cloud of dust that billowed up behind me.

I arrived deliberately early.

The yard in front of the house sloped down to the lawn just as I remembered it when I'd taken Stevie to a birthday party there several years previously. A post and rail fence had been newly erected around the front lawn. Sheep and goats grazed there and judging by the trampled flower beds, I gathered Saul Vermaak didn't plan on growing and selling organic flowers. I climbed the front steps, worn by centuries of footfall, and reached for the brass door bell. A Medusa, with a rope hanging down that twisted round and round. It seemed strange when the air felt so still.

From within, I heard someone shout. 'Dad. The door.'

'Answer it then,' came an impatient reply.

'You get it.'

A long silence followed and just when I thought I might turn around and wait in the car, I heard footsteps approach and the door finally opened.

I looked up. Saul appeared taller than I'd imagined. His brow furrowed in surprise.

I held out my hand. 'Anya Kubik. I'm a bit early. Sorry.'

He shook my hand, warmly. 'Anya! Of course.' He kept hold of my hand which felt unusual.

'I was expecting a Ms Marsden from the newspaper.'

'She's coming,' I said, and eased my hand back. 'I spoke to her after I'd seen the fracking article.'

'Come on in.' He smiled and stood aside.

His jawline was strong and he had wide set hazel eyes and a dimple in his chin. His arms were a deep conker brown beneath a slim fitting T-shirt.

'My apologies for not recognising you from your profile picture,' he said, and tilted his head.

'And you probably weren't expecting me,' I said. 'If you didn't read my last message.'

'Afraid I missed that.'

The sun emerged from behind the clouds and spilled through the door and onto the tiled floor. Saul closed the door behind us and the hall was pitched into near darkness.

Saul gestured for me to follow him. 'The living room's habitable.'

We walked along a stone-floored corridor with freshly painted white walls and tall curtainless windows. Tubs of tomato plants sat on each windowsill, each laden with ripened tomatoes. I felt tempted to pluck one as I passed, but instead, I inhaled their scent.

Saul turned to me. 'I do the same each time I walk through.'

'Invites a whole new meaning to vine ripened,' I said.

'Let me pick you a few before you leave,' he said.

'That would be lovely,' I said. 'I grow roses and a few herbs but that's about it.'

We walked into a vast, high-ceilinged room at the end of the house, which in contrast to the entrance hall was bright with sunlight from tall windows that reached to the ceiling. I noticed large framed photographs propped against the wall and I paused to look out at an orchard. There were some drawings and charts piled on the windowsill, and a map lay open. Beside it was an aerial photograph of a farmhouse with gardens and fenced paddocks. I assumed it must be their previous home. What an upheaval it must have been for them to leave Africa and move their belongings all the way to England.

Saul joined me and looked outside. 'We have Gala, Discovery and Cox's apples, Greengage and Victoria plums, Damsons and Comice pears,' he said.

'How lovely to have such a variety.' I touched the photo frame. 'And is this your previous home?'

'It is. In some ways I was sorry to leave it.'

'But your new home is as beautiful,' I said.

'Yes, it really is,' he replied.

A corner leather sofa and matching armchairs furnished the living room. Seagrass rugs covered the floorboards, flanked by two bookshelves - half-filled.

'Whereabouts in South Africa were you?'

'Cape Town.'

'Quite a move,' I said. 'And I imagine, a big change.'

'We needed a change. There are droughts and water shortages in South Africa due to changes in the climate and made worse by how the water supplies are managed. And organic farming works in the UK.' He paused. 'At least I was hoping so.'

'I hear you're concerned about the fracking,' I said. 'Polly in the grocery store mentioned it.'

Saul nodded. 'Not only am I concerned, I'm fuming. Our sellers made no mention of it. Nor any of the locals when I spoke to them.'

'No one knew until this article broke. And I hear all the gossip.'

His brows wrinkled. 'It's hard to believe no one knew anything.'

'It's obviously been covered up,' I said, then added. 'By a few players.'

His eyes darkened. 'I want to know the names of these players.'

'I'm as shocked as you are.'

His expression softened. 'Of course. My apologies. Now tell me, do you prefer tea or coffee?'

'Tea would be lovely.' The sofa sighed as I sat down and the leather felt cool against the backs of my legs. A shiver ran through me. There was something about Saul that put me on edge. He had an intensity about him. Serious one minute and then it was as if he remembered he should be courteous the next. He had a presence about him, that was bold and self-assured and I wondered if he was aware of it. In short, there was nothing small about Saul Vermaak.

When he returned with a tray he glanced round for somewhere to put it. He set the tray on the floor in front of me. 'I don't have any biscuits. The gannets have guzzled them.'

'But you have strawberries,' I said, looking into the brimming china bowl. 'And the gannets are two boys, I hear?'

'Two hungry boys.' He paused. 'And did you know I was widowed?'

'I'm afraid so. Like I say, most things worth knowing round here soon become common knowledge.'

Saul's expression grew serious. 'As I thought. Often the case in rural communities,' he said and held out the bowl of fruit.

I picked a strawberry and bit into it. It was sweeter and juicier than from any supermarket.

'Do people know how my wife died?' he asked.

I felt I'd crossed an invisible line. 'I didn't come here to pry.'

A silence fell between us and I picked up my cup of tea and took a sip.

Saul sat on the armchair. 'You're our first real visitor,' he said and then turned to look out of the window.

'I'm sorry if I sounded intrusive,' I said.

He leaned back into the chair and stretched out his legs. 'Do you have children?'

'Two girls. Stevie, eighteen and Rose, sixteen.' I rubbed my finger and realised I'd forgotten to put on my wedding ring. 'And I'm married to, Toby. You'd like him.'

Saul raised an eyebrow. 'I'm sure we'll meet, some day.'

A knock at the front door echoed from the hallway. Saul glanced at me before he set down his cup and left the room.

A woman's voice rang through and she entered the room like a bird in the breeze. Saul followed her in. Her face was lit up and she carried a notebook and pen. Her red leather handbag swung on the crook of her arm.

79

She quickly spotted the bowl of strawberries. 'Oh, how lovely. You must have known they're my favourite. Did I tell you when we spoke?' she asked Saul, her face perfectly serious.

Saul looked confused.

Her face broke into a broad smile and she laughed. 'Of course I didn't.'

Saul didn't smile.

She held out her hand to me. 'Anya.' She tilted her head. 'I recognise you from somewhere.'

Nicola looked unfamiliar to me. 'I often shop in Richmond.' I offered.

'You've a distinctive face.' Her expression remained curious.

'Do you ride?' I said.

'A bike?' she asked.

'Horses. I manage the livery yard at Willows End.'

She shuddered. 'Not at all. I'm allergic. Horses... and certain people.'

I liked her humour and I laughed.

Saul picked up his cup of tea and sat down next to me on the sofa.

'Let's talk,' said Nicola as she settled beside Saul with her bag at her feet. 'Is that my cuppa?'

Saul picked it up and passed it to her.

'I don't generally take milk,' she peered into the cup, 'but this looks good and strong. Builder's tea.'

'I know how important tea is here,' said Saul. 'So I've been practising. In fact, I'm beginning to prefer it to coffee.'

'How thoughtful.' Nicola gave Saul a flirty smile and crossed her legs in an exaggerated fashion.

Her manner lacked subtlety but she was refreshing.

'I have half an hour, max,' she said. 'Can you believe, I must photograph a rare breed cow that's about to give birth? Apparently, she's having triplets and is the size of a whale. She may need a C-Section. No such thing as natural labour nowadays. Women, cows - we're all on a production line.' She clicked her pen. 'Righto. Let's share what we know.'

Saul nodded his approval and I noticed Nicola shuffle a little closer to him.

She wasn't as I'd imagined. Everything about her seemed curved; the roundness of her shoulders, her cheekbones, her owl-like eyes and enormous bosom, long, dark curls, and she wore a cream fitted shirt that accentuated her incredible figure.

'Earlier this week I received an anonymous tip off from a woman who said she'd heard Quadrillum had obtained a license to drill for shale gas in locations across Wensleydale,' said Nicola. 'Apparently, surveyors had done all the necessary preliminary investigations. Some landowners must have known, but I imagine it was hushed up to avoid resistance. Backhanders, I've no doubt.'

Had Toby known about this, I wondered again?

'Thanks, Nicola.' Saul looked from Nicola to me. 'Here are my initial thoughts. I propose a local, and national online petition through social media and we'll link up with other fracking protest groups on their social networks. We'll hold demonstrations in public places and protest at the proposed sites. We'll call a community meeting asap. We'll lobby politicians near and far and invite any councillors that we can be sure are opposed to fracking to come to the meeting.'

'Brilliant,' I said. 'I should have taken notes.' I felt a spark of adrenaline. 'We'll need people. I'll invite masses of people. Everyone will be up in arms so I'm certain we'll get support.'

'I believe we'll make a good team,' said Nicola. 'I'll dig and scrape to get a list of those involved.'

My stomach churned. I suspected Toby may be connected in some way, and hoped Nicola could unearth some clues, whilst I'd discover what I could.

'Can you think of anyone who might have a vested interest in this?' Nicola looked from Saul to me in turn.

'I don't know many people here yet.' Saul turned to me.

'I know most of the farmers and landowners,' I said. 'And if money is involved I can think of a few who are either blinkered or struggling enough to be a party to this.'

'Write down any names and addresses. Any at all,' Nicola urged.

Then I thought, what if I suggested names and I was wrong or they found out I'd implicated them? I had a hunch that Toby's involvement may have been down to naivety rather than collusion. At least, I hoped that to be so.

'I wouldn't feel comfortable giving out names of possible suspects without at least some evidence,' I said. 'Better if we find out what we can first. I imagine you could persuade the councillors to supply names.'

'I'll try.' In a theatrical gesture she placed two fingers on her temple. 'My powers of deduction and intuition lie somewhere on the scale between Sherlock and Superman.'

I didn't doubt her for a second.

'Nicola's quite a force,' Saul said, after he'd shown her out.

'Which is precisely what we need,' I said.

'I'd better get off too,' I said. 'I'm sure you've masses to do.' I picked up my handbag and hooked it over my shoulder. 'Are you breeding livestock or mostly growing crops?'

'Both. If you've time I'd like to show you around. I'm interested to know what you think,' he said. 'As you know Wensleydale so well.'

'If you've got horses I'll have an opinion.'

'No horses, but I won't keep you long. And you'll be doing me a favour.' The corners of his mouth turned up, and I needed no further persuasion.

'Then I'd like that very much.'

We walked through to the kitchen which felt comfortably cool, despite the heat of the day. A couple of the old units had been painted duck egg blue. On the walls, I noticed discoloured patches where old pictures had been taken down and a large gilt-framed mirror, with scratched bevelled surface.

'What a beautiful colour,' I said, with a nod to the painted units.

'My youngest's idea. He's artistic so I suggested the kitchen could be his summer project. We'll see if he can see it through.'

A china vase of tall daisies stood at the centre of the kitchen table, a pretty addition for a house of men. As we headed outside into the courtyard where buttercups and poppies sprouted between the stone slabs, the sun burned down, hot and high and with no hint of a breeze to offer relief. A black cat sat on the edge of a stone water tank and as its tail twitched back and forth its eyes followed us. On either side of the path there were two raised beds - one full with rhubarb and strawberries and the other with gooseberry bushes.

I put on my sunglasses.

'How old are your boys?'

'Dom's sixteen. Starting Richmond High in September, and Alex is nineteen and my business partner. He's done two years at agricultural college, so technically he's better qualified than me. He's a planner, too, like his mum, was. He's written a challenging annual plan with financial projections.'

'Important to have objectives,' I said. 'Especially in farming. I know the hurdles farmers face.'

'I have my faults, but head in the clouds isn't one of them. I'm a staunch realist. What's thrown me is that fracking hadn't entered my head.'

'Mine neither. Wensleydale is renowned for its natural beauty. I thought we were safe. How naive.'

Saul paused and turned to me. 'I'm grateful for the support. When I read the article I wondered how locals would react. Whether they might be apathetic.'

'No, Saul. People will be furious. Angry enough to stand up and protest.'

'I hope you're right. Numbers count.'

'What about Dom?' I said. 'Does he know what he wants to do?'

'He's not sure yet...' Saul's words trailed off.

'Are you, or was his mum creative?' I asked.

'Tara was a psychiatrist. She helped people.'

We continued on through an archway in the wall to a lawn that swept down to a lake where patches of lily pads bloomed with pink and white flowers. Beyond the lake lay deciduous woodland and further still, Great Shunner Fell, its peak softly golden in the sunlight. It was a breathtaking view.

'Tara sounds like she was a good person.'

'And still would be if it hadn't been for one of her clients knifing her.'

I spun round to face him.

Saul's brows drew together. 'The bastard's paying for it now.'

'That's terrible, Saul. I'm so sorry.'

83

'Tara warned me he was dangerous,' he said. 'If I'd known how dangerous I'd have got to him first.'

I knew well how grief could twist the soundest of minds. Grief as a result of murder had to be one of the hardest causes to come to terms with.

'I'm sorry,' he said. 'I shouldn't be burdening you with all this.'

'When bad things happen, we should talk,' I replied. 'If we don't our emotions can fester.'

Saul gazed down to the lake - his back rigid. 'I've barely spoken to anyone. And not about how angry I feel.'

'I realise you barely know me, but I am a good listener.'

He turned to me. 'I can see that.' He gave a heavy sigh. 'I don't like to upset the boys, so I keep it to myself.'

'You might find they want to talk about her,' I suggested.

'You're probably right. I think it's me - I don't know where to start,' he said.

'I... we lost someone. My brother-in-law, Euan. He drowned in the river on our farm. Gemma, his wife and I have shared many tears.'

'You were close to him then?'

'We all lived together on the farm. We were a close knit family. We still are.'

As we strolled along the edge of the lake Saul described his plans for the farm - where and how he wanted to sell his produce, his plans for a farm shop to sell seasonal fruits and vegetables and how he wanted to set up a home delivery service in the area.

'The supermarket in Richmond say they'll try my produce. If they offer a contract it'll be a steady income. Plus there's the twice weekly market. Popular, so I hear.'

We skirted around a flock of Canada geese. Some rested at the water's edge and others paddled in the shallows. The young birds pecked the grass or nestled against their mothers. I watched two fly down in tandem and with a great whoosh of wings and splashes as they landed.

'Our Canada Geese stay by the river, thankfully,' I said.

'I knew they were here but I'll keep an eye on numbers. They're beautiful, but if they interfere with the crops or chickens I'll have a rethink.'

'My guess is you'll barely notice them, in time,' I said.

An hour later as I drove home over Orben moor, the sun dazzled my eyes and the bracken and gorse shimmered in luminous shades of green and yellow. The heather, bright and abloom, spread its lilac blanket like a protector of the earth beneath. And as I reflected on the morning, my mind buzzed with ideas. At least we had a plan. As I continued down the hill into Riseham, I shivered as I pondered Toby's involvement and contemplated the potential ramifications. If I sounded him out about the health risks and environment factors, surely he'd be anti-fracking. How might he react when I questioned him about my concerns, and why, when I thought of doing so, did my insides twist and churn?

Chapter 14

The air felt close and the bedsheets warm despite the open windows, and ribbons of moonlight flitted between the blinds. After drifting restlessly in and out of a twilight sleep for hours and glancing at the clock every so often, I gave up trying and lay still with my eyes closed, but my thoughts churning over and over. When the dawn chorus sounded I slipped out of bed. I zipped up my jeans and buttoned up yesterday's blouse. Toby muttered a few words then turned onto his side.

Downstairs, I plucked a pear from the fruit bowl and with Freda eager at my heels, I headed out to the stables to groom Pepper, who was in desperate need of some exercise. The grass sparkled with dew and down by the river the mist swirled beneath the willows and drifted like a silk scarf in the breeze.

Across the yard, some of the horses looked over their stable doors when they heard me approach. Pepper whinnied his greeting.

I reached into my pocket for a carrot stick and held out my hand. 'Good morning, my beauty.'

He leaned out and with a gentle turn of the head he lapped the carrot from my palm and crunched as I stroked his velvet muzzle.

I unbolted the door. 'Stay here, Freda.'

We'd lost our previous dog, another Jack Russell, to a carelessly placed hoof in a stable, and since then I'd insisted no dogs in the stalls. When we were out riding, Freda nimbly kept a safe distance.

In the tackroom I pulled Pepper's saddle from the rack and heard familiar footsteps on the cobbles.

Gemma appeared in the doorway. 'You're up early.'

'I couldn't sleep,' I said. 'Besides, why waste a beautiful morning?'

'My thoughts exactly,' she said. 'Where are you riding to?'

'I haven't decided.'

'I'll come if you can wait.'

'No rush,' I said. 'Stevie and I made some jumps in the woods the other day. We could do those?'

'Sounds good,' she replied.

After I'd saddled Pepper and picked the dirt from his hooves I led him round to the front of the house. Toby came through the front door.

I waved and called over. 'You're early.'

He didn't wave back or smile. 'Says she.'

'What time will you be in tonight?'

'Got an evening meeting. So I'll be late.' He climbed into his new Maserati and slammed the door shut.

My heartbeat shuddered. Maybe I'd kept him awake with my restlessness. His moodiness made me feel anxious as well as annoyed - tiptoeing around him wasn't something I was either used to or enjoyed.

Gemma and I trotted the horses up the stony track and as their hooves click-clacked on the flintstones, Pepper tugged at his reins, desperate to pick up speed. Despite Ebony's size and strength, he'd always been an easy ride and unused to Pepper's energy, my arms and legs quickly grew tired. Part thoroughbred and part Arabian, Pepper was tall and fine-boned but with a fiery spirit and speed that made him an exhilarating ride. Before the accident, Rose had picked out a bitless bridle for him, in the belief it would discourage him from fighting for control. I hadn't resisted her choice, though I had insisted I watch her ride him in the paddock before she went out on a hack. Her theory had appeared to work. So, where was I going wrong?

I relaxed the reins, but he only saw this as his signal to break into a canter. 'Steady!' I pulled him in hard as we approached the five bar gate at an alarming speed. He skidded to a halt and I steadied him and leaned over to reach for the latch. Pepper pranced and Freda sprang out of the way.

'Why didn't you use the snaffle bit?' said Gemma. 'He's the wrong horse for a bitless bridle. Too young and flighty.'

'I realise that now,' I said, as Pepper snorted and spun round in another circle. 'I wonder if it caused Rose's accident. I shouldn't have allowed her to swap bits.'

'Pepper looked under control with Rose, but he was being ridden every day,' she said. 'Here, let me.'

Gemma edged Maya, her appaloosa mare, alongside the gate, undid the catch and we rode through into the meadow.

'I used the snaffle bridle last time I rode him and he seemed easier.'

'Do you want to go back and swap?' asked Gemma.

'It's OK, I'm sure he'll calm down once we get going.'

We rode on and I inhaled deeply. 'I never tire of the scent up here.'

'It's the corncockles and harebells,' said Gemma.

'And the grasses,' I added, as a cloud of butterflies, disturbed by our appearance, lifted in front of me.

Gemma took her feet out of the stirrups and stretched her long legs. She loosened Maya's reins, who took the opportunity to snatch a mouthful of grass and buttercups as she moved.

'I'm so relieved Rose's feeling is returning,' said Gemma.

'I can finally breathe,' I said. 'And Rose's whole mood has lifted. Only now I can see she was slipping into depression. Understandably so.' I pulled on the reins and Pepper threw his head up in defiance. 'I've organised for her physio to come daily to speed her recovery along.'

'Good move. Keep up the momentum.' Gemma patted Maya's neck. 'So, what's keeping you awake?'

I hesitated for a moment. Too many things buzzing around in my head.

'If it's not Rose, it's the fracking.'

'Surely, it can't be allowed,' said Gemma. 'Not here. Everyone I've spoken to is going mental over it.'

'I know, but there's a difference between feeling annoyed about it and doing something proactive.'

'They'll come to the meeting though,' said Gemma.

'I hope so. But apathy could settle. People will shout loud enough, but will their voices transfer to action?'

'It's not like you to be negative,' she said.

'Maybe I've got my reasons,' I replied.

'What does Toby think?'

'We haven't discussed it properly yet,' I said, unsure whether to share my suspicions.

'Why?'

'He's barely been in. Out early, home late.'

'Surely you talk in bed or when you're alone?'

I hesitated. 'The past few weeks he's been up and down and moody. It's worry about Rose. He's tired and busy too.'

'Do you reckon?'

There was something in her doubt and her tone that deepened my concern.

'Rose's accident has been an ordeal. For all of us. But we do need to talk.'

'Surely Toby supports the campaign?' she said.

'Honestly, I don't know. I'll pick my moment.'

'You have to pick your moments with him?' She asked, incredulous.

'He's stressed, that's all.'

My inner voice nagged me once more to stop being a coward and to broach the matter, even if it did cause conflict.

'Come on, Anya. This is Toby we're talking about.'

'I will. Tonight.'

As we reached the path into the woods a bird of prey called, sharp and shrill.

I turned to Gemma, 'The Red Kites.'

We gazed skywards and two circled the air high above us - great winged shadows against the blue sky.

'Haunting and so beautiful,' Gemma replied, as the bird called out once again.

'The jumps are in a figure-of-eight. I did them fine on Pepper so they'll be a breeze for Maya,' I said. 'If you follow me we won't collide at the centre.' I gave a slight laugh.

Pepper knew what was coming and pranced with excitement. 'I'd better go first,' I said, and sat deep in the saddle.

The second I eased my hold on the reins, Pepper snorted and broke into a brisk canter with his ears pricked forward. He adjusted his pace at the first jump, a two foot high stack of branches, and leaped clean.

'Good boy!'

Rose had been right about one thing; Pepper had huge eventing potential. As we approached the second jump, I checked his speed and with a giant leap that almost unseated me, we made it over and then onto the first bend in the track. I reined him in to an extended trot and then relaxed again as we approached the third; a branch propped between trees on either side and filled in with sticks and bracken. I pushed forward and he timed his jump to perfection. But, as we landed his front legs buckled. The following seconds became a blur as I was shunted forward, then flew over Pepper's neck and landed smack in the undergrowth. The air filled with a horrendous squeal and I scrambled back up to see Pepper lying on his side. He thrashed his legs and his eyes, wide like black orbs, looked full of pain and fear.

Within moments he became unnervingly still, save for his breaths which seemed unnaturally laboured.

Gemma leapt off Maya and hurried around the jump. She knelt at Pepper's head and stroked his ears.

She glanced up at me. 'Are you hurt?'

I shook my head and pulled at a bramble stem tangled in my hair.

I crouched beside Pepper and placed my hand on his cheek. 'What have I done to you, boy?' His nostrils flared blood red as he gasped for breath.

I stood up and cast my eyes over his form, then I squatted and with caution moved my hand down his nearside foreleg. I turned to Gemma and my eyes told her all we needed to know.

'No, Anya!'

Suddenly, Pepper screamed out in pain and his legs flailed. We scrambled backwards.

'Do you have your phone?' Gemma's voice shook.

I reached into my pocket. 'Damn it!' The screen had shattered. I pressed the power button, but it remained lifeless. I cast it aside.

'I'll go back,' she said, then paused. 'Are the bullets still in the safe?'

I nodded - too choked to speak. Could we be about to euthanize Pepper? We'd never had to do that to an animal here, not even to any of our dogs or cats. I felt physically sick. And if I felt this way, how would Rose feel? Worst of all, I could have avoided the accident altogether. Reckless of me to be jumping a young novice that wasn't even my own horse.

'Ring Toby. But please don't tell Rose.' My voice trembled and I reached out and held Gemma.

I drew away again. 'Go. Be quick.'

Gemma jumped onto Maya and for a brief moment she held my gaze. Then she swung Maya round and in seconds they'd disappeared from sight.

I crouched beside Pepper who lay still once more and I stroked his neck which was slick with sweat. His breathing had slowed, but seemed unnaturally forced and his mouth frothed.

He grunted and I rested my cheek upon his. I felt the rise and fall of each breath.

I'd seen a horse be euthanized after a fall at a cross country event. The memory of it returned - the speed at which the vet had arrived on the scene, the devastation on the rider's face, and the tears of onlookers, myself included. Such a needless waste of a beautiful creature because humans chose to take risks with them. A risk I'd taken with Pepper.

Pepper's wild eyes seemed to plead for an explanation and I heard the sound of gurgling from his abdomen. He hadn't only broken his leg. I pressed my ear against his side and the sounds suggested he was bleeding internally. But I could do nothing to ease his pain and I felt his life flow weaken fast. I knew his final breath approached and the futility of trying to prevent it.

I wrapped my arms around his neck and spoke softly. 'You are a noble and brave horse, Pepper.' I choked on my tears. 'Rose will miss you so much.'

A bitter cocktail of anxiety and guilt welled up within me. An effective bridle could have saved him. I'd have had proper control. This was my doing.

Pepper lay still and I placed my palm on his muzzle. No further movement came from his abdomen and no breath of air upon my hand. I heard only the creak and rustle of the trees, as though they watched over us.

I buried my face in his mane and wept as I felt his blood cease to flow. How could I tell Rose after all that she'd been through?

I don't know how long I lay there beside Pepper, but some time later I felt the earth murmur beneath me and I listened to the thunder of hooves as Gemma returned on Maya. I stood up and watched her through the trees as she galloped up the hill and alongside the edge of the woods. But then I spotted something else. Something I'd previously missed, only a few feet away. A wooden stake, freshly snapped, that jutted up from the ground at an angle, and right in the middle of the track. Pepper landed there, so I had no doubt that it had caused him to fall so violently.

I gripped the wooden stake and it came away in my hand. Freshly cut, it looked precisely the sort used on building sites. The sort that Toby also owned and used. It could only have been placed there since Tuesday or we'd have spotted it as we'd built the jumps and ridden round.

When Gemma reined in Maya they both breathed hard. Gemma's eyes and cheeks had stained with tears and dust.

'He's gone,' I said. 'He ruptured something, too. I heard fluid.'

She jumped down, placed the rifle on the ground and held me close. Then she hunched down and ran her fingers tenderly through Pepper's forelock. 'I'm not sure I could have pulled the trigger.'

I held up the broken stake. 'This is what killed him.'

She took the stick from me. 'What the hell is this doing here?'

'I've a damn good idea,' I said. 'And what's more, I know the bastard responsible.'

Chapter 15

'I'll take care of Pepper. You look after Rose,' said Gemma.

We stood together in front of the house and I felt another wave of horror at what I had to do. What Rose had to hear.

'I love you,' I said.

Gemma hugged me once more, and with an ache in my heart, I walked to the front door.

Outside of Rose's bedroom door I stopped and I tried to frame my words. There was nothing I could say that could soften the shock but I must remain calm and sensitive to her reaction. As I turned the door handle, my palms felt damp and my head throbbed. When I entered, Rose was sitting in her wheelchair beside the bed.

Her eyes searched mine. 'I've been ringing you, over and over,' she said.

I sat on the edge of her bed. 'I'm sorry. My phone's broken.'

'I've been worried,' she said.

I took her hand and waited for her to continue.

'I heard a horrible scream.'

'Oh, baby,' I said and my voice cracked. 'You heard?'

Her eyes filled with tears. 'It was Pepper. Wasn't it?'

I nodded once.

Her face crumpled and tears spilled down her cheeks.

In between her questions and her cries I explained as simply and as sensitively as I could to try and minimise her pain and sadness. But I hesitated and stumbled over my words and all the while I loathed myself for knowing that I was partly the cause.

It felt heart-rending to look upon Rose's grief, and despite my efforts to comfort her, I had to sit back and allow her to cry and try to come to terms with it. At this stage, reassurance would have been a lie. When after some time, her tears subsided I helped her back into bed and she curled up beneath the covers, emotionally spent.

My head and body ached, and despite the hour, I poured myself a shot of whisky and sat on the bench at the front of the house to await Toby's return.

When I rang him it went straight to voicemail. A minute later I received a text.

'Got Gemma's and your message. So sorry. Back soon.'

He was obviously too busy to even call me. Furious tears stung my eyes.

I returned to the kitchen and poured another small whisky. The alcohol acted as a crutch but I needed it. When I popped my head round Rose's door I saw her wrapped beneath the covers and silent. Softly, I closed the door.

I ran through recent events in my mind. Our luck couldn't get worse. Rose's accident, the fracking and now Pepper. One of these would be more than enough to handle. And on top of it all the anniversary of Euan's death loomed in a few days, which was always painful. How would it be this year? Would it churn up everyone's emotions again? We'd always tried to make it into a celebration of his life. To remember him, his love and generous nature. But, inevitably, despite our best intentions, we ended up regurgitating the whole terrible event; conducting our very own post-mortem analysis.

Then there was Toby's mood swings which had become more frequent. He was undoubtedly less predictable than he'd ever been.

The last time I'd attempted to discuss the fracking with him, he'd been dismissive. 'You're worrying about something that will never happen.' As though that automatically solved the problem.

And when I'd persisted he'd stormed into the bathroom. 'We've finished this conversation,' he said and slammed the door.

In his mind, case closed. His reaction concerned me. Was he simply too stressed to be able to cope with the fracking too? Nevertheless, I was no longer prepared to avoid the subject for the sake of not rousing his anger.

I'd always known that Toby reflected on things, but that he preferred to resolve conflicts in his mind and in his own time, as opposed to open them up for discussion. In many respects this suited me well, as he didn't bother me with trivial problems. And in some ways I was the same. I'd inherited this from Mum, who had not been typical of most mothers from what I could gather. She'd never been the sort of parent who asked me how I felt about things or how my day had gone. She'd been distant and uninterested in many ways, compared to some of my friends' mothers. But this hadn't mattered because Dad had always stepped in when I'd needed to talk. Even with boy stuff.

From as early as when Rose could speak, I'd seen the same trait in her. Quite different to Stevie, who tended to speak, and then think.

That being said, there was a difference between considering one's words before speaking and not saying anything at all. How could I get through to Toby, so we could talk freely and attempt to resolve our issues?

I swallowed the last drop of whisky and placed the tumbler at my feet. The minutes crawled by as guilt continued to churn through my insides.

The clattering sounds of people and horses echoed from the yard and I wondered if Gemma had shared the news yet. I assumed so. Pepper's death would unsettle and upset everyone.

I couldn't face talking to them about it or admitting that I was the one riding him. Gemma – always the strong one – offered to do it instead. I admired her strength and resilience and knew she'd also do so sensitively.

There were many times I wished I could be more like her.

At last, I watched as Toby's car pulled in from the lane and proceed slowly up the drive. When he turned off the engine it seemed he hadn't noticed me and instead he looked at his phone for a minute before he opened the car door.

'Important message?' My words came out laced with sarcasm.

'As a matter of fact, yes.' He didn't elaborate but reached into the back of the car for his briefcase and jacket.

He hung his jacket over a chair and sat next to me. 'Needed a drink, I see.'

I felt close to tears again, but my anger prevented me from succumbing. 'What do you think?'

'Come here.' He held me close but briefly. He drew back and his eyes searched mine. 'Were you hurt?'

'Poor Pepper took the brunt of it,' I said with a sharpness I knew he'd notice.

He stroked my hair. 'Poor you. It must have been horrific.'

'I'm fine.'

'I can see you're not fine,' he said. 'How has Rose taken it?'

'She heard Pepper scream. All the way from the woods.'

His brows rose in surprise. 'How?'

I nodded. 'When she told me, I was freaked out too.'

'So she already knew?'

'Not that he'd died, but she knew something bad had happened.'

Toby looked thoughtful for a few moments. 'I've heard teens can hear high pitched sounds.'

'His screams must have travelled in the wind. Poor Rosie, sitting in her room wondering what had happened. Frightened and alone. This is the last thing she needs.'

'Where is she?' he asked.

'She wanted to be alone. She's resting.'

'I'll go talk to her.'

'We need to talk first,' I said.

'Oh?'

'About what caused his fall.'

'You said he fell at a jump?'

'I said we'd been over a jump. He'd already cleared it.'

'What then?'

'He landed on a wooden stake in the path.' I watched Toby's face closely. 'A surveyor's stake.'

Toby rubbed his stubble, thoughtful.

'And,' I continued. 'It wasn't there when Stevie and I built the jumps the other day.'

His brows knitted. 'Have you told Rose?'

'Not yet. I didn't want to start laying the blame anywhere. She's had enough to take in.'

His eyes fixed on mine. 'You know I didn't put it there.'

And my resolve strengthened. 'Please, Toby. Let's not skirt round this.'

96

'I didn't know they'd stick it in front of a jump where my daughter's horse would fall and break a leg.'

My tone accused. 'Who did put it there?'

Toby's mouth twitched before he replied. 'You know I authorised Atkinsons to conduct a ground survey. I've had two emails since. The first illustrated their findings and the second said they may want to revisit to complete their work. When I replied I said they must let me know if and when they wanted to return.'

'Can you forward those emails to me? When we first discussed this I asked if you'd include me in any correspondence.'

'I forgot.' He shrugged. 'You know how busy I am.'

Inside, I raged. I swung round to walk away but as I did I kicked my glass. It shattered upon the gravel.

'You did not forget. You didn't want me interfering.'

'Stop overreacting,' he said.

'Rose's horse is dead,' I said. 'If you'd kept me informed, as you promised you would, I'd have made sure they came nowhere near our land.'

'I didn't know they were coming back for definite,' he said.

'Send me the emails, Toby.'

'It'll be easier on the laptop.'

I knew he was stalling. 'Now, Toby. We need to sort this out. Atkinsons are liable for Pepper's death.'

'We need to support Rose first.'

'We need to do both,' I replied and lowered my voice, despite my frustration.

'Fine,' he said, with impatience. 'After I've seen Rose, I'll find them.'

As Toby stepped off the decking he stumbled and fell. 'Jesus Christ!'

I moved to help him.

He got up and brushed his knees. 'Fucking ruined.'

I looked down at the tear in his trousers. 'I'd say it's preferable to a broken leg. Wouldn't you?'

I picked up his briefcase and jacket. Without a nod or a thank you he took them from me, turned and walked into the house. I heard Freda bark her welcome. A moment later she whimpered and I jogged up the front steps. Toby was already halfway up the stairs and Freda skulked in the corner with her tail drawn between her legs.

'Freda.' She trotted over, but still cowered. I picked her up and rubbed her ears and carried her into the kitchen for a treat.

'Let's go check on Rose.'

Rose was sitting up in bed.

'Freda!' Rose reached out her arms. 'Oh, let me cuddle her.'

'Watch her on your leg,' I said, and placed Freda in her arms.

Freda licked Rose's face, grateful for the love and attention.

'Was that Dad home?' she asked, and rocked Freda like a baby.

'He's coming in to see you.'

Freda curled up on Rose's lap as she continued to stroke her.

'Mummy?'

I sat on the edge of her bed. 'Yes.'

Her lips trembled. 'Did Pepper continue screaming?'

'No, my darling. He lay still.'

'Did he land awkwardly?'

I took her hand. 'I'm afraid so.'

'Pepper's so sure footed over jumps.'

'Yes, well…'

'It must have been the hard ground,' Toby said, as he walked in and stepped round to the other side of her bed. 'We've had no rain for weeks and it's probably unwise to jump where the ground is like concrete,' he continued.

I stood up. 'Pardon?' I was aghast at his blatant lies that implied I was responsible.

Toby glowered at me. 'Shall we talk after I've seen how Rose is?'

I kissed Rose on the crown and avoided Toby's eye. 'I'll be in the kitchen.'

He focused his attention on Rose.

I felt lightheaded as I strode out. Furious with Toby's snitchy comments I slammed the kitchen door behind me and leaned against it. I took some slow breaths. The last thing Rose needed right now was to hear me arguing with her Dad.

She needed to eat properly too, and her appetite had never been brilliant. I went to the fridge. Warm falafels, waldorf salad and buttered crusty bread might tempt her. She generally refused any meat dishes, and the more she spoke about the way animals were reared and slaughtered, the more I veered towards a vegetarian diet.

Rose made a persuasive argument, I thought as I cut into the loaf.

The last time she'd broached the subject in Toby's company, he'd snickered. 'But a farmer's daughter can't become a vegetarian. It's not in your genes.'

'Technically, Dad, you're not a farmer. And, this isn't a farm, it's a livery yard where people care for their horses, not cut them into steaks and grill them on the barbecue.'

'Mmmm.' Toby thought for a moment. 'Most horse owners aren't vegetarians and your Mum and I are busy enough without having to prepare separate meals.'

'Dad,' she'd said with a smile. 'I'm almost sixteen. I can make my own food.'

I heard footsteps in the hall and Toby walked in.

'She'll be OK,' he said, with a nod of reassurance. 'I've offered to buy her a young horse when she's back on her feet again.'

'Pardon?' I said.

'I said…'

'Jesus, Toby.' I stabbed the knife into the bread. 'I've never told you this but it's way overdue. You're a tactless and insensitive bastard sometimes.'

He regarded me with mouth agape.

'Your daughter's horse has died because of something you agreed to, and your magic solution, on the exact same day, is to replace him, like a broken bike. I'm speechless.'

'Hardly speechless.' Toby snorted. 'And I was only trying to soften the blow of losing Pepper.'

'What was her response to your generous gesture?'

He squinted as he worked up a suitable answer. 'She said she'd think about it...'

'Really? It's a good job I wasn't there.'

'Too right,' he said. 'Your bizarre behaviour will upset her more. You're being weird. And she can probably hear you.'

Suddenly worn out and unsure, I wiped my hands on the tea towel. 'That's unfair,' I said, quietly. 'I watched Pepper die through no fault of his own, or mine, for that matter. And only weeks after our little girl almost died in an accident where you were driving.'

Toby looked back at me but didn't retaliate.

'I can't even look at you…' I turned away and sliced into the loaf.

'Anya…' He paused.

'Forward those emails, Toby,' I said.

'Don't you trust me still? After all we've been through.'

I spun around. 'How can I? Pepper's dead because you haven't communicated with me. You said you'd include me in any communications. But conveniently, you forgot.'

'I've told you, I'll bloody send them.'

'When I've read those emails we'll talk.' This was one argument I'd save until then.

Chapter 16

Days later Toby still hadn't forwarded the Atkinson emails.

'I must have deleted them. My laptop was running out of space.'

'Why should I believe you?' I said.

'Because I'm your husband. Because we've been together twenty years. Because you know me and love me.'

'Sometimes you make it hard for me to trust you, Toby.'

He protested too much and my will to argue it out, grew thin. My offer to go through his emails had been met with resistance and I began to mistrust anything that he said.

'If you don't trust me. What can I do?' He sniffed and turned away.

Where had our trust gone? And when I thought about it properly, had I ever fully trusted him?

And to make things worse still, in bed at night I grew detached and felt irritable when he touched me.

'I want to read,' or 'I've still got my period.' Sometimes I didn't even make an excuse, but brushed him off, such was my frustration. He didn't understand, or at least, he pretended not to. He grew resentful at my physical rejection which only increased the tension between us.

I read a couple of pages of my book even though I couldn't finish a paragraph without my mind wandering. Beside me, Toby scrolled endlessly through his phone. After a few minutes I turned off my bedside lamp and slipped on my eye mask. Out of sight, out of mind.

I considered moving into the spare room. The only thing stopping me was that I knew it could unsettle Rose just when she was beginning to make progress with her mobility.

One night I woke up and my thoughts began to rattle endlessly round. I slipped out of bed, pulled on my robe and went down to the office. Silently, I shut the door, and sat at Toby's desk. I opened his laptop and recalled his password, hoping he hadn't changed it recently. The screen cast just enough light for me to see the keyboard. If Toby was hiding something, he may well have changed his password. Surprisingly, I logged in without a problem. I clicked on the email icon. His inbox was full of unread messages, some dating back a couple of days. Clearly, he was struggling to keep on top of things, workwise. I scrolled back a few weeks worth of messages but there was nothing from a David Atkinson or anything I could link to the fracking. He'd obviously deleted them and I clicked on the bin.

I started when I heard the door open and I spun round to see a silhouetted figure in the doorway.

'So this is what you do when I'm not looking,' he said. 'Find anything of interest?'

'Toby.' I flipped the lid shut and my heart thundered.

'Well?' He took a step closer.

'No, I didn't find anything. Though if you'd given me a few more minutes I'm sure I'd have found what I was looking for.'

'Maybe so. I told you I had a clear out. Nothing sinister about it. What is bizarre is that you still think I'm hiding something. So here you are sneaking around to try and catch me out.'

'How many times have I tried to talk to you about the fracking, Toby?'

'Once or twice. Usually when I've just got in from work or I'm knackered and falling asleep.'

I stood up. 'But each time you deliberately change the subject. You always dismiss my concerns. I feel like I'm doing this without you. Relying on others for support.'

'Maybe it's a good job you have others who'll support you.' His voice sounded bitter.

'Yes,' I said, and marched past him to the doorway. 'Too damn right it is.'

'No apology then?' Toby called after me as I ran up the stairs.

I leaned over the bannister and whispered loudly. 'Not until you find those emails. Get the bastard to resend them if you need to.'

I didn't care that he'd caught me poking around. It might even make him understand how important this was to me. I headed to the spare bedroom.

The following morning, I didn't even see Toby as he'd left early for work again. Rose and I sat at the kitchen table to eat eggs on toast.

'Are these from the Davies' farm?' she said, and eyed her scrambled eggs with suspicion.

'We get all of our eggs from them,' I said, patiently.

She picked up her knife and fork. 'I'll only eat free range.'

Normally, I would have said something, such as, 'Please don't be too finicky about your food.' But, like anyone faced with a demanding person who was either ill or emotionally delicate, I held back.

'I could do with your help today,' I said.

'Sorry, Mum. I've already got plans.'

'What plans, darling?'

'I'm organising a memorial service for Pepper and then I need to call a friend.'

'That's a shame,' I said. 'Not that those things aren't important. But I could do with some help.'

'What is it and I'll let you know,' she said.

'You know the fracking?'

'Yes, Mum,' she said. 'Dad says it'll never go ahead.' She looked at me to gauge my reaction.

'It could well go ahead. Especially if we sit back and do nothing to resist it.' I felt a flash of anger towards Toby. 'I'm meeting with Saul Vermaak to finalise plans for the community meeting and I wondered if you could write the minutes on your laptop.'

'Minutes?' she said. 'Aren't you getting a bit carried away?'

'This is serious,' I said. 'We need to decide our strategy for the community meeting, create more interest and build awareness, as well as action every item. The community meeting could be the deal breaker for fracking going ahead or not.'

She sniggered. 'Hold on. I need to tick off my business bingo card.'

'Come on, Rose.' But I couldn't help but smile.

'Sorry.' She set her face straight. 'I'm all ears.'

'Thank you. I've told you about Nicola from Richmond News?'

'You have.'

'She's coming today, and apparently, she has urgent news.'

I figured a cause might be what Rose needed to motivate her to get better faster and it might also help to take her mind off Pepper. I knew she was as concerned about the fracking as I was, and she was savvy too.

As we headed up the drive to Hollow Grange, the three tall chimneys of the house appeared above the cluster of Scots Pine trees. I eased my foot off the accelerator and drove through the archway in the boundary wall.

'Are they nice people?' asked Rose.

I thought about Saul; physically striking, intelligent and with a strong social conscience.

'I haven't met the boys yet, but Saul is smart and has big plans.'

'Has he got any horses?'

'Horses aren't their thing.'

A pheasant scurried in front of the car and I braked to avoid it.

'Why do they always do that?' I said.

'He'll be shot soon and served up for some rich man's dinner,' said Rose.

'Well, shooting birds is definitely not one of Saul's plans,' I said.

'Good. I wouldn't talk to him if it was,' said Rose.

'How are you feeling today?' I asked.

'Sad still. I keep thinking about Pepper and how much I loved him. And it feels worse because I hadn't had a chance to make peace with him after my fall.'

'I understand. And I still feel responsible,' I said.

Rose turned to me. 'It wasn't anything you did.'

'I blame the surveyors, too,' I said. 'Even so, I never should have been jumping him.'

'Pepper was always so loyal,' she said. 'He'd come trotting over whenever he saw me.'

'Do you know why he was so loyal?' I asked.

'I'm not sure,' she replied.

'Because you were gentle with him. You never rushed him to learn. Patience with horses is the most valuable quality in horsemanship. And ultimately, horses reward us for it. As do most animals, for that matter.'

'I'm not sure I want to train a young horse again.'

'I'm not sure I want you to either,' I said. 'Wait until you're better, and then decide what sort of horse you want. If any.'

During her last physio session, Lisa, her therapist, estimated three months until Rose would be walking securely. That was more optimistic than I dared to hope. Despite my disbelief in God, I still said a silent prayer everyday. Superstitious, but it gave me comfort.

'Whoa! It's massive,' said Rose, as she gazed up at the Grange. 'Big for three of them?'

'It is impressive,' I agreed. 'The land and river were an important factor but the house needs a lot of work.'

'And his wife was murdered? How awful, and kind of exciting, too,' Rose said.

I couldn't help but smile. 'Not so exciting for those involved, perhaps.'

'Sorry. I'm feeling nervous.'

'No need. Saul's lovely.'

'What's his accent like?'

I switched off the engine and pulled up the handbrake. 'You've that to look forward to.'

As I helped Rose into her wheelchair, I heard raised voices. A door slammed from somewhere inside and I turned around and saw a tall boy with a mass of straggling hair appear in the open doorway.

He turned and shouted back inside, 'Mum hated you. And so do I.' He jumped down the steps in one leap, paused when he saw us then sprinted in the direction of the barn.

Rose looked at me, and nibbled her bottom lip. 'Awkward.'

'They've been through a terrible ordeal.' I pushed her forwards.

'Wait.' She gripped the wheels. 'I'm not going in yet. Mr whatshisname might need to calm down.'

'Don't be daft. Teenagers fall out with their parents all the time.'

'We don't.'

'That's because your dad and I are especially tolerant.'

'It's 'cus they're boys,' she said, scornful.

'Alex is nineteen, so a grown man. And I think that must be Dom, the younger boy,' I added.

Saul came into the doorway and jogged down the steps. 'Ahh. You've met Dom?' He raked a hand through his hair. 'Which way did he go?'

Rose pointed.

'He did look quite upset,' I said.

'I'll leave him to calm down,' Saul said, and gestured for us to come in. 'You can meet Alex. He's joined the campaign. And without undue force.'

Rose chortled. 'Like me, Mum?'

Saul and I exchanged a smile then each took a side of Rose's chair and lifted her up the steps.

'It's your future's we're thinking of. Isn't that right, Saul?'

'Everyone's,' he said. 'Including the entire planet.'

'Is Nicola here?' I said, as I pushed Rose into the hall.

Saul turned to me and his nose crinkled. 'I've just received a text to say she can't make it. No explanation necessary, apparently.'

'That's odd,' I said.

'I'll ring and update her later. Though I am curious as to her reason.'

'Let me know what she says,' I said.

'I'll make us a brew,' Saul called up the staircase. 'Alex? The Kubiks are here.'

'In the kitchen,' a voice called.

'You're getting to grips with the Yorkshire dialect then,' I said.

Saul raised his eyebrows. 'Ahh. Brew.' The corners of his mouth turned up.

As we entered the kitchen a striking looking young man with wavy brown hair stood leaning against the worktop. I glanced at Rose whose eyes fluttered in surprise.

He set his cup on the worktop. 'I'm Alex.' He came over and shook my hand and then turned to Rose.

'I'm Rose.' Her cheeks flushed as she held out her hand.

106

Alex had clearly spent time outdoors and he showed off a toned physique in black vest and khaki shorts. Rose's eyes followed him as he reached into the cupboard for some cups.

I sat at the table and watched father and son prepare tea and a plate of biscuits. They stepped around one another as though in a smoothly choreographed dance. The occasional nod or passing of a utensil revealed a closeness in their relationship.

'I've got the names of councillors from Nicola and key players from Quadrillum and Atkinsons. The main fracking bod is Hugh Plant and he's agreed to come along. I rang him yesterday and after finally speaking to him - quite an achievement, he didn't sound in the least fazed by our campaign. He was an arrogant twit. But it'll put us in a stronger position if he assumes we'll roll over and submit.'

'From what I've seen and read online, these people expect resistance, but they secure support from local government and top lawyers which makes it tough for protestors to get around legislation. And I had a thought; endangered wildlife or natural habitats might help our case.'

'Yes! I'll look into that,' said Saul.

'I will too,' I replied.

'You'll speak at the meeting?' he asked me. 'You're persuasive.'

'Wouldn't you like to?' I asked.

'Of course. We both will.' Saul looked from Rose to Alex. 'What do you think, Rose?'

Rose nodded, enthused. 'Mum's very persuasive.'

'Thank you for the vote of confidence,' I said, although I didn't relish the thought of talking in front of an audience that included pro-fracking experts.

We sat around the kitchen table for half an hour and outlined our defence arguments and any counter arguments we might face. Saul had done considerable research, particularly on the properties of the chemicals used by fracking companies.

'Studies from Australia and America make terrifying reading for anyone unaware of the dangers,' said Alex.

Rose's face filled with concern. 'I'd no idea,' she said.

'Not many do,' said Saul. 'Most have heard about tremors and minor quakes, but it's the chemicals in our waterways and

107

drinking water and related health problems people should worry about.'

'Virtually everyone I've spoken to is coming to the meeting and most are up for protesting, should it come to that,' I said.

'Shall we finish up the notes?' Alex said to Rose, and moved around to sit with her.

Rose adjusted her laptop so they could both look at the screen.

'I'd better find Dom.' Saul put his cup in the sink and turned to me. 'Fancy helping?'

'If I can.' I'd rather have declined, but Saul also had a quietly persuasive manner.

'I'll check his bedroom first,' he said.

What teenage boy would want some stranger interfering, I thought as I waited in the entrance hall?

Saul came back down stairs and sighed. 'Nope. All quiet up there.'

We walked down the steps and stood at the front of the house.

'Dom was close to his Mum,' he said. 'I'm worried about him.'

'Have you considered counselling or a support group?'

Saul looked thoughtful. 'Maybe I should have.'

For a moment, he dropped his guard and in doing so he appeared vulnerable. I tried to imagine how I'd feel if ever the girls lost their Dad. It wasn't something I wanted to contemplate.

'Don't be too hard on yourself. Becoming a single parent is bound to be difficult. And to lose their mum in such a way, too.'

He nodded. 'Alex appears to be coping OK but he and Tara were never that close.'

'My mum and I have always had a, how can I put it - a strained relationship,' I said.

Saul nodded. 'When Alex was born I became the main carer, as well as running the farm, whilst Tara continued to work. It was her choice and I was happy to combine the farm and being a Dad to Alex. Then when Dom came along Tara seemed to bond more easily with him and decided she was going to give up work to be with the boys full time. I was surprised but pleased. The boys needed their mum. Things were good for a while and we were happy. Or at least I thought we were. When Dom started school Tara itched to get back to work and once again, given no choice,

I was their main carer. We needed extra help on the farm and my stress levels rocketed. Tara would often stay away all week in town to save on the long commute and at weekends she'd spend hours working and often seemed distracted by her other life. But she was successful and made a lot of money - more than the farm ever brought in. She was the breadwinner and although I respected her for it, I can see the boys missed out.'

'And how about you? Did you miss out?' I asked.

'Truthfully, Anya - I got used to her absence. But now I can see just how much Tara's absence - her detachment, has affected Dom.'

'We think parenting should be the most natural thing in the world - that mothers and fathers automatically bond with their babies, that parenting shouldn't be complicated, but it's really not the case,' I said.

'Not in my experience. But thinking about supporting Dom now, maybe counselling is something we should try. How do I go about finding one?'

'I know one. I went through a tricky period, a few years ago.'

'Really? You seem so sorted,' Saul replied.

'I am more so these days.'

'Sorry,' he said. 'Stupid to make assumptions on appearances.'

'It's fine. And I'm glad I appear relatively normal. I'll maybe explain some time.'

I heard footsteps approach from behind and I turned around.

Dom stood with his hands in his trouser pockets and his hair flopped over his eyes. He swept his fringe away and appeared embarrassed.

Saul walked up to him, and rested a hand on his shoulder. 'You all right?'

Dom nodded, slowly. 'Sorry, Dad.'

'Don't worry, mate. Come here.'

As Saul embraced his son, I looked out across the paddock. What an openly affectionate and demonstrative father he was.

'This is Anya,' said Saul. 'Our fracking campaign leader.'

'Good to meet you, Dom. My daughter, Rose, is inside. She's starting at Richmond sixth form, too.'

'That's cool.' Dom broke into a smile. 'I might go say hello to her.'

'That's great,' said Saul.

Saul watched Dom until he was safely out of earshot. 'That's a relief. His behaviour has been so up and down recently.'

'And he seemed so mature and sorted,' I said.

'Touche!' said Saul, and gave a small laugh. He looked up at the house, and his shoulders relaxed.

After a moment he turned back to me. 'You're easy to talk to. You know?'

I felt my face flush. 'I'm not sure Toby would agree with you right now.'

'Mmm. Sometimes, it's those we're closest to who're the hardest to understand.'

'Maybe we're less tolerant than we should be,' I said, and wondered if that had been the problem between Toby and me. But then I reasoned, that wasn't strictly true. I'd held back in saying what I really wanted to say to him for days and he continued to drive me mad with his unpredictable and evasive behaviour. He was out most days and late into the evenings, which for someone who worked from home, struck me as odd. Though he always seemed to have a good excuse. Had any of his consulting work been fracking related? Or an affair? I didn't want to consider either, especially the latter.

'Was Tara easy to understand?' It seemed a natural thing to ask.

Saul blinked as he thought. 'Not always, and I suspect this worked both ways. Sometimes we gelled but as time went on it often felt as though I barely knew her.'

'I think I understand,' I said, and felt a stab of guilt at my disloyalty.

'Tara was intuitive and would openly analyse me and the boys. She said I was complex. I should have told her I thought the same about her, but she didn't take criticism well.'

'I don't think any of us appreciate being told we're imperfect,' I said.

'But aren't we all multifaceted and different from day to day?' Saul said.

'Far more than we care to admit,' I agreed.

'Tara was selective with what she shared. And in the trial, things came out that I hadn't known about her.'

'Oh?' I said, intrigued.

'I'll tell you, sometime.'

Saul's face was inches from mine and I watched as the blackness of his pupils seemed to flare. When his hand brushed mine it seemed intentional and I felt something alter within me. And although it was a sensation I knew to be wrong, I didn't resist.

'Yes,' I said. 'Sometime.'

When he held my gaze, I felt my heartbeat quicken.

Voices sounded from inside.

'I should probably get back. The horses…'

'Yes,' he said.

'Life is unpredictable,' I said. 'Rose's accident. Pepper's death. Tara…' I felt a rush of emotion as everything around me blurred. In contrast, Saul's features sharpened in the sunlight.

He put his hand on my arm. 'Perhaps, we should accept the unexpected. Good and bad. Some we can prevent, some we should embrace.'

His words made so much sense to me.

'And it's about being open to change and new possibilities,' I said. 'Or we may walk on by, oblivious.'

His eyes locked onto mine. 'Your eyes are wide open, Anya.'

'And you, Saul, are observant.'

He continued watching me, his gaze sharp and unblinking.

I heard voices and turned to see Alex with Rose at the front door.

Instinctively, we stepped apart and Saul jogged up the steps to help.

'Dom was nice,' said Rose, as we drove away from Hollow Grange. 'He's completely different to Alex.'

'In what way?' I asked.

'Alex is down to earth, funny, confident. Dom talked a lot, but seemed intense. We listened to some really cool jazz, then as he chatted he made an amazing model horse out of plasticine. I took a photo of it.'

'His dad said he was artistic.'

'I can't wait to tell Julie how brilliant he is. She's doing art.'
Rose paused. 'Maybe I should, too.'

I suppressed a smile at her fickle reasoning. 'You can still change your options. See what grades you get first.'

She groaned. 'Don't remind me, Mum.'

'I have every faith in you,' I said.

She replied. 'I'm glad someone has.'

Chapter 17

When we arrived home, I settled at my desk to carry out some fracking research. I'd hoped Nicola would offer a date the councillors could attend the community meeting but until Saul had spoken to her that was still an unknown. Her absence that morning concerned me.

'Hey there.'

I swivelled round in my chair. 'Hi, Gem. You OK?'

I'd been worried about her since she'd, in effect, been drug raped. We'd spoken about it a few times, but Gemma wanted to try to forget about it and already had a date lined up with someone she'd met at The Black Horse that previous weekend.

'I'm surviving. Still angry about Rob. I've thought about talking to him to let him know I know what he did. It might make him think twice before trying it again with anyone.'

'I think you should. What he did was despicable and criminal. You can still prosecute, you know?'

'I've arranged a checkup at the clinic. I want to see if it comes back clear or not. Then I'll think again.'

'Good idea. And if you want me to come with you to talk to him, just say.'

'Course,' she gave a thin smile. 'Anyway, Rose has just told me about your meeting with the Vermaaks. Sounds as though it was productive.' Gemma's tone grew provocative.

'Pardon?' I said.

'Rose mentioned they're about the best looking men she's ever set eyes on.'

'You know why we're working together, don't you?'

'Maybe I should come along and meet Mr Vermaak.'

'I'd love you to,' I said. 'Besides, Rose's hormones are running riot and therefore not to be trusted.'

Gemma sat on the sofa and tilted her head to one side. 'Because once you hit forty, desire fizzles and dies.'

'Oh shush and say something useful,' I said, but I couldn't help laughing. 'Anyway, I'm not forty yet.'

'Not long, though,' said Gemma. 'Do you fancy a ride?' she said.

'That's more like it.' I placed my pen and notepad in the draw and pushed my chair back. 'Precisely what I need.'

'I'm desperate for a decent ride too.' A flickering smile appeared on her lips.

'You get more horny with age, not less.'

'Hey you. I'm not old.'

'Mmm.' I looked at her askance. 'It's all relative.' I took her hand, pulled her up and we ran through to the hallway.

Stevie walked out of the living room, threw us a pained look, and turned right back round again.

As Gemma and I set off on horseback my high spirits scattered and the weight of my worries returned to blacken my mood. Beneath clouds that seemed to have settled for the afternoon, the air felt oppressive - an apt reflection of my state of mind.

I sensed change lay ahead and I wondered if in life we could only expect the normal order of things to last for so long. I recalled reading somewhere that our lives passed in seven year cycles, and it had been more since Euan's death. It seemed we had reached a crossroads, and the decisions that we made over the coming months would determine which road we travelled onwards.

The horse's hooves rang hollow upon the cracked earth, whilst all around us the birds persisted in their song as the occasional one dipped and dived overhead. The bridle path narrowed and I reined Ebony in to follow Maya between tall hedgerows lush with summer berries, foxgloves and yarrow. My thoughts settled once more on Toby. What reason could he have for colluding with the frackers? He'd always been as pro-environment as me and especially so considering his profession. Furthermore, I'd never known him compromise his principles for financial gain. We'd gone through a couple of rough patches in our marriage and the last 'patch' had all but broken us. The prospect of facing a repeat of it was something I didn't want to contemplate.

'Anya,' Gemma's voice broke my thoughts. 'Are you with me?'

'Sorry?'

'I said, I don't know how you can ride in shorts.'

'I'd rather have my skin pinched than swelter in this heat. And my legs tan.'

'I prefer mine from a bottle.'

'Far healthier,' I replied.

Gemma spurred Maya into a trot and without encouragement, Ebony sprang forwards to keep up. Despite the incline and narrowness of the path we broke into a canter and the hedgerows and trees passed by in a blur.

'Branch! Duck.' Gemma called over her shoulder.

I leaned over Ebony's neck and the leaves overhead brushed across my back. Up ahead, the open skies greeted us and the path opened out to moorland and rocky outcrops with the distant hills hazy upon the horizon. We reined in the horses.

Behind me came a sudden flurry of wings. Ebony started and I gripped tight with my thighs and shortened the reins. I turned to see a grouse rise up from the gorse and fly away with a squawk.

I drew alongside Gemma, turned to her and grinned. Then with a squeeze of my calves, Ebony took his cue and launched into a gallop. Maya soon thundered up beside us and we raced along the track side by side, free flowing into the wind, breathless, wild and heady. My mind cleared of everything but the moment - the freedom, myself and Ebony as one, neither of us controlling the other.

As we sped towards the far edge of the moor, where heather met farmland, I pulled Ebony up.

We jumped down and left the horses to nibble the grass as their sides sweated and heaved from exertion. The breeze ruffled Ebony's mane and he gave a snort of contentment.

I lay back and crossed my arms behind my head and the dry grass crackled beneath me. I breathed out - long and slow. 'Nothing much beats that.'

Gemma lay down beside me and beamed. 'It's the ultimate in freedom. It's what I was born for.'

I took Gemma's hand. 'Me too.' I squinted up at the clouds as they ballooned, tumbled and merged above us. 'Better than loving a man?'

'I wouldn't go that far,' she said.

'Me neither,' I said. 'But damn close.'

When we arrived back at the yard, I hosed the sweat from Ebony's coat and he snorted and quivered as the water poured over his back. I rubbed his ears and produced a carrot from my pocket.

'Anya?'

I spun round. 'Hi.' It wasn't often Toby came to the yard and his appearance surprised me. 'Is Rose OK?'

'She's fine.' He folded his arms. 'Facetiming last time I looked in.'

'Oh, good.'

'Will you be in soon?' His eyes narrowed.

'What's happened?' I asked, and the distance between us seemed to have grown.

He turned to leave. 'I'll see you shortly.' And walked briskly out of the yard.

Clearly, something had upset him.

Rather than turning Ebony into the paddock, I rubbed him down and shut him in the stable.

I found Toby in the office. 'Everything all right?'

He sat and stared at his computer screen and without turning around, he held up my phone. 'I was trying to work and your phone kept ringing. After the fifth consecutive call, I could hardly ignore it.'

'Who was it?'

'Saul wants to speak to you.' His tone was laced with scorn. 'It's urgent, apparently.'

'Did he say what he wanted?'

'Oh, he wouldn't tell me.' Toby heaved an exaggerated sigh. 'Must be too personal.'

'You know we met yesterday about the fracking,' I said, taking my phone. 'It'll be about that.'

'Obviously. At least he's got your new mobile number.' Toby's sarcasm didn't mask his irritation.

Annoyed by his petulance, I turned and walked out.

'Don't mind me,' he shouted and I heard a drawer slam.

I phoned Saul.

'Nicola's in hospital,' he said. 'But she's going to be OK.'

'Why?'

I heard Saul take in a sharp breath. 'She was driving alone and run off the road by another driver. She'd been aware of a car up her bumper for a mile or so. They kept honking then overtook and cut her up sharp. She swung away to avoid hitting them, crashed through a hedge and down an embankment. Ended up in a stream.'

'What are her injuries?'

'Whiplash. Cuts and bruises. Several stitches.'

'Has she any idea who was driving?'

'None at all.'

I sensed it must be related to our campaign.

'What are you thinking?' Saul asked.

'I'm not sure.'

'It's obvious,' he said. 'Nicola's publicly against fracking and the industry is corrupt as hell.'

'We shouldn't jump to conclusions,' I said. 'Did anyone see it happen?'

'Psycho driver drove off, pronto. Nicola said the woman who stopped to help told her she was passed by a lunatic.'

'Maybe psycho driver was having a bad day or Nicola's working on other controversial stuff.'

'There's nothing else she can link it to. And she's pretty astute.'

'I don't like it, Saul. This is getting serious,' I said.

'We should go visit her.'

We agreed to drive over to Nicola's the following day then hung up.

By the time I returned to the office, Toby had already put his laptop away and gone. I hurried upstairs to our bedroom as butterflies wreaked havoc with my gut, but desperate to make things right with Toby.

He was laid on the bed, with eyes closed and one arm flung across my pillow.

I sat on the edge of the bed and took his hand. 'You all right?

He didn't reply.

'Talk to me, Toby.'

'About what?'

'You're upset with me.'

He sighed and opened his eyes. 'I'm not the one receiving multiple calls from some woman.'

'It's only fracking business.'

'Is it more important than me? Than us?' He pulled his hand away and massaged his temple.

'That's a bit unnecessary, isn't it?'

'Is he good looking?'

I traced his brow bone with my fingers. 'Nowhere near as handsome as you as it happens.'

Toby had never been the jealous sort and I imagined he must be joking.

'Not what Gemma said. And she hasn't even met him.'

He ground his teeth then without speaking got up and walked into the bathroom.

Toby was generally easy going, but something had wound him up. Yes, he'd caught me snooping on his computer, but he knew the reason for that. I'd blamed his behaviour on guilt over Rose's accident, but she was recovering. Perhaps he was genuinely suspicious of my relationship with Saul.

The bathroom door flew open and cracked against the wall.

Toby unbuttoned his shirt.

I glanced at the bedside clock. 'Isn't it a bit early for bed?'

He sat down on the bed and pulled off his socks. 'Join me then.'

I walked round the bed and sat beside him. 'I'm worried.'

'You're not the only one,' he said, but he wouldn't look at me.

I took his hand. 'You don't seem yourself.'

'Me? I'm not meeting up with strangers in secret.'

'Saul isn't a stranger. But he does have a vested interest in preventing the fracking. As do we. His business is organic and will never get off the ground. And think of the health implications for our children, the horses.'

'The risks aren't proven,' said Toby. 'If you've bothered to read the research.'

I snatched my hand away. 'No, Toby.' I marched across to the window, looked out and took some slow breaths. I turned back round. 'I've read about everything there is to read on the subject, from both perspectives.'

'You need to be careful, Anya,' he continued, unphased. 'I advise you to think long and hard about this and back off and leave it to those who don't have a business and a reputation to protect.'

'You're not serious?'

He opened his palms. 'Show me the proof.'

'The only people who deny the health and environmental impact from fracking are those considering their bank balances,' I said. 'We won't even have a livery business if they frack near here.' I walked towards the door. 'You know what, Toby? I can't even look at you.'

'Go look at Saul then.'

I spun around. 'Think about what you're saying.'

'You mean like you do?' He laid down on the bed and turned his back to me.

Chapter 18

I gazed out at the cornflower blue sky as a breeze swept in through the open windows. Then I went through the hangers in my wardrobe, picked out a sleeveless blouse and denim skirt, and stepped into a pair of wedge heeled sandals.

Stevie walked in, still wearing her pyjamas.

'Rose says you're going out. Shall I stay in with her?'

'Is she all right?'

'She's a bit tearful.'

I buttoned up my skirt. 'Did she say why?'

Stevie whispered, 'I think it's a boy.'

I picked up my hairbrush. 'If I think back to when I was her age, there was always a boy.' But what chance had Rose recently had to meet up with any boys?

I applied some lip gloss. 'Social media confuses things these days,' I said. 'Or so I hear.'

'It's true,' said Stevie. 'A like given to another girl, a compliment or a flirty reply. A comment that seems short, or even worse, being ignored. We read way too much into everything.'

'Oh dear,' I said. 'I'd better talk to her.'

Rose already had so much to cope with. She could do without boy trouble. If Stevie's hunch was correct.

'At least you don't need to worry about me,' said Stevie.

I considered her; happy, relaxed and oblivious to heartbreak.

'Enjoy it, my darling, wh…' my words trailed away.

'Oh, it'll last all right,' she said, her tone breezy.

'I'm sure it will. I'll see Rose before I go, but I shouldn't be too long. Thank you for caring for her, Stevie. You're a kind sister.'

'You look pretty, Mum,' she said. 'I hope I look as good when I'm old.'

'Thank you,' I said, and ignored her jibe. I picked up the body spray, squirted it in the air and walked through the mist.

Stevie said, 'You're supposed to spray it before you put your clothes on.'

I laughed lightly. 'You're wise in many wonderful ways. Do you know that?'

'I've got good teachers,' she said, and kissed my cheek.

When I popped in to see Rose, she was laid in bed, blowing her nose and without either a book or her laptop. She never had been good at hiding her feelings.

'Your sister said you seemed upset.'

'Stevie should keep her big fat nose out.'

'What's happened, darling?'

'Nothing really. Only someone I like who I thought liked me hasn't messaged back.'

'I'm sure he will.' I plucked a tissue from the box and gave it to Rose. 'And if he doesn't then it's his loss.'

'It isn't that simple.'

'No, of course it isn't.'

'I'll be fine. I feel fine, now.'

'Sweetheart. I want you to promise to talk to me. Or Stevie or Gemma, if anything's upsetting you.'

She blew her nose again. 'I will, Mum.'

'Good.' I gave her a big hug. 'Stevie's staying in, but I've got my new phone if you need me.'

As I turned the key in the ignition, my phone rang. I reached across and rummaged in my handbag. It was Saul.

'Can I ask a favour?' he said.

'Of course.'

'Alex needs the car today and I wondered if I could have a lift?'

'Sure. I'll drive over.'

'You're a gem.'

I rang off and smiled to myself.

Saul slid his seat back and clipped the seatbelt. 'Thanks for this.'

As we drove to Richmond, he re-played his conversation with Nicola. 'She's terrified. I heard it in her voice.'

'I'm pretty scared, too,' I said. 'And I wasn't the one targeted.'

121

'We need to be hyper vigilant when we're out. Even if you're riding,' said Saul.

'Maybe I'll avoid the lanes for the next few weeks. I'll mention it to Stevie and Toby, too.'

'Good idea,' he said.

We pulled up on Beech Avenue. It was a pretty road with a mix of three-storey townhouses. As per its name, Beech trees lined the pavements and many of the front gardens had colourful flower beds and neatly trimmed lawns.

'Are you sure she's in?' I said, after I'd knocked twice.

'She's home from the hospital and I can't imagine she'll feel like going out,' said Saul.

Through the frosted glass I watched Nicola approach the door and the latch clicked.

She opened the door with the safety chain still on.

'Nicola, it's Anya and Saul,' I said.

She unfastened the chain and opened the door wide. 'I appreciate you coming,' she said, and stood aside.

Nicola wore a neck brace and I concealed my shock at the angry bruises on her face and arms.

'Apologies for looking like Quasimodo,' she said.

'Please don't apologise,' I said. 'And your bruising will fade.'

We followed her down the entrance hall and through to the sitting room. Their living room had a large bay window and it had been beautifully updated and furnished with emerald velvet sofas and armchairs and colourful cushions. I cast my eyes around the artwork that adorned the walls.

Nicola saw me admiring them. 'They're my husband's. Philip Marsden?'

'I thought they looked familiar. They're fantastic. I went to his talk and exhibition at the Town Hall. He's a witty man as well as talented.'

She forced a smile. 'He's quite the comedian. Or piss artist, as I like to call him.'

Saul and I chuckled, and the atmosphere in the room lightened.

'He's having some success, finally. It's taken him years.'

'I like them. Very much,' I said.

'I'll tell him,' she said. 'Can I get you some tea?'

'I'd love one,' I said. 'But please let me. I'm sure you've been told to rest.'

'The doctors are wasting their breath,' she said.

'Even so,' I insisted.

She smiled and sat down. 'Thank you, Anya.'

I left them talking and walked down the corridor where more of Philip's paintings hung, and through to the kitchen at the back. I filled the kettle and as it boiled I searched for tea bags and mugs, both of which I found tidied away into cupboards.

Their home was uncluttered, tastefully furnished and homely. It was clear they paid more attention to design and aesthetics than Toby or I did. Colourful pieces of pottery and art dotted the kitchen. A painted tile of a fish hung above the sink, a framed replica section of the Bayeux Tapestry hung on a cupboard door and the handmade cups hooked beneath the walled units looked far too good for everyday use. The painted wooden units looked charming.

As I carried the tea tray into the sitting room, I said. 'You've a beautiful home…'

'I could kill the bastard,' said Nicola through her tears. 'When I find out who it was.'

Saul stroked her back, and mouthed, 'Help.'

I set the tray on the coffee table and sat beside Nicola.

I reached for a pack of tissues in my handbag.

'Do you really think it was someone involved in the fracking?' I asked.

Nicola blew her nose. 'At first it didn't occur to me. Then afterwards, the more I thought about it, something clicked. I've no proof, of course. But from the moment I came home our phone keeps ringing and when we answer it, no one speaks.'

'That's scary,' I said.

'They're trying to scare me,' she said. 'And it's bloody working.' Nicola stood up, walked across to the mantlepiece and picked up a packet of cigarettes.

'Maybe you should take a back seat?' said Saul. 'For a few days. You need time to recover and we can handle the council contacts.' He looked across at me. 'What do you think, Anya?'

Nicola lit a cigarette and sucked sharply on it. With her face swollen and bruised, she looked smaller and vulnerable.

'Seems sensible.' I nodded. 'And maybe psycho driver, whoever he is, will back off. We'll keep you in the loop.'

'But our community must frighten them off.' She tapped her cigarette into the ashtray. 'You should be on high alert too. We've all been publicising the protests so we're all potential targets. You can guarantee they'll know your names and where you live.'

'Of course.' Saul looked at me. 'You're right.'

'It's your call,' I said. 'And we'll be hyper-vigilant, too.' I knew that in her position I'd have felt angry and vengeful too. Bullies wanted their victims to cower; too terrified to pick themselves up and fight back.

We drank our tea and set a date for the meeting - only a week away. We now had the names of the councillors and members of staff at Quadrillum who we thought would attend.

'I'll see what I can dig up on these guys,' I said, 'And forward it on to you both.'

A while later, as I pulled up at Hollow Grange, Saul said. 'Fracking is a filthy business, in more ways than one.'

'And I'm with Nicola,' I said, turning off the engine. 'No way am I sitting back and leaving this to chance.'

He turned to me and his eyes had an intensity that explored more than my face. 'I'm grateful for your support,' he said. 'Genuinely. We need numbers to tackle these monsters.'

'They want us, the public, to back down to their intimidating and underhand ways.'

His expression grew thoughtful and in the pause between us I felt the blood pulse in my ears. His gaze swept over my face, and as I waited for him to speak, I lowered my eyes to the broadness of his shoulders that filled his t-shirt to perfection and then down the full length of his arms to his hands and fingers.

Saul leaned nearer and I felt his breath warm upon my face. 'Will you come in?'

If I accepted, what was I going in for? There was Rose, Toby and the yard.

And yet, without speaking, I unfastened my seatbelt.

Chapter 19

With all the time I'd devoted to garnering support for the campaign, Gemma and Stevie had put in endless extra hours in the yard. I was surprised not to have been called on to help resolve any problems but I imagined that Gemma was too busy dealing with things on her own and didn't want to add to my burdens.

After a day of fracking related calls, messages and delivering protest flyers, I walked over to Walnut Cottage to see Gemma and to ask how her day had gone.

The sun had already set, which left an orange glow above the woods as though a fire burned up on Orben moor. The bats darted and swooped and the crickets chirped in surround sound. As I passed the living room window the television lights flickered upon the walls. The front door was ajar and I called through, 'Only me.'

It remained quiet, except for the murmur of the television.

'Gemma?' I called, louder.

'I'm at the front,' she called back.

I walked through to the kitchen and on through the back door. I found Gemma sitting beneath the arbor with a glass of wine in hand.

She lifted her glass. 'Want one?'

I sat on the woolen blanket draped over the bench. 'I'm tempted, but no. I need a clear head tomorrow.'

'Ahh. The big meet.' She raised the bottle of wine and refilled her glass.

'I only hope the right people turn up,' I said.

'Oh, they will,' she said, and her face grew animated. 'Too much money involved for the oil mongers and too risky the consequences for the community.'

'I can't understand why Toby is so non-committal,' I said. 'He isn't coming, you know?'

'I need to tell you something.' Gemma paused to rest her glass on her knee. 'About Toby.'

'Oh?'

'It may be nothing to get too worried about, but when I was riding down by the river, he was sitting at Euan's memorial stone.'

'Did he say anything?'

'He was crying and didn't see me, so I turned around. I was riding with a couple of the girls and didn't want to embarrass him.'

I tried to recall if Toby had mentioned Euan recently.

'After my ride I was concerned enough to seek him out,' Gemma continued.

'And?'

'I mentioned I'd seen he was upset. Initially, he was defensive. Told me to mind my own business. But you know me, takes a lot to make me back off. So I told him that I, too, was feeling anxious about Euan's anniversary. He was quick to dismiss he was upset about Euan. Too quick. He said it wasn't so much Euan but too many difficult thoughts to deal with.'

'I think he is upset about Euan,' I said. 'He muttered his name in his sleep the other night.'

'Really? I probably do that most nights. No wonder none of my boyfriends last,' she said.

'No, Gemma. That's because you end it with them before you get too close.'

'I know, but I'm not ready. I'm not sure I'll ever be ready.'

'One day you will be.'

'Maybe.' Gemma's eyes glistened. 'I thought grief was supposed to lessen over time. It's been eight years.'

'Grief doesn't have a time limit. It takes as long as it takes,' I said.

For a few minutes, we sat in silence, each with our thoughts and memories.

In the light cast from the kitchen, I watched a bee hover then settle to feast on a rose. It struck me as unusual for this time of day.

When I turned back to Gemma I found her watching me.

'Do you have times where he isn't in your thoughts?' I asked.

126

'When I'm busy I might not think about him all day,' she said. 'But when I'm alone, he returns. His voice, his face, so vivid still. And then I feel guilty, as if I've been avoiding him.' Tears formed in the wells of her eyes.

My throat tightened. 'Don't feel bad for being alive. Euan would want you to move on.' And I thought how many times I'd repeated those words.

'No one lives up to him, Anya. However much I want them to. And then I feel more guilt because truthfully, I'm desperate for someone to take his place.'

'Oh, Gemma.' I reached out my hand, all the while looking into her eyes. 'Not to replace Euan, but someone for you to love.'

But she was right. She'd never meet a man to compare with Euan.

I wondered, did we always glorify those who died young to the extent that it hindered us from ever moving on? Was it because our memories had been cut short and those missing became exalted in our minds? How different our lives might have been if Euan had still been alive.

Despite our difficulties, I resolved to give Toby the opportunity to talk. Though I doubted he'd be in the mood to share anything honest or real with me right now.

My phone buzzed in my pocket.

'Sorry,' I said to Gemma. 'Hello Saul.'

'Bad news,' he said. 'Nicola's heard from a reliable source that Quadrillum are setting up their operation at the back of Hesketh Common.'

'When?'

'It's imminent. So while we're meeting with the big nobs, their guys are preparing.'

'We're running out of time, Saul.' A feeling of panic rose in my chest.

'We need their timings,' he said.

'Should we say at the meeting?'

'Too right,' he said. 'Hopefully there'll be a riot.'

My mind's eye filled with angry locals shouting and hurling chairs.

There was a pause. 'Why don't you come over early… and we can travel to Riseham together?'

'I'd like to but I'll have the girls and Gemma with me.'

'OK. I understand. See you at the hall.'

Saul hung up.

Gemma said, 'That sounded serious.'

'This could sink our entire campaign,'

After leaving Gemma's I went to the office to check my emails. Stevie sat at Toby's desk.

'Everything OK?' I asked her.

'Dad's rung to say he won't be home tonight.'

'I wondered where he'd got to.'

'He said he tried to ring you but couldn't get through.'

'Did he say why?'

'A client's cocktail party. In Leeds. He's annoyed because he'd forgotten and doesn't have an overnight bag.'

'It'll maybe do him good,' I said.

She got up and hugged me. 'I'm off to bed.'

'Sweet dreams, darling. Is Rose still up?'

'Dunno. I've only just got in,' she replied. 'Night, Mum.'

'Sleep well. See you bright and early.'

I read my emails and went to say goodnight to Rose.

When I turned her door handle, it was locked.

'All right in there?'

'Yep, fine,' called Rose.

'Want a hot chocolate?'

Silence.

'I'm having one,' I said.

'No thanks, Mum,' came her reply.

'See you in the morning.'

She sounded happy enough and I remembered how much time I spent in my room as a teenager. Locking us out was a new one. Still, I must respect her privacy.

Freda scratched at the back door and when I opened it, she charged out barking. I filled the kettle, then rang Toby. He didn't pick up and I'd had no missed calls, after him telling Stevie he'd tried ringing me.

I texted. 'Give me a call when you can. Hope you're having a lovely evening.' Then another. 'I miss you, A xx.' And I did miss him. I also hoped it might persuade him to call back.

'Freda,' I called into the darkness. Without a second call she trotted back in. 'Come here, girl.' I picked her up and gave her a cuddle. 'You can sleep with me tonight.'

Delighted to be given the freedom of the house at night, she bounded in front of me and up the stairs. She leapt onto the bed, and shuffled around in circles before she rested her head upon Toby's pillow.

'My beautiful girl. You won't be grumpy, will you?' I stroked her and she rolled over for me to scratch her tummy.

As I undressed, my thoughts blackened and I slumped onto the bed. I knew Toby had been dishonest. And I also realised it could have been my fault. And that hurt. Was I driving him away, like before?

My phone buzzed and I reached for it on the bedside table.

It wasn't Toby, but a message from Saul.

'I've discovered something that'll help.'

I messaged back. 'Call me if you can.'

My phone rang with an incoming video call.

I hadn't expected him to facetime and almost naked, I dashed to grab my robe.

'Sorry,' he tilted his head back and laughed lightly. 'I pressed video call by mistake.'

'It's fine. Toby's away tonight.'

I listened as Saul explained his discovery. His eyes grew wide and danced with enthusiasm.

'This'll throw them a spanner,' I said.

He shook his head. 'If only I'd read the loopholes I'd have looked into it sooner.'

'Of course, the protection of animal habitats is a big thing with any groundwork operations.' I knew this because Toby had encountered delays many times in his consultancy work.

'I'll never sleep with all this in my head,' said Saul.

'I'll just be glad when tomorrow's over.'

'I hope you manage to sleep,' he said.

'If I can't I'll practice my words.' I felt a flutter of nerves each time I thought about speaking.

'No need to be nervous,' he said. 'I'll be right next to you.'

We talked about other stuff and I knew it was to prolong the call. He seemed in no hurry to end it, and neither was I.

Saul laid down on his bed and turned on the bedside lamp. I lay my head back too and felt myself relax in his company.

'I love the way your mind works,' he said. 'Wise beyond your years.'

'I'm not so wise, or young.' I sighed. 'And believe me. I've done some stupid things in my time.'

'Then I'm even more intrigued,' he said, with a crinkle of his eyes and nose.

'I'll spare you the details,' I said, and felt my cheeks burn.

Freda snuffled in her sleep and I glanced at the clock. 'It's getting quite late,' I said.

He made steady eye contact. 'I'm not tired.'

I wasn't either, but what we were doing felt wrong. 'I'll see you in the morning.'

He blew me a kiss. 'Sweet dreams, Anya.'

I blew a kiss in return then hung up.

I stroked Freda's back. Saul liked me and I knew I ought to make it clear I was happy with Toby. But Saul knew my situation and it hadn't deterred him from pursuing me. If only he didn't engage me or look at me the way he did. Maybe I'd been too transparent, and he'd responded to my obvious interest. He didn't seem the womanising type. I'd met plenty of them before. No, if anything, Saul appeared reserved and even modest. So unlike Toby, whose confidence and enthusiasm overflowed.

And my Toby, who'd turned me beautifully crazy with love from the moment we met. But was our breakdown in communication too big? Toby's failure to support me seemed too significant to push aside and continue on regardless. What did it say about his respect for me and the things I cared about? And what did it say about his concern for the natural environment? I had too many unanswered questions and my mind whirled with them all.

I checked my phone. Toby hadn't messaged back. It left me feeling confused rather than aggrieved. Perhaps I should phone him? And then I thought, Toby or Saul?

As though someone had heard my thoughts, my phone buzzed.

Text message. 'So sorry I forgot to say about stupid drinks party. I'll be home first thing.'

I typed my reply. 'I probably won't be here. It's the meeting. Remember?'

I waited for his reply. After ten minutes I messaged again. 'Stevie, Rose and Gemma are coming. I'd like you to be there, too.'

Still no reply. I searched my phone for some relaxing music, switched off the bedside light and shut my eyes.

I am lying on the riverbank beneath a willow tree with my head resting in the summer grass and the sound of acoustic guitar echoing all around. The tree's leaf laden tendrils fall and dip into the swirling water below and flickers of sunlight drop, feather soft and warm upon my skin.

Softly, a hand covers mine. Cool yet assured. I trust the touch. My skin shivers as hidden memories reemerge. The depth in his eyes. His mind. The tenderness of his words.

He whispers in my ear. 'You must talk to Toby.'

'But you know how stubborn he is,' I say.

'Set aside some time. He'll listen if you explain the importance to you.'

'Will you talk to him?' I plead. 'He misses you. I miss you.'

'I can't.' His voice is full of regret. 'You know why.'

My eyes hurt and my throat contracts. 'What happened to you?'

'Leave it to the past. I have.' His voice floats all around me.

'I need to know. Gemma needs...'

He squeezes my hand. 'No, Anya. Let Gemma move on. And you must, too.'

'If only I could.'

I open my eyes and lift my hand. Now empty.

'Why, Euan? Tell me Euan...Euan?'

There's a glimmer of light in front of me which is vibrating as fast as it recedes. I reach out to keep him here, but already, he's gone and I'm alone once more.

'Mummy. Are you OK?' Like an angel, Stevie appeared at my bedside.

She sat down and I looked at her face, gentle in the light cast from the landing.

I sat up and turned on the bedside light. 'I had a strange dream.' I wiped away a solitary tear that fell upon my cheek.

'Was it the bogeyman or the frackers coming for you?'

She took my hand and she paused before she whispered. 'You were calling Uncle Euan.'

My dream lay thick and silent. My mind still heavy and confused with sleep. 'Euan?' I asked.

She nodded. 'Is it because of his anniversary soon?'

'I still find it hard. And I worry about Gemma.'

Stevie drew up her legs and sat cross legged. 'I have an idea for his anniversary.'

'Tell me about it?'

'Let me think it through properly first. Then you and Gem can give me your thoughts. We'll make it even more of a celebration.'

Her eyes looked heavy with sleep.

'I love you.' I hugged her. 'Have I told you recently?'

'You have.' Her mouth curved into a smile. 'And I love you.'

'As much as Jake?' I raised my brows, playful.

'Stop it.' She nudged me, smiling. 'But I really do love him.'

'I can see that,' I said. 'Enjoy being together. Don't worry about the future. Simply care for his feelings, and your own.'

'I've never felt like this about anyone. I want to be with him ALL of the time.'

'I remember that feeling. But keep some independence. Freedom for both of you to be yourselves.'

'Like you and Dad?'

I thought for a moment. 'Your dad was the first man to show me that love isn't about possession. Before I met him I had a jealous boyfriend and I grew scared to be me. Even down to the clothes I wore or who I spoke to. He'd watch me and find fault.' I sighed. 'From the day we met your dad let me be myself. Never controlling or possessive.'

But even as I spoke, I realised that I was no longer convinced this was true and that the dynamics of our relationship had recently changed. And symptomatic of this was the way that he spoke to and behaved towards me.

Stevie nodded. 'I was worried about Jake returning to Uni. But he loves me as much as I love him.'

132

'It's OK to worry,' I said. 'If we didn't we wouldn't be human, or we'd repress a part of ourselves that we shouldn't. But, try not to allow your worries to overflow into jealousy. It makes us feel insecure and ultimately, it's destructive.'

'Mmmm,' she said, thoughtful. 'Some of my friends torture themselves over their boyfriends or girlfriends. They make themselves miserable thinking about all the things that could go wrong.'

'Such a waste of emotional energy,' I said. 'Yet on the other side of the coin, we shouldn't be naive. Things can go wrong. The important thing is not to preempt problems that might bring them into existence.'

She brushed her hair back and lifted her chin. 'I don't think I'm the jealous sort.'

'Good. Then we're alike.'

'You and Daddy seem the perfect match. How old were you when you met?'

'Only nineteen. But I knew, instantly.'

She thought for a moment then stood up. 'We should probably sleep.'

I drew back the duvet. 'I'm sure Freda won't complain.'

'No thanks, Mum. She's annoying when she licks and scratches.'

'Oh, yes. I'd forgotten about that.' I lay down and pulled up the duvet. 'Sweet dreams, my darling.'

Chapter 20

Anya - Age Eighteen

Henry Ebbotson was my Statistics lecturer at the University of Leeds. He was also my personal tutor. Statistics, a subject I'd been dreading, turned out to be my favourite area of study and the only one where I successfully completed all assessments and achieved decent grades. Even during my first lecture with him I was astonished how he managed to make statistics sound a crucial and exciting part of accountancy. He was also deeply engaging. Henry was one of the younger lecturers, and at thirty-four he'd already had papers and books published. By all accounts, he was a brilliant and gifted rising star in his field and I felt privileged to be under his tutelage.

When I received my first assignment back from him, I read his feedback. It finished with a date and time for me to come to his study to meet him. I was more than happy with my grade and so was mystified as to the reason for the meeting. I imagined it was because he was my tutor, though when I asked around, he hadn't asked any of his other tutees to meet with him.

The old part of the University campus was like a rabbit warren and it took me some time to find his study, on the uppermost floor of what appeared to be the oldest building on campus. The staircase spiralled up three floors and the long, narrow corridor was lit only by the occasional window on one side. In my floral pumps, I walked noiselessly down the parquet flooring and felt nervous at what I might be expected to talk about. Outside his office door I paused and listened. From within came the lilt of classical music and a man's voice humming along.

I knocked.

'Come in,' he called.

I entered and pushed the door shut behind me.

'Anya, welcome to my humble study.'

Henry Ebbotson sat behind an antique desk set in front of the window. There were piles of books and papers at either end of the desk and a tiffany lamp - lit up to reveal the delicate wings of gold and blue dragonflies. Sunlight streamed through the window which caused me to squint, and also meant that Mr Ebbotson appeared almost in silhouette.

He gestured to the chair in front. 'Please, take a seat.'

I settled in the chair, crossed my legs and felt a flutter of nerves as I swept the hair off my shoulders.

'I enjoyed reading your essay,' he began.

'Thank you, sir. Is that why I'm here?' I asked.

He pushed back his chair, and my eyes followed as he walked to the far end of the office. He turned down the music on the stereo then opened the cupboard and brought out two glasses and a bottle of wine.

'I wanted to congratulate you on achieving top marks in the class. In fact, on achieving the highest mark I've ever awarded on this particular question.' He paused. 'I found it wonderfully insightful.'

'Gosh. I did try really hard.'

'I can tell. And as I'm your personal tutor and will be for the duration of your course, I wanted to introduce myself less formally.' He set the glasses on the desk. 'Elderberry wine. Weak as milk, but refreshing. Would you like a taste?'

I nodded. 'Yes please.'

He filled two glasses and placed one in my hand. I brought it to my lips and took a sip. It was cool, fruity and delicious on my tongue.

He asked me a few questions about my essay and for a moment I wondered if he doubted I'd written it.

'I shall use it as an exemplar answer,' he said.

I felt a warm glow inside, which I suspect the wine contributed to.

'How are you finding being away from home?'

Without hesitation, I said, 'I've never been happier.'

'I see,' he said, with a nod of understanding.

It was true. I might not have been enjoying the course, as a whole, but being away from my parents I felt freedom and independence had beckoned at last. There was no way I'd ever return, at least not for more than a night or two.

'You're squinting,' he said. 'Is the sun in your eyes?'

I shielded my eyes. 'A little, yes.'

He picked up his chair and carried it around to my side of the desk. I turned my chair to face him.

'How's that?'

When he crossed his legs his foot brushed against mine.

'Better,' I said, and shifted back in my seat.

We talked about my other subjects, my housemates, what I did in my spare time, my favourite bars and he listened without taking his eyes off me. He knew most of the bars and as the wine took effect, we laughed and joked and it felt as though I were talking to a fellow student rather than a professor with a doctorate.

He refilled our glasses and the minutes melted away, until eventually, Henry looked at his watch and said my session was over.

'I hope you've found this helpful...Anya.' His tongue lingered over my name.

'Oh. Extremely helpful,' I said, and felt dazzled by his intelligence as I floated in a drunken afternoon haze.

'Then if it will help with your grades, we can meet again?'

'I think it would help,' I said.

He walked with me to the door. 'Allow me,' he said.

But instead of opening the door he looked intently into my eyes. He rested his hands on the tops of my arms, leaned over and kissed me slowly and softly on the cheek. I knew perfectly well this wasn't how a tutor behaved with his students. And he knew I knew this too.

For the first time, I was in love. Not some childish, teenage infatuation, but a love that made me want to burst into laughter and cry tears of joy, all at once. A love that induced in me a feeling of ecstasy and an all consuming desire that gnawed at my insides whenever I thought of him. I felt hypnotised by his presence and whenever we were in his study my eyes followed him as he moved, his lips as he spoke, the graceful movements of his hands as he gestured or if he picked up a pen to write or

136

pour a glass of wine. And despite everything that happened subsequently, in some way I felt indebted to Henry Ebbotson for helping me understand what it felt like to be a real woman.

In the weeks that followed we'd meet in his office, kiss long and deeply, hold and touch one another lying together on his fireside rug and make love late into the evening. I didn't share anything about our relationship with my friends. I knew it would be frowned upon and I didn't want Henry to get into trouble. He said he wanted me all to himself, and that was why we never went to bars or to watch a movie at the cinema. I was so utterly intoxicated by my desire for him that I didn't question why he'd never asked me round to his place. I didn't even know where he lived, and likewise, he never asked for my address.

In my mind, he was crazy about me because he'd ask what I got up to when I wasn't with him. Were there any boys I liked? Did I get chatted up in bars? Initially, his jealousy reassured me.

'I ignore them,' I'd say. Although I wasn't lying about seeing anybody else. I barely noticed any college boys once Henry had made love to me. His every word flirted with my senses. Everything he did turned me on. He possessed me in every sense of the word.

With his words he consumed me and with his lovemaking he drove my mind and body beyond anything I'd ever experienced. It wasn't sex; it was a fucking love drug I was hooked on. So much so that he'd cover my mouth to hush my cries at the peak of our passion. I'd send him crazy too, and I'd tease and tantalize before I'd submit and let him devour me completely.

A fellow housemate, Jerry, was also on my course, and we'd sit together in lectures. He was kind and handsome and I suspected he was sweet on me. He'd insist on buying me a coffee between lectures and often asked if we could study together. As he was super intelligent I was more than happy to pick ideas from his substantial intellect.

It wasn't long before Henry noticed this innocent friendship and after one particular lecture he asked me to stay behind.

'Shall I wait?' asked Jerry.

'No worries. I'll find you in the library,' I replied.

Henry waited for the auditorium to clear before speaking. 'I can see your nipples through that sweater.'

'Do you like it?' I said, teasingly.

'Are you even wearing a bra?' His lips twitched.

'I'd never get away without one.'

'Then, were you aroused?' he asked, his voice thick with lust.

'I can't help but be when I see you.'

'And what do you think it looks like to all those impressionable boys?'

I was beginning to feel uncomfortable and I folded my arms across my chest.

'I hadn't considered it,' I said.

'I think you have. And bare legs with that skirt...' he shook his head and heaved a sigh in response.

'But I thought you liked me in short, tight clothes?'

'Oh, I do.' He pulled my hands away and his eyes lingered upon my breasts.

Suddenly, he took my hand and led me behind the drapes at the back of the auditorium.

He pushed me against the wall. 'I want to fuck you.'

'We can't. Not here,' I protested, weakly.

He pulled up my sweater. 'You lied to me.'

'Only a small one,' I giggled, and jiggled my breasts. I figured this was another one of his games he liked to play.

His expression softened. 'Kneel down, my love.'

I knew what he wanted. What I wanted. And I turned around and got down on my hands and knees. He knelt behind me, lifted up my skirt and peeled back my knickers.

And for the briefest moment as he eased himself inside of me I felt I wasn't the only girl to have been here. Like this. Behind this curtain. With Henry. I pushed the thought from my mind.

Afterwards, I smoothed down my clothes and stood on my tiptoes to kiss him.

He pecked me on the lips and as he zipped up his trousers, he said. 'I can't stay. I've organised a one to one with Pixie.'

Pixie was one of the girls in my class. She was Finnish and funny, petite and pretty. I liked her.

'Oh, OK,' I said, but felt disappointed that we couldn't cuddle and talk like we usually did.

'Next time, I want to see you dressed appropriately for class. I can see the boys watching you and it makes me doubt where our relationship is heading.'

'I will. And I'm sorry,' I said.

And with that, Henry walked away, leaving me feeling fragile, used and close to tears.

Henry had sown the seeds of mistrust and as I left to find Jerry, I realised I'd let him down, but more importantly, I'd let myself down.

'What did letchy Ebbotson want?' asked Jerry when I found him.

'He's not letchy.'

'Not what I've heard.'

I suspected Jerry was jealous and dismissed his words.

After that, I toned down my attire which seemed to satisfy Henry. He suggested I leave a mini skirt, vest and some high heeled sandals in his office so I could dress for him. He even bought me some new clothes and lacey underwear.

It wasn't long before I began to lag behind in my other subjects and missed assignment deadlines. The crunch point came when I received a letter from the Head of Faculty which asked me to meet with her to talk about 'prioritising my workload'. I hadn't met her yet but had heard she was a brilliant Maths lecturer. My enthusiasm, other than for Statistics and Henry, had worn dangerously thin and I arrived at her office not caring a great deal what the outcome would be.

When she opened her door I recognised her instantly from seeing her around campus. She was tall with short straight mahogany hair, and impeccably beautiful in a distant way that made me feel scruffy in comparison.

She held out her hand. 'A pleasure to meet you, Anya.'

Did I imagine she looked me up and down?

She gestured for me to sit in the moulded plastic chair in front of her desk and the moment I was seated she got straight to the point.

'I understand from Mr Ebbotson,' she paused, 'my husband,' she paused again and watched me closely, 'that you are excelling in statistics.'

My head swam and my vision blurred. Why hadn't it clicked that Mrs Ebbotson was Henry's Mrs Ebbotson? I'd vaguely considered they may be related - cousins or siblings, perhaps. I took some slow breaths to steady myself.

'In contrast, your other teachers inform me they're concerned you're missing classes and not completing assignments, even when extensions are granted.'

'I'm sorry, I haven't been feeling well recently.'

'I see,' she said. 'And are you well now?'

'Much better. Thank you.'

'Is there any other reason for your lack of commitment to your other subjects?'

She waited, but I couldn't think of a suitable answer.

'I'm confused,' she continued. 'Why is it that you show such enthusiasm in Mr Ebbotson's classes and little elsewhere?'

'It's more interesting,' I said, feebly.

'You will fail your exams unless you improve your focus and complete all assignments,' she said. 'Do you understand?' Her tone left no room for manoeuvre.

'Yes. I understand.' Though my thoughts were in a whirl.

She came and sat on the edge of her desk and crossed her long stockinged legs.

'Can I share something with you, Anya?'

I nodded and writhed uneasily in my seat.

She picked up a framed photograph from her desk and brushed the glass with her perfectly polished fingertips. She turned it around to show me.

'I have a one year old baby daughter and a four year old son.' She watched for my reaction. 'And there's nothing my husband and I like more than going home after a long day at work and spending time together with our young children.'

For several seconds I forgot to breathe as I looked at the perfectly imperfect model family before me.

'How lovely,' I said, but the walls staggered inwards.

'And one day, you too can have that. A fulfilling career, a devoted and loving husband and even children. If that's what you want.'

'I do want a career,' I said.

'A career in accountancy?'

'I thought so,' I said.

'Then might I suggest that you think about what it is you really want.' She leaned over and smoothed her hand down the endless length of her calf. 'I find an honest reality check is vital sometimes.' She looked directly at me. 'Is this making sense for you?'

'I think so.' I began to cry. 'And I'm sorry.' It was obvious she knew, or at least harboured suspicions about my relationship with Henry. He never wore a wedding ring. I'd thought he was single. How stupid I had been.

As I walked home through the park, my cheeks soaked with tears, something inside of me switched. I realised I was only a part of a sordid tradition. A tradition whereby Henry picked out a student he fancied, seduced her and made her fall in love with him and then treated her with disdain the deeper she fell. And when I thought of him, instead of feeling deep desire and love, I felt foolish, guilty and enraged.

In the days that followed I swung from tears one minute to fury at my naivety the next. After I missed our arranged rendezvous I ignored Henry's texts, phone calls and voice messages. I was dreading my next statistics lecture and considered missing it, but given that I was trying to make an effort to at least pass my first year exams I decided I must attend. Such was my fury with him that at the last minute I dressed in an angora crop top, suede mini skirt and knee high stiletto boots. I took my seat in the front row of the lecture theatre. Even Jerry asked what the power dressing was in aid of. When Henry spotted me he was unable to hide his shock at my appearance.

I leaned over and whispered in Jerry's ear. 'You were right about letchy Ebby.'

Jerry turned to me, drew his lower lip between his teeth, then whispered back. 'Bet he'd like to lick your boots.'

I threw my head back and dissolved into laughter.

I caught Henry's eye and he glared.

'May I ask what the joke is, Miss McGregor?' he asked.

'Sorry, Mr Ebbotson,' I said. 'Jerry's so funny I couldn't help myself.'

'See me after the lecture,' he said, visibly restraining his anger.

As we packed away our books I said to Jerry. 'Please wait with me. He might be nicer with you here.'

After the other students had vacated the auditorium, Jerry remained seated and I walked across to Henry who stood with arms folded and back straight as a rod.

'Jerry,' called Henry. 'Please go to your next lecture.'

Jerry stood up and swung his rucksack onto his back. 'I'll wait for you outside, Anya.'

As the door swung shut behind him, Henry grabbed my arm.

'I love you, you stupid bitch. Why are you being like this?'

I pulled his hand off me. 'Why didn't you tell me you were married?'

'Because I thought you knew,' he said.

'You mean because you dropped it into the conversation? And you wear a wedding ring?' I mocked. 'I'd never have slept with you.' I burst into tears. 'I'd never have fallen for you.'

'But I don't love her,' he said. 'I love you. You're the most perfectly beautiful girl I've ever seen and I want you to be mine forever.'

'But I don't want you. Everything's changed.'

'You can't simply switch off a love as powerful as ours,' he said.

'It never was love. It was pure lust. Only not so pure because you were never mine in the first place.'

He gripped my shoulders. 'I'll leave her. I want you so much, my sweet girl.'

He tried to kiss me and I ducked and pushed him away. 'You have children,' I said through my tears.

He shook his head as if to deny their existence. And I hated him even more.

'I've fallen in love with Jerry,' I said, defiantly.

Henry sneered. 'He's a boy.'

'Yes, he's much younger than you and he's honest and funny, too.'

Henry ran his tongue slowly across his bottom lip. 'But does he make you wet like I do?'

'Stop it.' I turned away but he gripped my shoulder. I kicked my leg behind, wrestled free and rushed for the door.

'You'll never stop wanting me,' he said.

As I opened the auditorium doors I called back. 'I already have.'

Chapter 21

The sound of tyres crunching over the gravel awoke me and I jumped out of bed and opened the blinds. I watched Toby slam the car door and glance up at our window. He scraped a hand through his hair and I glimpsed a smile. I waved down and he gave a wave back. Relief flooded through me.

Later that morning, when we arrived at Riseham village hall, Saul, Dom and Alex had already set out the chairs leaving an aisle down the middle.

Rose turned to Gemma. 'Thanks, Gem. I'll manage now.'

I looked at Rose with affection. 'You won't need that chair much longer.'

She stretched her legs. 'I can't wait to get this pot off. The itching is unbearable.'

'That means your feeling is returning fast, my girl,' I said.

'Then I'll stop moaning,' she said, and folded her arms. 'Right now.'

Saul waved from the far end of the hall and marched over. He called back to Alex and Dom. 'Guys, come and say hello.'

I caught Gemma's eye and she cracked a smile.

Saul wore a navy suit, white shirt and tie and had shaved his usual stubble. The boys too, looked tidy with smart shirts and trousers.

'Saul, meet Stevie,' I said.

Saul shook her hand. 'You're like your Mum.'

'I guess that's a compliment,' said Stevie with a quick grin.

'It certainly is,' Saul said and looked my way.

'And this is Gemma,' I said.

They shook hands and exchanged smiles and greetings.

Alex and Dom joined us.

'Alex.' He gave a salute to Stevie and Gemma. 'And little bruv, Dom.'

Dom frowned. 'I can introduce myself, you know?'

Stevie tucked a strand of hair behind her ear and her eyes grew wide as she looked from one boy to the other.

Eight chairs had been arranged at the trestle table on the stage. Four for each side of the camp.

'Let's take our seats and sort out the paperwork,' I suggested.

'Nicola's bringing Paul Mahoney, our council insider. But remember he's supposedly here as an unbiased observer,' Saul said. 'He's Senior Planning, lives locally and dead against fracking,' he added.

'I've got a list of who's who amongst the enemy, and in brief, what I could find out about them,' I said.

'Good stuff,' said Saul.

I looked around as people that I did and didn't recognise filtered into the hall. I spotted Marianne and Tim.

'Hey guys.' I beckoned them over.

Marianne weaved her way through the throng and hugged me.

'Feeling nervous?' she said.

'Literally quaking, which is why I need you and Tim at the front,' I said. 'Cheers for the good guys and jeers and rotten tomatoes for the bad.'

'If you want me up there beside you, give me the nod.' Marianne turned her attention to Saul. 'Mr Vermaak.' Her eyelids fluttered and she tilted her head a touch.

How terribly unsubtle, I thought.

His eyes crinkled at the corners. 'We've met, I believe.'

She chortled. 'Oh, you remember.'

I spotted Nicola as she entered the hall with a portly middle aged man.

I stepped nearer to Saul. 'Let's talk tactics with Nicola and Paul.'

'There's so much riding on this,' he said.

And in his face I saw he felt the weight of responsibility. As did I. We had to perform well and make an impact.

'Turnout is encouraging,' I said, as yet more bodies filed into the hall.

Nicola introduced us to Paul. Most noticeable about him was his salt and pepper beard, more salt than pepper. When I shook his hand it felt warm and clammy. He released mine and proceded to wring his hands together.

His eyes appeared startled as they darted around the hall.

He turned back to Nicola. 'Do you want me right at the front?' A sheen of perspiration gleamed on his forehead and the bridge of his nose.

'Of course,' she said, her tone brisk. 'Right between us and the enemy, I should think.'

'You mean, like piggy in the middle?' he gave a nervous laugh and headed off to find his seat.

'Is he all right?' I asked Nicola and lowered my voice.

'He doesn't know how he's going to contribute. He can hardly admit to leaking stuff, neither does he want to defend the frackers,' she said. 'He doesn't want to blow it.'

'I think we're all feeling like that,' I said.

'Bring it on, I say,' she replied.

And I felt braver. If Nicola could be bold, despite the threats made to her life, so could I.

'Have you spotted the enemy?' I asked her.

'In the car park. Vaping and chatting as if they were off for a pint.'

'Do you know any of them?'

'I recognise Hugh Plant, the CEO. He's got a reputation for being loud and arrogant. No surprises there.'

In front of us, the seats were filling and my stomach did a tumble.

We'd booked the hall for three hours, and according to protocol, each side had been given a total of forty minutes to state their case. We were first. Or rather, I was first.

Saul called a start to the meeting.

I took a breath, pushed my chair back and stood up.

'Good morning everybody. Some of you here will know me - Anya Kubik from Willows End Livery. With your support today and in the coming weeks and months, I'm confident we can prevent what would be catastrophic for Wensleydale. To our land, water supplies, our children's and our own health as well as the wellbeing of our animals and livestock.

Wensleydale is an area of outstanding natural beauty and the chemicals used in the fracking process are not selective where they spread from the water table. This will sound alarming, but I guarantee the carcinogenic chemicals used will contaminate our soil and water for years to come. We drink the water, and therefore, we too are at risk of being poisoned.'

I realised I was speaking too quickly and I took a breath and slowed down.

'Furthermore, tourism in Wensleydale is essential to the local economy. To our hotels, restaurants, shops, art and cultural venues, and visitors will stay away for fear of ingesting the chemicals and methane released during the fracking process. Quadrillum will tell you the chemicals are contained, but we only have to look at America and Australia to see how the lives and businesses of those close to fracking sites have been devastated. Burns to children's skin from water supplies, respiratory problems, children fainting, people being confined to their homes for weeks on end because of the noxious fumes outside. Ponds, streams and rivers have been decimated and animal and plant life killed off. In many cases, the value of residential properties fell by well over half.' I paused, and a murmur spread throughout the hall.

I watched people's expressions as they registered the information, then as they exchanged whispers with those around them. I glanced over at Hugh Plant and he caught my eye. His eyes narrowed and he pushed his tongue into his cheek. I knew exactly what he was hinting at and my anger blazed.

He looked like a beast of a man, with eyes that sliced through his prey. He ran his thick tongue between his lips and turned back to the audience. As the sun burned down on the roof and with the hall full of people, the air grew uncomfortably warm. The sweat shone on Hugh Plant's face, and suddenly becoming conscious of this, he mopped himself with his handkerchief.

Undeterred by his attempts to intimidate me, I continued. 'Can we afford to risk the health of our families and our animals? When shale is split to release natural gas, trapped methane is also released and inevitably this rises to the surface. It rises through the aquifer and surface water and into the air and through our water channels. There have also been numerous cases of wells exploding and sending heavy machinery flying. Can you imagine if there was a methane leak close to, or in our homes? This is a genuine possibility and we cannot allow anyone to suggest otherwise.'

I glanced at my timer. I turned to Nicola and Saul who nodded their agreement.

'I could cite numerous examples of drinking water turning murky brown due to poisonous chemicals leaking into the natural water supplies. Some of you may have heard about the flaming tap. When drinking water is contaminated with methane and a splint is held next to the flowing water, the water ignites. The methane ignites.

'And finally, if we allow Quadrillum to drill in Wensleydale, tremors will begin immediately. Larger tremors will pause fracking temporarily, but won't prevent damage to infrastructure - our roads, farm buildings, your homes. Do we really want that risk hanging over us?'

I stopped and looked around at people's reactions.

'Thank you for listening. I'll hand over now to Nicola Marsden, Richmond News, and Paul Mahoney, from Richmond Council, who'll fill you in with regard to the fracking license, proposed sites and timings.'

The audience applauded loudly and I glanced to my left to see the CEO and his colleagues whisper to one another. Hugh Plant glared at me and faked a smile. Smug bastard. I turned to the audience and Marianne gave me a thumbs up.

Still in her neck brace, Nicola hadn't attempted to hide her bruises with makeup.

'Good morning all,' she said. 'I've been investigating Quadrillum's intention to frack here in Wensleydale. I've left copies of my articles and reports at the entrance. Please do read or take a copy. My apologies for my appearance today. You may be wondering why I'm bruised and wearing this neck contraption. One week ago I was the victim of a road rage crime. Wholly unprovoked. I was driving at an average speed along a main road near Richmond when I was overtaken by a silver car driven by a man. He cut me up and slammed on his brakes. I had no option but to swerve off the road which resulted in these injuries. I could have been killed, but I was lucky.'

Hugh Plant stood up, his face flushed and failing to hide his anger. 'Young lady. Are you accusing Quadrillum?'

She glared at him, her voice dry. 'Did I specify names or businesses?'

He coughed. 'It seems you're working up to it.'

'And should I be?' Her question hung in the air.

'This is ridiculous,' he finally spluttered. 'Typical wo…' He stopped.

'Typical woman?' Nicola prompted, her expression incredulous.

He turned to the audience. 'This woman's behaviour is bordering on hysterical.' He rounded on Nicola. 'For all we know you were driving atrociously, and the frustrated driver was merely trying to pass and move on.'

'I can assure you, Mr Plant, Richmond police know precisely what happened. It was a deliberate attempt on my life. Thankfully, I'm still alive to warn these good people here that some will stop at nothing to get what they want.'

She sat back down and the audience mumbled their disquiet.

'You won't get away with this.' A man stood up in the second row and shouted over to Hugh Plant. I recognised him as Philip Marsden, Nicola's husband. 'None of us will allow fracking here. Trust me, you ain't seen how determined Yorkshire folk are when deceived or crossed.'

Hugh Plant stood up. 'Will you sit down. There will be time for questions later. And you will hardly be able to stop us if we go through the proper channels.'

Marianne stood up. 'Proper channels? You're having a laugh. You mean expensive lawyers who weedle round regulation and offer backhanders?'

'Here here!' 'Frack off!' Voices began to echo around the hall. 'Fuck off frackers.' People got up off their seats. There were jeers and taunts and someone threw a pen which was well aimed and caught Hugh Plant on the arm. He stood up and stamped on it. There were more taunts from the audience.

I stood up, as did Saul. Nicola appeared particularly pleased with how the meeting was progressing and gave me a sidelong look of approval.

'Please everybody,' I called above the hubbub and the shouting dropped to murmurs. 'Thank you. I fully understand your concerns. But please let's allow all of the speakers to say what they came to say and I assure you there will be time for questions as well as answers.'

'Paul?' Saul said to Paul Mahoney on his left.

Paul pushed back his chair. He picked up his papers which rattled in his hands.

His eyes darted here and there as he spoke too quietly and too quickly about timings; just weeks away, as though all had been decided and given the go ahead. He failed to mention the imminent plans to set up their operation.

'These are proposed plans that have not yet been signed off,' he finished.

Our insider lacked conviction, and judging by the snarl on Nicola's lips, she thought the same.

What a lily livered sock puppet, I thought. We should have vetted him thoroughly first.

Hugh Plant stood up, and slid his tongue along his bottom lip once more. The room silenced. 'It's time I brought some solid facts to the table and set straight exactly what this exciting industry can bring to you, your community, and, let's not be coy about this, your pockets. Firstly, you should know the anti-fracking movement are doing hardworking families a huge disservice. The boost from extracting your natural gas will refill the county coffers. Your council tax goes up each year. How many of you despair at the funding cuts in your children's schools, for local childcare provision, for keeping open community centres and libraries?'

I knew he spouted bullshit. The local council wouldn't see a penny; only Quadrillum, central government and maybe a small cup of snake oil for the landowners.

'We've been granted a license to drill in areas that will least impact housing and farmland. And without affecting any protected nature reserves. We'll recruit local labour and if any of you or your family members are seeking work, this could benefit you directly. Our country needs to secure additional energy sources. Without cheaper energy the British economy is under threat.'

I'd done my research and knew these were lies, poorly disguised as flimsy facts. Shale gas could only be used to fuel lorries and buses, not the average petrol car. Not even diesel. Hugh Plant continued on and on in that vein until Saul stood up to inform him his allotted time was up.

Hugh Plant brought his spiel to a close. 'Extraction of shale gas is essential to the UK economy. Shall we delay and pass it over like we did with North Sea oil? Or shall we allow future generations to profit from our innovation and business acumen?'

Murmurs rippled through the audience, followed by a few nods of interest. I turned to Saul who was already on his feet as he waited to speak.

He stood tall and lifted his chin.

I felt another rush of adrenaline.

'There isn't much I can add to what Anya and Nicola have already explained. But I would like to draw your attention to two major problems. This week I've been speaking to the British bats conservation trust and following a visit from one of their experts, I must inform Quadrillum that they've located at least two sites where bats are roosting and where Quadrillum have put in plans to drill. The eaves of the barns are thick with bat dung which means they've been there for some time. Their habitats are protected by law. Secondly, I have received a sample of tap water from the East coast of America, where fracking has been taking place in numerous wells for several years.'

He reached into a bag, lifted out a bottle of water, held it up for the audience to see then placed it onto the table. The water looked crystal clear.

'This water is from my outdoor tap fed by a natural well,' he said to the audience.

He caught my eye and I raised a brow.

Saul reached into the bag once again and produced a second bottle. He held it up, similarly. The audience gasped when they saw the murky brown water.

Hugh Plant stood up and walked around to the front of the table.

'This is outrageous slander.' He snatched the bottle from Saul, unscrewed the top and poured it onto the floor until the bottle was empty. 'You can no more prove that water came from a tap near a fracking site than from a muddy pond.'

'Oh, but I can,' said Saul calmly. And he pulled a letter from his pocket. 'This is a letter from a Mrs Joan Riddleston, the farmer and landowner I mentioned. It's her testament, also signed and stamped by her lawyer, to confirm the sample is from her kitchen tap. Anyone in doubt is free to read this letter, including yourself, Mr Plant. And I have another water sample currently being analysed for a full breakdown and analysis of chemicals; the results of which will be available in a day or two. We will be publishing the results in local and national newspapers. This water came from a farm three hundred metres from a fracking well.'

Marianne rose to her feet. 'May I ask a question?'

'Please, go ahead,' said Saul.

She looked directly at the other end of the table. 'Would you allow your wife or children to drink the filthy contaminated water, Mr Plant?'

He glared at Marianne and the silence dragged as we waited for his reply.

Finally, he spoke. 'My dear woman. If you're naive enough to believe this ridiculous claim, then I can assume you come to this meeting as ignorant as many others. I suggest you read the booklet I give out at the end of the meeting.' He waved it over his head. 'This contains facts, not fanciful fiction.'

Anger flared in Marianne's eyes. 'Excuse me, you pompous, greedy, fool of a man. You have called me, my friends and Yorkshiremen here, ignorant. I think we can all safely conclude you've dug your own pit to lie in regarding plans to frack in Wensleydale.' She remained standing and resolute.

Beside Marianne, Tim stood up and then one or two other members of the audience stood up behind them. Tim began to clap slowly and the others joined in. When Saul and I stood too, virtually everyone else in the hall did the same. And as the clapping intensified and a cacophony of angry voices grew, Mr Plant's mouth set tighter and his cheeks grew redder.

Chapter 22

The nature of the post presentation questions made it clear that no one bought into Quadrillum's story and I felt relieved the meeting had gone well, if not better than I could have anticipated. We headed down to The Black Horse for a post mortem analysis and much needed drink.

Set to the north of the village, the Inn looked onto a green with ancient Oaks and a pond circled with bullrushes, slim and velvet tipped. Beyond the pond and through iron gates, stood the picturesque church of St. Wilfrid's, small but proud amongst the gravestones, mounds and furrows. Beneath one twisted yew were three graves that remained close to our hearts, and at which we'd periodically leave flowers and clear away the weeds and detritus brought to rest by the wind.

Like many of the buildings in Riseham, the Inn dated back to Tudor times. Beams criss crossed the Yorkshire stone, and since Marianne, a keen gardener, had taken over ownership, clematis and pink roses grew colourful and abundant up the walls.

A warm fug of people hit me as Saul and I weaved our way through to the bar.

I touched his arm. 'You were quite brilliant,' I said.

He lifted a brow. 'I was merely fortunate with my research.'

'A bit more than that, and you know it.'

'OK. I guess I know more about these things now.'

'It's been a steep learning curve for both of us,' I said.

'If it hadn't been for my chancing upon those bats, we'd have all been none the wiser.'

'Funny thing is, I see them all the time, but had no idea they were protected,' I said.

'It was Dom who told me. So it's him we should thank.' Saul looked over to our teens as they chatted with triumphant and smiling faces round the table. 'Anyway, it was your speech that had everyone enthralled. Even the enemy,' he said.

'Hardly. They were laughing at me.'

'It was nervous laughter,' he said.

'Stop it.' I giggled.

'I was slightly in awe, too,' he added.

'I'm only glad I prepared well,' I said.

Marianne stood watching us from the other side of the bar.

'Would either of you like a drink?' She had a cheeky glint in her eye.

'Is something in your eye?' I replied.

'It's called a twinkle,' said Saul.

'Well observed,' said Marianne. 'Now, what can I get you? On the house, as you've brought a crowd along.'

'Did you see their fat ugly faces when you showed them that revolting water?' Rose said to Saul, as he placed the drinks on the table.

'I didn't have much choice when Mr Plant grabbed it from me,' replied Saul, and he drank a mouthful of beer with obvious satisfaction. 'This looks and no doubt tastes infinitely better.'

'Is that really what our tap water will look like if they start fracking?' asked Dom, who picked at his finger.

'It genuinely happens,' said Saul, 'to some households.'

'Can you imagine being burned by chemicals in the shower and having to buy drinking water to avoid swallowing chemicals?' asked Stevie, aghast.

Saul set his pint on a beer mat. 'Which is why we'll fight until we see them off, whimpering with their tails between their legs.'

'Hey Mum,' Rose said. 'You could talk to the sixth formers at school. You'd get their support and they might come to the protests.'

'If you wouldn't mind,' I said.

'If you gave the speech you gave today, I'd be proud.'

'Then I'll call Mrs Barrows,' I said.

The new head teacher of Richmond High, Mrs Barrows, had proved to be a popular and inspirational leader. I hoped this would be evident in the girls' upcoming exam results.

Rose looked over my shoulder and her face broke into a smile. 'Hey, Dad.'

I turned around.

'Mind if I join you?' asked Toby.

Dark shadows lurked beneath his eyes and he didn't smile.

'Darling,' I said. 'Come and hear all about the meeting.'

'Looks like I came at the right time,' Toby said, with a glance at our glasses.

'Can you buy some crisps?' asked Rose. 'No meat flavours.'

'You know none of them have actual meat in?' said Stevie.

'That's not the point,' Rose replied. 'I don't like the thought of chicken, or bacon. Becoming a vegetarian makes you think about how humans treat animals like products, not living creatures with as much right to be here as us.'

'We eat meat to survive,' said Stevie. 'It's in our genes.'

'Earth can't sustain the world's growing population on meat. We have to adapt and it could mean leaving meat behind and using our land to produce enough crops to feed more, not to keep the likes of McDonald's stocked with fatty burgers to make us unhealthy.'

I smiled at Rose riding on her high horse and intervened. 'Get a selection, please, Toby.'

While Toby headed to the bar, Saul pulled up another chair for him. I was surprised to see Toby, but happy he'd made the effort to come. This was a genuine show of support.

When Toby returned, he and Saul shook hands and made some polite exchanges, though Toby's reticence felt palpable.

Toby drank his pint as Saul and I described our successes and Saul's trump card.

'Anya is giving me too much credit,' said Saul. 'If anyone swung the case in our favour, it was her.'

Toby slapped his empty glass onto the table. 'Indeed. I know only too well how persuasive and charming my wife can be.'

Saul didn't respond with a smile, but stood up to return to the bar. 'Then it's charm put to excellent use.'

'Still, you haven't yet prevented the fracking. Perhaps only stalled it, while they look into the bat situation,' Toby said to Saul. 'If they even bother.'

'The bats won't vacate their home,' Rose interjected.

'You realise Quadrillum will select another site where there are no bats,' said Toby.

My frustration rose in response to his negativity. 'Hey, whose side are you on?'

154

'Yours, obviously. I'm merely stating the counterargument and obvious next move for Quadrillum. I'm doing you a favour by not congratulating you before you've won. Be prepared for a backlash, that's all I'm saying.' His mouth set in a hard line.

'Let me get you a drink,' said Saul, and reached over to take Toby's glass.

Toby placed his palm over his glass. 'I have work to do, unfortunately.'

I rested my hand on his. 'Stay for a bit, darling.'

He thought for a moment. 'A half then,' he said to Saul. 'Thanks.'

'Let me help,' I said, and stood up.

Saul leaned on the bar. 'I'll head home after this one.'

'I thought we were celebrating.'

He leaned in close. 'I'm sensing Mr Kubik might prefer I wasn't here.'

'Not at all,' I said.

He rubbed his chin as he thought. 'I know men aren't supposed to have intuition, but it's a feeling I'm getting.'

I nodded. 'OK. Toby is jealous. It's a recent thing.'

'If you were mine, I'd be suspicious of any man befriending you.'

'Oh.' I felt a rush of blood to my head.

'Sorry. I shouldn't say...'

Toby walked briskly up to my side and as he turned to face Saul his lips drew back in a snarl. 'Forget the drink, mate. I'm leaving.'

'Stop, Toby,' I said.

'And you and the girls are coming.' He grasped my arm, and turned to our table. 'Stevie, Rose. We're leaving.'

The girls looked over and I watched confusion rise in their faces.

'Stop it,' I hissed.

'Do you want everyone to hear?' He glared, and paused for an answer. 'Or shall we talk in private?'

I turned to the girls and Gemma. 'I'm so sorry.'

'Why are you leaving, Dad?' Stevie came across and stood in front of Toby. 'You've only just got here.'

'Let me drop the girls home later,' offered Saul.

155

Toby turned and with his face inches from Saul's, he spat, 'You tosser!'

Toby released my arm. As he stormed towards the exit he barged his way through a group of people causing one man to spill his drink over the woman next to him. I'd seen them at meeting.

'Oi! Watch it mate.' The man grabbed Toby's shirt and yanked him back. 'Apologise to my wife.'

'It wasn't me spilled my pint, matey,' said Toby. Not in the least intimidated. 'It's you who should apologise.'

The man – tall and built like a mountain gorilla, swung his fist at Toby, who ducked and neatly avoided the punch. Toby jostled through the throng and dashed to the door. Uncool, but I was grateful he didn't want to join the fight.

The entire pub fell to silence as everyone looked on.

Marianne leaned across the bar. 'Oh my God, Anya.'

Stevie took my hand and her voice shook. 'What's up with Dad?'

'I don't know, but I need to find out. I'm so sorry.'

I looked across at Rose who was trying to manoeuvre her wheelchair. 'Please look after Rose,' I said to Stevie, and releasing her hand, I hurried to the exit.

Toby was already reversing out of the space and I ran round and opened the passenger door. He kept reversing as I scrambled into the front seat and pulled the door shut. Toby didn't acknowledge me and without looking he pulled out into the road, with a squeal of tyres.

My stomach did somersaults as Toby put his foot down and drove stupidly fast out of the village and with jaw set and eyes fixed on the road ahead. His mobile pinged. He glanced at the screen and the wheels rumbled off the side of the road.

'Jesus Christ, Toby. Are you trying to kill us?'

Without replying, he slipped his phone into the door pocket and as he focused on the road again, he adjusted his speed.

I switched over the stereo channel and as a violin piece played, I stared out across the moor. Feeling confused and scared, I watched the heather and sky melt into one another in a passing blur. The silence between us lengthened.

As Toby parked up at home and yanked on the handbrake, a wave of nausea sent my head spinning. And for a moment I tried to conjure up an excuse to go to the stables - something that couldn't wait.

Toby rammed his door shut and stormed into the house without a backward glance. He left the front door wide open.

With fear ripping through me, I followed him into the kitchen. 'Let's talk in the garden,' I suggested. 'I've got fresh rolls and there's salad and cream cheese.'

Toby didn't reply but stood and stared out of the French windows.

'I don't know about you, but I'm starving,' I continued, and loathed myself for sounding so timid and desperate. 'Do you want anything?'

In truth, my appetite had vanished.

Toby turned around, slowly. 'Anya, please sit down.'

'I'll make us a coffee first.'

He gave an audible sigh before he pulled out a chair for me. 'Sit down.'

Resigned to hear him out, I leaned against the worktop, and folded my arms.

'My laptop was doing an update that was taking forever so I borrowed yours,' said Toby.

'And?'

He glared at me with an unnerving intensity.

I turned away, picked up a glass from the draining board and ran the cold tap.

'Is there anything you've forgotten to tell me?' he asked.

I sipped from the glass. 'Nothing that springs to mind.'

'Then let me jog your memory. I don't imagine it'll come as any great surprise.'

My legs weakened. Had I even logged out yesterday?

'Tell me about your relationship with Saul? You owe me that, at least.'

I drank another mouthful of water and held it in my mouth until it became warm. I swallowed. 'We're friends. Acquaintances, really.'

He regarded me for some seconds with eyes that grew dark and unyielding. 'I think you and he are far more than that.'

'We've chatted a lot.' My voice cracked. 'But only because of the fracking.'

'Nothing to do with him being easy on the eye and a tight arsed slimeball?'

'And what precisely have you done to support our community against the frackers?' My nerves switched to anger. 'Nothing! You even colluded with the surveyors to 'check out' our water supplies and our land. Thankfully, Saul cares about the area, the wildlife, the water that irrigates our crops, feeds our people and animals.'

Toby walked over, then slowly and deliberately he took the glass from my hand, raised it above his head and launched it at the window. I turned and placed my palms over my ears as the collision sprayed shards of glass in all directions. I dashed to the back door and turned the handle, but found it locked.

His hand clamped onto my shoulder. I yelped and ducked but he kept his hold and pulled me against him while he clasped his other arm around my chest.

'I'm not going to hurt you.' His voice grew deep and controlled. 'I only want to talk.'

'Let-me-go!' I hissed. 'Then we'll talk.'

But he squeezed even tighter - his chest rammed hard against my back.

'You're scaring me,' I whimpered.

'You're only scared because I've found out about your affair with Saul.'

'There is no affair.' I struggled to breathe and get my words out.

He gripped my arms and turned me round to face him then shook me back and forth. 'Tell me the truth, Anya.'

I raised my knee to his groin, but missed. 'Get the fuck off me, Toby.'

He stopped, lowered his face to mine. 'Then explain the messages.'

I felt his spittle on my face.

'Messages?' And inside, my guts liquefied.

Toby pulled a mock thoughtful expression. '"Are you free tomorrow? I can come over. I really want to talk to you." Your words, Anya.'

'"Can't wait to see you. Kiss, kiss." Saul's words,' Toby said, in a sing-song voice. 'The kisses are a sweet touch.'

'If you let me go and calm down I'll try to explain.'

He released me and his hands fell to his sides.

I only wanted to run away from him; from his accusations.

I rubbed my arms. 'You've hurt me. I hope you're pleased with yourself.'

'So, tell me.' He cast a glance at the gaping window. 'I'm waiting.' Then he pulled out a dining chair, sat down and drummed his thigh with his fingers.

I leaned against the worktop. 'OK,' I said. 'You deserve to know what has, and hasn't happened.'

He nodded. 'Indeed I do.'

'Saul and I have grown close and it's my fault. You know his wife was murdered, so he's vulnerable. I should have kept a distance and said the right things when he showed an interest.'

'Is he good in bed?' Toby's nostrils flared and his eyes welled with tears.

'We haven't slept together, silly.'

'Why should I believe that?'

'Because I'm not you. I can show restraint,' I said.

'And here we go again. I wondered how long it would be before you brought her up.'

'I don't want to, but you need reminding it was your past behaviour that almost destroyed us.'

'You know why and how it happened.'

'I know your version,' I said.

'And you know, Anya, that I've regretted the affair ever since. There's not a day goes by when I don't remember how much I hurt you.'

'Good. And I wouldn't have brought her up again, but I haven't slept with Saul and you did have sex with Diane. Several times, in fact. Find out the truth before you go smashing windows like a thug and throwing me around. What's the matter with you?'

'I don't care about the window. And I'm sorry if I hurt you. But I love you,' he paused. 'If he's touched you I'll...'

'I'll tell you. If you swear not to threaten him, or hurt me.'

159

Toby's eyes blazed, but after a moment he nodded his acceptance.

'OK. I admit Saul and I have grown to know one another. And perhaps this was driven by a physical attraction. But more on his part. A week ago, after we'd visited Nicola, following the road rage attack on her, I drove him home and he asked me in for a coffee.'

'Jeez! What a cliche,' Toby snarled.

'Not a cliche. That was my only intention.'

'Self-delusion is a curse,' he growled.

I ignored him and continued.

'He showed me around the house. It needs work but has some lovely features.'

'How about his etchings?'

'Please, Toby. Let me explain.'

He rubbed his forehead with his fingers then exhaled.

How could I truthfully relay to Toby, my husband of twenty years, what had happened? It would destroy him. It could destroy our marriage. I'd forgiven his affair. Once. I would never tolerate another. But, Toby? There was no way he'd accept what I'd done as a mere mistake.

I recalled the afternoon. My emotions had been heightened by the attack on Nicola. It surprised me how supportive and strong Saul had been towards her and myself. I'd felt a chemistry develop between us from the moment we'd met. That afternoon when I dropped him home, I knew he'd invite me in, and I also knew I would accept. We both knew 'coffee' was an excuse. And as we climbed the stairs, side by side, I'd felt his fingers brush mine. On the landing, he took hold of my hand and led me along the corridor - anticipation fluttering in the pit of my stomach because I knew where he was taking me. Our hands remained laced together, and as he'd told me about the attic rooms above and the old relics left behind by the previous owners, I felt the blood pulse in his hand - fast and heavy.

In the bedroom, he drew back the velvet drapes and sunlight filled the room. 'See that view, Anya' he said. 'It captured me from the start.'

I stood before the window and gazed down at the summer brushed lawn and to the lake and wild woodland beyond.

I swallowed. 'I can see why.'

'It isn't only that view that's captured me,' he said, with a rasp that caught in his throat.

I sensed him move closer behind me. The warmth of his breath. The scent of his unique essence that burrowed into my skin. And when his hand fell upon my shoulder I lifted mine and placed it over his. He moved closer still then leaned down and kissed my fingers. He gathered my hair, drew it aside and hot spikes of desire fired through me, making me tremble. And when he planted the softest kisses upon my neck, his breath hung like static silk across my skin. I moaned. He turned me round to face him. By then I didn't question what I was doing, or the consequences. I felt driven by an energy that had stirred into life and was sweeping me along with gigantic force.

His eyes held mine with an intensity that enthralled me and as he cupped my chin with his hand, he parted his lips. The thirst in his eyes fuelled my need for love and connection, and I pressed my lips upon his. As we kissed and touched one another, my blood was flooded with an uncontrollable longing. We pulled at one another's clothes, hands and skin upon skin, our eyes, and senses driving our desire. He clasped my waist and led me over to the bed. Slowly, we undressed one another, and as we did we drank in one another's bodies, each curve and angle, the textures and hues of flesh and form. Being naked together felt natural and incredible all at once, and seeing every part of him, the exposure of muscle and darkness, shocked all of my senses, sending them reeling into a state of reckless craving.

Saul, gazed down at me. He cupped the fullness of my breasts leaned down and licked and kissed so that a fluttering swelled between my legs and wet warmth spread through me.

He held my face. 'Each time I see you, hear your voice, and probably from the moment we met, the thought of touching you and loving you... I've thought of nothing else.'

I don't recall my reply. I was lost and beyond rational thought.

As we kissed again, we fell onto the bed and our limbs moved together and slipped skin against skin, instinctually. Our bodies clasped and entwined and shuddered in a rapturous frenzy.

*He pulled away and looked at me - his eyes drunk with lust.
'I want you, Anya,' he whispered. 'And If we make love now I'll
want you forever.'*

*My senses feasted upon his physique which was pure and
perfect. If I fell in love with looks alone, I'd fall in love with Saul
and never let him go. And when he slid his fingers between my
thighs and into the softness of my core, desire poured through
me. I sighed and opened myself to him.*

'I need you.' I breathed.

*But then I heard something else over the sound of our
combined breaths and the blood pounding in my ears.*

Footsteps and then a voice. 'Dad?'

*'Jesus.' Saul fell away and as he did, he smacked his head on
the headboard. 'Alex,' he mouthed.*

*I reached for the sheet and pulled it over me. 'I thought you
said he and Dom were out all day,' I whispered.*

*Saul rubbed the back of his head. 'I'm getting changed,' he
called.*

'Can I come in?' Alex was right at the door.

*'Only if you want to see your old dad naked.' Saul forced a
shot of laughter.*

'Ughh, no thanks,' came Alex's reply.

*I listened as Alex's footsteps retreated and finally, there was
silence.*

*We waited. Neither of us daring to speak. My heart still
thundered. Saul jumped up and walked to the door. My eyes
followed him. His legs were long, lean and strong. Above a slim
waist his shoulders were broad and tanned. His buttocks were
round and toned to perfection. Slowly, he turned the handle and
peered through. He closed it again and turned back to me. 'Lucky
the door swings shut.'*

'No it doesn't. You shut it,' I said, and giggled.

He chortled, without embarrassment. 'So I did.'

*He walked back to the bed without a hint of shyness at his
arousal and nakedness. He lifted the sheet away from me and his
eyes ran the length of my body. He shook his head. 'You are the
most insanely beautiful woman I've ever seen.' He leaned over
and kissed my mouth. His lips felt warm and sensual.*

'Stop. Please.' I sighed.

'Do you mean stop, or...?'

'Maybe. Maybe not.' I pushed him onto his back.

'My dear lady. Your reputation would have been in tatters.'

I giggled. 'It's not funny, Saul.'

'I should have bolted the doors. And the windows,' he said.

'Maybe Alex has saved us a whole lot of trouble,' I said, but felt frustrated that we'd been interrupted.

'Maybe he's just ruined his Dad's day, week, month and year.' Saul sighed. 'My entire life.'

'Stop,' I said again and jumped up.

I picked up my discarded knickers and stepped into them.

'Let me help.' Saul jumped off the bed retrieved my bra and held it up. He wet his lips with his tongue. 'Although every fibre in my body is screaming not to.'

I put my arms through the straps and he placed the cups over my breasts and slowly turned me around to hook the back.

He kissed my shoulder. 'Do you always wear such pretty lingerie?'

'Mostly, yes.' I lied, and turned around. Pretty lingerie and riding horses didn't go well together. In the saddle, a thong sliced me in two and lacy bras offered little support.

Saul smoothed the palm of his hand down my ribs and rested his hand on my hip.

'You have a new scar,' said Saul. 'Are you well now?'

I nodded. 'Yes, it was a problem for a little while, but no more.' I hadn't even thought about revealing my new scar. If I had, I might have been more coy.

He looked down at me for a moment or two - silent. 'For someone so slender, you are deliciously curvy.'

'Now you're making me blush,' I said, but laughed.

He wound a lock of my hair around his finger. 'But it's true.'

I gasped. 'The boys will know I'm here,' I said. 'My car.'

Saul inhaled – slow and deep – and thought. 'Don't worry. I'll get you out and I'll think of something.'

'Something?' I asked.

He kissed me briefly then whispered into my ear. 'Something plausible.' He shook his head. 'You are lovely. You know?' And he kissed me once more.

Toby waited for me to speak.

'Don't hold back,' he said. 'I want to hear it all.'

'I tripped down a step on the landing, and Saul helped me up. He kept hold of my hand and then he kissed me.'

'A peck on the lips or a long smooch?'

'I suppose more than a peck, but less than a smooch. A few seconds.'

'Christ, Anya. I don't need all the gory details.'

'You said you wanted to know it all. And you're making me nervous.'

'Good,' he said.

Toby's eyes narrowed, but I sensed a softening in his tone.

'That's all that happened. I reminded him that I was married and, more importantly, that I love you.'

'What did he say to that?'

'He apologised profusely. Way over the top, actually.'

I wasn't proud of my lies, but I had no choice but to save the situation from spiralling out of control. How might he react if I allowed myself to be honest with him? I didn't dare risk it.

'I'll still kill him.'

I walked over to Toby and leaned against the table. 'I know you don't mean that,' I said. 'There wasn't an affair. Never would be. And despite some mild attraction that's completely gone on my part, that was all that happened. We've been conscious not to cross that boundary again. Truthfully, I don't find him overly attractive. I love you.' I lay my palm on his cheek. 'I've always loved you.' But I felt him flinch.

What a fool I'd been. I felt sick at my dishonesty. But, at the same time, what choice did I have?

I heard the front door open then Gemma and the girls as they talked quietly in the hallway.

When Rose came through she looked down at the shattered glass.

She turned to us. 'What's happened?'

'It was broken when we got in. Possibly a bird.'

Gemma's expression said, who are you trying to kid? If the girls hadn't been there she'd have demanded an answer.

I retrieved the dustpan and brush from under the sink.

Toby pushed back his chair. 'I'm going for a lie down.' He looked at me. 'My head is pounding.'

Clearly, I was to blame.

'I'll bring you a cup of tea,' I said.

'Don't bother,' he said, rubbing his temples. 'I'll be asleep.'

To avoid further discord, particularly in front of the girls, I didn't react to his tone.

Gemma stepped aside as Toby walked past. His shoulders stooped and his hair flopped over his face.

Rose came closer. 'Why's Dad behaving so strangely?'

Her eyes watered and she looked confused.

'I think,' I said, choosing my words. 'I think the past few weeks have been a huge strain on him. And I know he always gets upset when it comes round to Euan's anniversary.'

'I thought it might be me,' she said.

'No, my darling. Trust me.' I hunched down in front of her. 'You've done nothing wrong at all. OK?'

'OK. But I'm still worried about Dad.'

'I am, too. But let's leave him to rest for now,' I said, and stood back up. 'I'll talk to him.'

I turned to Stevie. 'Do you want to help me sort out lunch?'

'Sure, Mum,' she replied, but without her usual ebullience.

'Let me clear up this mess and you have a look in the fridge to see what you fancy,' I said.

As I swept the glass into a heap, I reflected on our argument. I'd been an idiot. After lunch I'd declutter my laptop; clear it of any incriminating evidence. My phone, too. Had I become the sort of woman who liked the sound of breaking glass? And I realised just how close I'd come to throwing our lives into chaos.

Chapter 23

Six weeks after her accident Rose was making incredible progress and each day her strength grew as she took a step or two closer to recovery. Despite my worries about the fracking as well as feeling continually misunderstood by Toby, Rose's recovery was the best reassurance that life was improving.

My alarm woke me at five-thirty and from the bedroom window I looked out at the horses grazing in the misty morning light and beyond to the pink pomegranate sun rising above Orben Moor. I'd organised for a delivery of straw and the only time the farmer could do it was an unearthly hour.

'I haven't even had a coffee yet,' complained Gemma when I'd knocked on the cottage door to rouse her.

'Come on. We'll soon get it done.'

As we heaved the bales off the back of the trailer, clouds rolled in and the air grew progressively warm. By the time we'd finished stacking them up in the barn, two and a half hours later, I felt hot and exhausted and I went inside to take a shower and put on some fresh clothes.

Halfway up the stairs I heard voices and turned to see Rose walk step by careful step across the hall. She hooked arms with Lisa, her physio, and used a crutch under her other arm. Rose had lost a lot of muscle tone in her legs and she looked too thin for my liking.

Rose beamed up at me. 'Hey, Mum.'

'Wonderful, my darling.' I jogged back down.

'Isn't she doing brilliantly?' said Lisa. 'We need to build up lots of strength and I reckon we'll have you running by October.'

'And riding?' said Rose, her face expectant.

'Only if you feel confident,' I said, 'And on a nice steady horse. Bombproof.'

'I miss Pepper so much. But I'm not sure I'd have the courage to ride a horse like him again.'

'A fall such as yours can cause the most confident rider to lose confidence. And if you decide you don't want to ride that's absolutely fine.' I didn't add that I'd be happy for her to give up altogether.

I followed them into the kitchen and helped Rose onto a dining chair.

'What's the latest on the fracking?' asked Lisa. 'Mum and I want to join the protest group.'

'We've pretty much got the entire local population on our side,' I said. 'However, I've recently found out that a couple of landowners, must be minus bats, have given permission for Quadrillum to lease their land.' I sat next to Rose. 'So ignorant and short-sighted. And they'll destroy their reputations locally. Who'd want to associate or do business with someone who's prepared to sacrifice their local environment? Not to mention the health of its people. And all for a few extra quid in their pockets. Quadrillum are setting up an enclosure next couple of weeks and we'll be there to protest and disrupt their plans.'

'Count me in,' said Lisa.

'I'm coming too,' added Rose.

I looked into her eyes, steely grey and determined. 'Of course you are.'

Lisa pursed her lips. 'Who are these landowners?'

'No names yet. But Nicola and Saul are meeting with our councillor today and we're hoping for names and locations. Forewarned and forearmed.'

'I can't wait to hear who these idiots are,' said Rose.

'Whoever they are they'll be hearing from many locals, once I tell them,' I said.

'It'll generate a lot of bad feeling,' replied Lisa.

'I agree,' I said. 'If their land is close by, the chemicals and methane could destroy water supplies. If it was close to Willows End, we'd have to give up the livery and sell the horses.'

'Would we have to move?' asked Rose.

'How could we?'

'Sell our house?' she replied.

'No sane person would buy it. Not whilst the fracking's going on. Even when they've gone who knows how long it takes for the poisons to leave the aquifer and the soil.'

Rose's mouth fell open and her eyes welled with tears.

I took her hand. 'Oh, sweetheart. I'm so sorry.'

'You're only being honest,' she said.

'It's too much information,' I said, and felt wretched for being so blunt.

She wiped her eyes. 'I'd really rather know. At the end of term we debated 'is ignorance bliss?' Most of us decided we wanted to know stuff, even if the truth is difficult to stomach.'

'Gosh, Rose. Sounds like a valuable lesson,' I said.

'That reminds me of a line, I forget who it's by,' said Lisa. 'Ignorance is a voluntary misfortune.'

For a moment, I considered what this meant. 'I do believe that, Lisa. Even so,' I turned back to Rose, 'I don't want to worry you.'

'But I'm getting stronger every day. My fall, Pepper, and all this fracking business is bringing me out of my cocoon. It's been a horrible summer, apart from the weather, but I feel different for it.'

I felt a stab behind my eyes. 'You teach me so much, Rose. I didn't have half your sense and maturity at sixteen.'

Maybe Rose was right. Despite all the painful things we went through and the obstacles that could hold us back from our dreams and planned trajectories, ultimately, they developed in us a resilience to withstand future difficult experiences.

I felt reluctant to ring Saul, for fear of encouraging any idea of 'us', but I sent him a brief text to ask what he and Nicola had discovered about the landowners. When he still hadn't replied by the evening I grew increasingly anxious and even annoyed. I checked my phone over and over and reread my reply. It had sounded rather abrupt and I wondered if I'd upset him. I typed another. 'Hi Saul. Not sure if you got my earlier message. I hope it went well with Nicola today. Any news? Hope all OK. Anya x.'

I pressed send and immediately regretted the kiss. Talk about sending out mixed signals.

I heard the front door and Freda's barks as Toby greeted her.

'Hello,' I called.

He walked in and dumped his briefcase on the table then hooked his jacket on the back of the dining chair.

He didn't look happy, but managed a greeting. 'Evening.'

'Hey Dad,' the girls said in unison.

'How was your day?' I asked and assumed a show of brightness.

'Nothing special.' He loosened his tie. 'The usual meetings with the usual bone idle morons unable to work to the timings they insisted on setting in the first place.'

'Frustrating then,' I said. 'Wine or tea?'

'Tea.' He went to fill the kettle and banged it back on its base.

Stevie pulled on her riding boots and left to help Gemma with the evening jobs in the yard while Rose went off to watch a movie in her bedroom.

Toby set his dinner plate on the table and eyed it with suspicion. 'An interesting combination.'

'I need to do a grocery shop,' I said, in explanation.

Toby picked up a falafel with his fingers and popped it in his mouth. He chewed and grimaced. 'Blimey,' he mumbled with his mouth full.

'What's the matter?'

He struggled to speak and reached for his cup of tea. 'Dry as a bone.'

'I had salad dressing. Don't eat it if you don't want it. Freda will appreciate them,' I said, but felt irritated by his complaining.

'I could have bought a takeaway,' he said, his cup poised before his lips.

'You never stop moaning, Toby. About everything. Is it the male menopause?' This was cruel, but I'd grown tired of his constant complaining.

'Men don't have the menopause. It's you women who lose the plot during the change.'

'In fact, you're wrong. When male hormones wane it can result in mood swings. It's called grumpy man syndrome. It's terminal, potentially.'

He turned on me and his tone accused. 'Do I seem as if I don't have enough testosterone?'

'Not at all. But I'm fed up of you whining about things that shouldn't bother you. Be happy I've prepared your dinner. Be grateful it's healthy and nutritious and not some processed crap. Appreciate that I don't send you out to buy salt and fat laden takeaways to clog your arteries and fill you with monosodium glutamate.'

He burst into laughter. 'I think you need to check your science.' His words jabbed me in the ribs.

I almost broke into laughter, too, but kept a straight face. 'I jolly well will. And I'll print you a report to prove it.'

He placed his knife and fork across the plate and picked up a cherry tomato. 'I look forward to reading it.' He threw the tomato in the air and caught it in his mouth.

'Stop it.' I bent over and kissed him on the cheek. 'You're maddening.'

'But I thought that was one of my charms,' he said with his mouth full. He bit into the tomato and its juice squirted onto my chin.

'Sometimes it's charming. Sometimes it's annoying,' I wiped my chin. 'Depends on my mood.'

'Remind me to ask what mood you're in next time I come through the door.'

I narrowed my eyes. 'Perhaps I'll be asking the same of you.'

'I'm always happy to come home to my beautiful wife.' He reached around and grabbed my bottom. 'Especially when I can feel your sexy arse in those shorts.'

He drew me close and my irritation melted away as I sank into his embrace; sensual and warm, and exactly where I belonged. I placed my cheek against his, and savoured the feel of his bristles against my skin and the subtle aroma of perspiration.

How could we so easily switch from fighting one minute to rubbing along well together, the next? It seemed that had always been our way. It was who we were, together.

I looked into his eyes and felt a familiar rush of love. 'I love you so much, Toby. Though sometimes I have no idea why.'

'I adore you too, Mrs Kubik.' He kissed me again. 'Fancy an early night?'

'I must help finish up in the yard and maybe we could take Freda for her walk first? Seems a shame to waste a beautiful evening.'

Freda jumped up the moment she heard her favourite word, and scampered over.

'A short stroll. If we must,' he said. 'I'll get changed and meet you outside,' he said and headed out of the kitchen.

'See you soon,' I called after him, and smiled.

Whenever I made an effort to put our problems aside, Toby was loving in return.

The evening felt warm and tranquil, and as I walked beneath the Lilac tree, I looked up at the flowers that swung in the breeze. A flower dropped from its stem and I threw out my arm to catch it in my palm. I lifted the flower to my nose and inhaled. Freda, who was in a playful mood, picked up a long stick and dragged it over.

'A bit ambitious, Freda.' I spotted a smaller stick and bent down and picked it up. 'How about this one?'

She discarded her stick and bounced up and down to grasp it from my hand. I threw it into the field and she jumped between the rails and dashed away to retrieve it.

When I entered the yard, Gemma and Stevie were sweeping the straw and dirt off the cobbles. 'Let me take over,' I said to Gemma.

Gemma straightened up and rubbed the small of her back. 'No need. We're done.'

'Good timing, Mum,' said Stevie. She swept the hair off her face and propped her broom against the wall. Her complexion looked pink and radiant.

'Are all the horses out?' I asked.

'Apart from Fizz,' said Stevie. 'Debra wants her fresh and clean for the show tomorrow.'

'I wonder which events she's entering,' I said.

'Dressage and jumping, I believe,' replied Gemma, quietly.

'Not the most sensible to stable before dressage,' I said. 'She pampers that horse and Fizz will be hyped up for tomorrow.'

Gemma grimaced and her brows shot up. Seconds later I understood why.

Debra appeared at Fizz's stable door. 'Is that right?'

'I didn't know you were still here,' I said, and cringed inwardly.

Debra banged and bolted the door behind her then swung round to face me. 'Evidently. I might pamper my horse, milady, but let me remind you that I pay a lot of money to keep her here. I pay on time and I pay more than most. And if I want to spoil her because she means so much to me and because I have no children, then I will.' She stood square to me, her arms folded. 'As you know, I was unable to have babies.' She paused and took a breath. 'Fizz isn't behaving badly or doing anything to upset you and your precious horses, so I'll thank you to keep your opinions to yourself.'

I felt nauseous and turned to Gemma who merely shrugged her shoulders and tilted her head inquiringly, similarly awaiting my reply.

I took a step towards Debra. 'My comments were tactless and unkind. I was insensitive and I'm sorry.'

'Thank you,' clipped Debra. 'Now if you don't mind I still have her tack to clean.' She marched away to the tack room.

Gemma sidled up to me and nudged me. 'I love you, sister, but sometimes you're your own worst enemy.'

'Yes, I'm aware of that,' I said. 'I appear to have an acute case of foot in mouth. Still, as the saying goes, always learning.'

'Which saying is that?' said Gemma.

'Actually, I'm not sure, but it applies to me.'

Toby walked through the archway. 'All done?'

I walked over and hooked his arm. 'I've just upset Debra. So yes, I'm definitely done.'

'Tell me all about it,' said Toby, and drew me close.

I called over to Stevie. 'We're taking Freda for a walk.'

'Have fun,' she called and gave us a wave.

The air was beginning to cool and I untied my cardigan from about my waist and slipped my arms into the sleeves. I didn't want to talk about my clumsiness with Debra but I did want to extend the good feeling I'd found with Toby. We clambered over the stile into the field and he took my hand.

I leaned against him. 'I can't remember the last time we did this.'

'Things have been difficult recently,' he said.

'I feel physically ill every time I think about them fracking near here.'

'Mmm...' he said, but didn't comment further.

The meadow grass had grown long and ripe for harvesting and this was the only field we used to produce our own hay. It brushed against my bare legs and I bent down and plucked a cornflower stem amongst the buttercups.

'Let me.' Toby took the flower, gathered my hair off my shoulder and slotted it behind my ear. 'There.' He cupped my face in his hands. 'So pretty.'

'Not really, but thank you.' I stood on tiptoe and draped my arms around his neck.

As we kissed, I listened to the steady hum of crickets amongst the grass.

Toby whispered in my ear. 'Shall we?'

I slid my hand down the front of his trousers. 'You mean, here?'

The hedgerows were full and green and the perfect barrier to conceal us.

Toby niftily unzipped my shorts and they fell to my feet. 'Yes, here.'

As I pulled off my cardigan and vest, Toby flicked his eyebrows playfully and rubbed his hands together. He reached around me and in one movement unhooked my bra. He took both my hands and lowered me to the ground.

'Relax there, my love.'

I folded my arms behind my head and the grass and wildflowers prickled against my skin. As Toby peeled off his T-shirt, trousers and boxer shorts we didn't take our eyes off one another. He lay down beside me and propped himself up on one elbow. He'd always been fit and muscular and he was as lean as today as he'd been in his twenties. Virile too. I don't think he'd ever refused my advances and he rarely failed to satisfy me completely. We were a great match still, despite everything. I stroked his warm skin and trailed my fingers down his ribs and over the curve of his hip.

I squeezed his buttocks. 'You feel so lovely,' I murmured.

He caressed my breasts then lowered his lips to kiss each in turn.

'How is it that you look and taste even more delectable than normal?'

'Must be the fresh air,' I replied. It wasn't like him to be quite so talkative whilst making love. Perhaps mother nature had brought out his romantic side. 'Do you remember any poetry?' I said, hoping to milk the moment.

'As it happens, I do.' He rested his chin on the heel of his hand and thought for a moment before leaning closer.

'Roses are red,
Violets are blue
We're naked in the grass, my love,
And I will devour you.'

I traced my fingers through his chest hair and on further down. 'You missed your true vocation, Lord Kubik.'

'You're my only true vocation,' he said.

He kissed me again then reached over to pick a buttercup. 'But first, I want to see if you like butter.'

I lifted my chin.

'That's not how I tell.'

'Oh?'

He slipped his hand between my legs. 'Will you bend your knees.'

Bemused, I followed his request.

He got down on his knees between my legs and held the buttercup up close. I felt his breath hot upon my skin.

'As I thought, my love. Butterlicious! I want to nip your velvet skin, just here.' He planted the softest kisses on the inside of my thighs.

I gave a blissful sigh.

We held one another and made love as nature's shadows lengthened around us. The daylight dwindled until the dew laden grass glistened in the moonlight and the sky above turned Indian blue. Content and breathless, we lay in one another's arms, warm and damp with satiated desire. As our breaths slowed to silence, the birds ceased their song.

Toby stroked my arm. 'You're chilly.'

'I hadn't noticed.' I sat up and pulled my cardigan around me. 'I'll remember this evening forever.'

He took my hand. 'We should make more time for one another. Sometimes, I think we forget. And that isn't good for either of us.'

'Tonight reminds me of that feeling when I couldn't get you out of my mind.' I kissed his shoulder then rested my head there.

'You've always been mine,' he said, stroking my hair. 'From the moment I found you in that car.'

'And you were my knight, Toby Kubik.'

'You've never needed a knight. But you're mine, and for that, I'll never need anything else.'

His words made up for all the doubts I'd recently had. Essentially, our love and our relationship remained as strong and deep as it had ever been. In fact, more so for all that we'd shared and experienced together; both the good and the bad.

'Look up there,' he said, and pointed to the sky.

I followed his hand between the silhouette of branches, their long black fingers against the night sky, to where two stars flickered, despite their distance light years away.

'That's you and me,' he said. 'Although we can't always see them, their radiance for one another is constant and timeless.'

'I heard that a star whose light we see, may no longer even exist.'

'But those two stars will exist for eternity, they'll share the same outer reaches of space, casting their brilliance to one another, and to us here on earth.'

And I thought, he was right. Nothing could ever extinguish the infinite light and love between us. We dressed in the afterglow of our lovemaking and I watched as he bent down and laced his shoes. He caught me looking and smiled. I reflected on my fling with Saul. To jeopardize our marriage had been crazy and I vowed to never let anything risk breaking us apart again.

Some people made marriage look easy, I thought. Not my parents. They hadn't been the best role models. Dad must have experienced a lot of pain because of Mum. She'd been work obsessed, too often offered unsolicited advice and seemed self-absorbed. Not least her affair, which I'd had the misfortune to witness, but I suspected there had been more. But, for some reason that only Dad knew, he stayed with her. And I could see they cared for one another enough to make it work.

Maybe we could never truly know what went on in our partner's mind. Toby and I rarely shared our deepest and darkest thoughts and if he was anything like me, he was selective. And maybe that was a good thing.

Almost all remaining light had gone when we climbed back over the stile towards home. We walked on in companionable silence until Toby's steps slowed and stopped.

'Anya,' he said, 'there's something I've been meaning to tell you.'

I turned to face him.

Despite the fading light, I could see the seriousness in his expression.

'I need you to promise that you won't fly off the handle.'

The sharpness in his eyes fired needles through me.

'What is it?' I said, my concern growing.

Scenarios flashed through my mind. He was having an affair and wanted to ease his bleating conscience, he'd accepted a job that would take him away for weeks at a time. Or was it fracking related?

'I need to remind you that Willows End - this land, belongs to me. That Dad left it to his children.'

I gave a nervous laugh. 'You're kidding me, right?'

'Hear me out. You may even approve.'

My mouth felt dry. 'OK. Talk to me.' I kept my voice calm.

'We have too much land,' he said. 'We don't need all this and we could benefit by selling a field.'

'No, Toby!' My voice rose. 'We use every inch and blade of grass. We could do with more land if anything.'

'I've received an offer for the meadow that's simply too good to turn down.'

'From who?'

'Maria, of course. Her land adjoins ours and because she wants to build her cattle herd, she needs more grazing.'

'Not our problem. She can try Geoff Plews.'

'His land isn't fertile enough and she'd have to cross the river downstream at Walden.'

'We can't,' I pleaded. 'It produces the sweetest hay, we all ride up here and it's perfect grazing out of season.' I gripped his wrist. 'The livery can't manage without it.'

'I've already agreed,' he said, and he removed my hand. 'The contract's almost ready for signing.'

176

'Rip it up, Toby. You've gone behind my back, knowing I'd object.'

'Not a chance.' He folded his arms. 'And what's more, you'll thank me for it. We need the money.'

'We don't. Your business is strong and the livery yard pays for itself and more.'

'Have you looked at our bank reserves recently?'

When had I last looked? I always assumed our substantial reserves, were just that, reserves.

'There's 50K,' I said. 'A sizeable cushion. We don't need more.'

'Listen to me, Anya. When we need to repair the roof on our listed home, that won't even begin to cover it. We've got Stevie starting University. Do you want the girls to have mountains of debt when they begin their independent lives and want to buy homes?'

Even if the money did help, why hadn't we discussed such an important decision first? It was deceitful - plain and simple.

'You knew I'd refuse,' I said, and my anger surged. 'So you've sneaked behind my back with Maria.'

'Because you never see the bigger picture.' He accused. 'You're incapable of thinking long term.'

'Says he who buys a brand new car every year while I still drive around in your twelve year old Volvo.'

'I have an image to uphold with my clients. You know that.'

'I know you love new cars and money. I don't want Maria looking down on us from up there. You're taking control when you have no right to. I'm your bloody wife and my name's on the deeds. And don't forget Gemma. Does she know?'

'When I explain, she'll see sense and be grateful I've taken the initiative.'

'You're delusional.' Nausea rose in my throat, I spun round and I stumbled on the rough grass.

'Don't walk away from me,' he ordered.

First he plays the romance card, makes love to me and then delivers his 'news'. I felt enraged that he'd manipulated me and I set off running.

I heard footsteps pounding closer behind me, and as I ran faster still, my breath came in ragged bursts.

He caught me by the arm. 'Will you stop?'

I pulled to get away. 'Get off me!'

He yanked me round. 'I swear to God. Shut up and listen.' He gripped my arms. 'You'll scare the girls if they hear you screaming.'

'Let me go,' I hissed.

'Not - until - you've - seen - sense.'

'Until I agree with you?'

He pulled me nearer and his eyes blazed as he demanded my compliance. 'Not what I meant.'

'You've lost it, Toby. You're behaviour has been unpredictable and weird lately. I've no idea who you are or what you've become.'

'Me being weird? Look at yourself. You've had a free rein for far too long. You give scant regard to how hard I work. I get no respect from you after an exhausting day. Then you repay me by shagging a neighbour.'

'What're you on about? Minutes ago I was in your arms,' I pleaded with him.

'I can't forget what you've done to our marriage.'

'Oh, so this is payback, is it? For something I haven't actually done,' I said. 'You're the traitor here, not me.'

His lips curled. 'And once again you bring her up.'

'I wasn't talking about her. I meant our meadow. But if you want to talk about her, go ahead.'

'You're impossible.' He shoved me and I fell onto my back. I lay there - winded and dizzy, and watched as he looked down on me with disgust before turning and walking away.

'I'll fucking leave you,' I screamed after him.

He came to an abrupt halt. I expected him to turn around, and part of me wanted him to so that we could continue to thrash this out. Another part of me was scared of what he might do and wanted him gone. After a second or two he continued walking and disappeared into the darkness.

This was a whole new level of madness and it terrified me. I touched my arm and a pain shot through me.

I couldn't go home in this state and I wouldn't risk seeing Toby. Gemma would understand and there wasn't much she didn't know about our marriage. My legs felt weak as I ran through the darkness, sobbing, all the way down the hill and around the back of the stables.

The kitchen light was on in Walnut Cottage. I wiped away my tears and knocked on the door. I heard a door slam from across the other side of the paddock. That would be Toby and I pictured the look on his face before he'd left me lying hurt on the ground. I knocked on the door again and after a few moments I heard Gemma coming down the stairs. She opened the door dressed in a silk robe.

Her eyes widened in surprise. 'Anya.'

'I take it you're not alone?'

'How did you guess?' She smiled lightly.

'Perfume. Attire.'

She looked out at me in the uncertain light. 'Have you been crying?'

'The pollen's sinking. I'm sorry.'

'Tonight was kind of impromptu,' she said. 'I can ask him to leave.'

'Please don't,' I said. 'I'll come and see you first thing.'

As I turned to leave, I saw the concern in her eyes.

At least Gemma seemed all right, I thought, as I walked the worn path across the paddock. Our lights were off but the back door was still unlocked. My handbag hung over the dining chair and I checked my phone. I was surprised to see a video message from Saul - sent late afternoon. I knew I should leave it until the morning, but If I didn't play it I'd lie awake wondering what he'd said. I'd barely heard from Saul for a few days, other than campaign emails, and I had no intention of messaging unless I had to.

My hands shook as I slotted in my earphones.

'Anya, I've wanted to message you for days. Believe me, I've tried not to. Delete it if you want.' He paused. But I couldn't delete it. Not yet. 'I want you to know that however hard I try to deny it, I have feelings for you. I know I should keep them hidden but I think you feel the same. I've seen it in the way you look at me. Not least during those incredible moments in my bedroom. You're the loveliest woman I've ever met and not only in a physical sense. It's your mind, the things you care about, how you speak to me, to other people, your smile, your intuition…'

he paused again and closed his eyes. 'You're perfect. But more importantly, I believe we'd be perfect for one another.'

My breaths became faster and my heartbeat shuddered in my chest. Saul was a lovely man and I couldn't deny that I found him physically attractive. But my heart belonged to Toby. It always had. And always would. Even despite his appalling behaviour which I hoped was temporary and which I had to deal with. Leaving him now or even considering an affair was an impossible idea. And not least because of our girls.

Saul had seen the way Toby treated me in the pub and I'd practically thrown myself at him in his bedroom. No wonder he thought we were a possibility. He'd be my rescuer and I'd be more than willing to be carried away to his castle.

I'd been a fool, and now I had to deal with the consequences.

My hands shook as I poured a whisky. I switched on Classic radio as the presenter introduced Adagio played by the cellist, Stjepan Hauser. A piece that Toby loved, too. How strange and timely for this song to be playing. As the melody began, a shiver coursed through me. I sank into the armchair, and sipped from my glass and when I closed my eyes the music and alcohol washed over me like rainfall.

Our lives had never been so complicated. Three months ago, life seemed easy, but the ache inside of me told me those days were gone. All that had happened recently had led to this moment and as if in slow motion, my thoughts shifted and reordered themselves. This was the turning point. Deep within me I knew what I wanted, what I needed. And equally as importantly, what I didn't want. Toby's image filled my mind then spun in circles and whirled through me until it felt as though he had swallowed me whole. Despite all that he'd done, and all the things that had been said between us, I had to see this through.

Chapter 24

The whisky lulled my senses and sleep closed over me like a blanket. I don't know for how long I slept before I was awakened by a persistent tapping. I blinked, looked around and turned to the French windows. The tapping grew more urgent, and still drowsy, I stood up and peered closer.

A face appeared up against the glass - a face I knew well.

'Anya. Let me in.'

I hurried to turn the key. 'Saul.' I recalled his video message. 'What is it?' I kept my voice low.

'We have to talk.'

If he was trying to get my attention, this was desperate. Not only that, it was dangerous.

I stood in the doorway unsure whether to let him in. If Toby knew he was here, he'd go ballistic. 'Tell me here.'

His skin seemed pale and his hands fidgeted. 'It's Dom. He's run away.'

I stood aside. 'Come in, but let's be quiet.' I shut the door and turned to him. 'Do you know why?'

He nodded. 'Dom came to find me in the barn earlier. He said he wanted to talk. I told him I was busy and I'd come and find him.' Saul paused and sighed. 'I was in the middle of messaging you. I assume you got it?'

"Yes, I did,' I said. 'And I will reply.'

Saul gave an almost indiscernible nod. 'I'd sensed an urgency in Dom's tone so I finished and hurried back in. But he'd already disappeared.' Saul scrubbed a hand through his hair. 'I'm a shit dad for not listening when he came to me.'

'Did he mention anything to Alex?'

'He left a note. Which is why I'm so concerned.' Saul pulled a scrap of paper from his pocket. 'It was brief.'

I took the note and read. 'Don't bother finding me. I need time to think.'

I looked up at Saul. 'Have you called the police?'

'I hoped he'd come home when he was hungry. I was wrong.'

'Then call the police now.'

Saul shook his head. 'But wait. Alex has just told me something. The reason why I'm here.' He paused. 'Dom's been facetiming and messaging Rose. Apparently, they've become friends.'

'Dom isn't here. If that's what you're thinking.'

'That's precisely what I'm thinking.'

'I talked to Rose earlier and she was alone. She hasn't mentioned Dom.'

'OK. But would you mind checking her room? If he isn't here I'll leave and call the police.'

I heard the click of the kitchen door opening.

I spun around.

Toby walked in, instantly clocked Saul and marched up to him. 'That's damned low. Turning up in the middle of the night to seduce my wife.'

They faced one another, nose to nose. Saul didn't step away and it was clear to see this was one standoff that would quickly get out of control.

Toby's voice deepened. 'You're even more of a moron than I thought. Now piss off before I see you off.'

I stepped in. 'Dom's gone missing. Saul thinks he may be in with Rose. They've become friends.'

Toby turned to me with eyes ablaze and jaw set firm. 'At this time of the night? He'd better bloody not be.' He whipped around and stormed from the kitchen.

I glanced quickly at Saul before rushing after Toby. 'For Christ's sake. Let me go in first.'

Ignoring my pleas, Toby turned the door handle. It was locked.

'Rose?' he shouted. 'Open the damned door.'

'Dad?' came Rose's shrill voice.

'Open up, or I'll kick it in.'

'Give her a minute,' I said. 'I don't want her falling.'

Toby folded his arms and tapped his foot impatiently. I detected voices and movement then the key turned in the lock.

Toby flung open the door and marched in. Rose was sitting up in bed and her eyes flickered nervously.

Toby switched on the light. 'Where is he?'

Rose pulled the duvet up around her. 'It's not what you think.'

The curtains in front of the bay window moved and Dom emerged. His hair flopped around his face and he shuffled his feet awkwardly. 'I haven't touched Rose.' He directed at Toby, and then to Saul. 'We were only talking.'

Toby stomped up to Dom, grabbed a fistful of his T-shirt and hauled him across the floor. Dom tripped and Toby hoisted him to standing.

'Toby, let him go,' Saul said, with his fists clenched at his side.

'Not until he's told me what he's doing in my daughter's locked bedroom in the middle of the night.'

'We've done nothing wrong,' cried Rose.

Rose wore her pyjamas and Dom was dressed in shorts and a T-shirt.

'It looks perfectly innocent,' I said. 'Let's talk this through, calmly.'

'Don't be so bloody naive, Anya,' Toby shot at me.

Saul lost his patience and strode up to Toby, latched onto him and after a short tussle the three of them fell into a heap of bodies and flailing limbs. Dom scrambled up and scurried round to the head of Rose's bed - probably the worst place to head for. Toby ran round to challenge Dom once more.

'It's your fault,' Dom shouted at Saul. 'I said not to look for me.'

Toby yanked Dom's arm and turned to Rose. 'Tell me the truth, Rose. Has this boy touched you?'

'We were talking,' she said. 'It got too late for him to leave.'

Saul approached Toby and Dom. 'You heard my son. They've done nothing wrong.'

'I want his explanation, not your excuses,' Toby fired in reply.

Saul jabbed his finger into Toby's chest. 'Don't assume every boy behaves like you did. Let him go, now.'

Toby squared up to Saul but tightened his grip on Dom's arm.

Dom's face paled and his legs trembled.

Stevie came into the room with Jake close behind. 'Daddy?' Stevie's eyes moved from the three men, to me.

'Let's stop and talk,' I said. 'Dom and Rose are the children. You're supposed to be grown men. There'll be an explanation if we allow them to explain.

Neither Toby nor Saul appeared to listen and the tension in the room magnified.

Toby made no move to release Dom, and Saul, tired of trying to negotiate, flung an arm around Toby's chest.

But then Toby's legs seemed to buckle beneath him, his entire body went slack, and he dropped like a brick on to the floorboards. As he landed, his head knocked the wall.

Saul stepped back and moments later Toby's whole body went into spasm.

I dropped to my knees and gripped Toby's shoulders to try to hold him still, but his legs and arms thrashed and his head rocked from side to side and banged against the floor. His eyeballs bulged and his neck arched.

Stevie rushed to his side.

'Somebody call an ambulance,' I screamed. 'Hurry!'

And then, as quickly as Toby had begun to fit, he became still. Disconcertingly so. The muscles in his face relaxed and his eyes closed.

Chapter 25

Saul held his hands up. 'I only wanted him to release Dom. Is he epileptic?'

I shook my head. 'Never before.' I touched Toby's forehead which felt cool and dry. I found the pulse in his neck. The beat raced fast and thready.

His eyelids fluttered. 'Toby?' I bent down and kissed his cheek.

He opened his eyes but stared out, vacantly.

'Do you hurt anywhere?'

But it seemed he could neither see nor hear me and after a few seconds his eyes flickered and closed.

The stillness and silence in the room merged as no one knew what to do or say. I couldn't take my eyes off Toby's. Lids shut and unmoving. The blood seemed to drain from his face. The edges of his lips tinged blue.

Cries and sobbing broke the silence and I turned round to see Stevie and Rose clinging to one another and looking down at their Dad. Then to Dom and Jake standing together, mute and frightened and watching from the far side of the room.

Saul got down on his knees and placed his palm on Toby's chest. He nodded.

I began to shake uncontrollably. I pressed his pulse which seemed steadier than before and some colour returned to his skin, although he was still unnaturally pale.

'Has somebody called an ambulance?' I said.

'Jake is,' said Stevie.

Had stress caused him to fit? Was it his heart? It didn't appear that Saul had done enough to cause this, but amidst the chaos I could have missed something. Saul got up and walked across the room to Dom.

Dom's voice shook. 'We didn't do anything, Dad. I swear.'

'I know. But you should have waited to talk to me.'

'You were busy.'

Saul's eyes searched Dom's. 'You can tell me anything. You know that.'

'I can't.' Dom looked away. 'You haven't wanted to hear anything I say. Not since Mum died.'

Saul put his arms around Dom and I heard him say. 'I've let you down. And I'm sorry.'

Stevie clambered off the bed and sat beside her dad.

'Help me down,' said Rose.

Stevie and I each hooked an arm and helped Rose onto the footstool.

Rose held and stroked Toby's hand.

My stomach continued to twist into knots. I'd never seen Toby this way. Why hadn't he come round?

Gently, I eased a pillow under his head and with Stevie's help, we turned him onto his side.

'Twenty minutes for the ambulance,' said Jake, as he came through the door.

I willed for it to hurry.

Saul and Dom left the room and Jake offered to wait for the ambulance at the front. All the while, Toby lay silent and unmoving as I checked his pulse over and over again, terrified he might still leave us.

'I heard everyone shouting,' said Stevie.

'This is my fault.' Rose looked at me, and her eyes swam with tears. 'I should have told you Dom was here.'

Rose had other friends who were boys and I'd never had any reason to think she'd jump straight into bed with one of them. If there'd been anything sexual going on with Dom, I'd have sensed something.

'Nobody's blaming you, or Dom. Your Dad's reaction was out of proportion. I've never seen him like this.'

Toby's behaviour had become ever more irrational and extreme. And unwittingly, I'd made things worse by igniting his jealousy.

'He was the same in the pub,' Stevie said, then paused. 'I think he's jealous of Saul.'

'But Mum and Saul are just friends. Like Dom and me. Oh, why is everything going wrong again?'

It seemed we sat with Toby for an age without any change in his appearance or consciousness.

'Stevie, please chase up the ambulance.'

But as she got up I saw flashing blue lights reflected through the curtains.

Gemma walked into the room, took one look at her brother and ran over. 'What's happened? And why are Saul and Dom here?'

'Dad and Saul had a massive fight. Dad collapsed and had a fit,' explained Rose.

Gemma crouched at Toby's side. 'Fighting?' She demanded an explanation.

'That's not strictly true,' I said. 'Dom was here with Rose. All perfectly innocent. Saul turned up thinking Dom was here, and Toby went into Dad defence mode.'

'Seems Toby has good reason to mistrust Saul.' Gemma's eyes bored into mine. 'First the pub. Now they're fighting?'

'No one is to blame,' I said. 'It was frayed tempers. Plus it's the middle of the night and everyone's exhausted.'

Gemma raised an eyebrow and pursed her lips - it was clear she mistrusted my version of events.

She lifted Toby's hand and spoke softly to him.

The sounds of voices and footsteps travelled from the hallway.

Jake returned with two paramedics - a young man and an older woman. Each carried bags and medical equipment.

I stood up. 'This is Toby Kubik. He collapsed and had a seizure for about a minute after which he opened his eyes briefly, but then fell unconscious.'

The woman set the bag and equipment on the floor. 'I'm Judith and this is Michael.'

We stood back and they began their examination. All the while they talked to Toby and asked me questions.

The woman placed an oxygen mask over Toby's mouth and nose. 'Has Toby ever suffered from epilepsy?'

'Never,' I said and looked at Gemma for confirmation.

Gemma shook her head. 'It isn't in the family.'

'Any history of heart problems, blood pressure, or other health concerns?' asked the younger paramedic.

'He's always been fit and healthy,' I said. 'I can't remember the last time he even had a cold.'

'We'll take Toby to Richmond General. See if we can find out the problem.'

I felt a rush of blood to my head and the room began to spin around me. I sat on the bed and closed my eyes. When the spinning sensation eased the paramedics were already transferring Toby onto the stretcher. They raised it to full height and placed a blanket over him. For a moment when I looked at him lying there it seemed his body was no longer inhabited by the man I loved - but a stranger, unrecognisable and distant.

As they wheeled Toby into the hall, I turned to Gemma. 'Take care of the girls. I'll call as soon as I know anything.'

'I'm coming too,' said Stevie.

I nodded. 'Run and get dressed.'

I hugged Rose. 'I won't ask you not to worry, but please try to rest.'

As they lifted Toby into the ambulance, Saul approached me. 'I feel responsible. Will you let me know what's happening?'

'I don't think this was because of you, Saul.'

But I could see the doubt in his eyes. 'It might have been stress, which is my fault.' He rubbed his hand across the back of his neck. 'I'll wait up until I hear from you.'

I nodded then turned around and climbed the steps into the back of the ambulance. Stevie and I sat beside Toby and when I touched his forehead I was relieved that he felt warmer.

As the ambulance turned towards Richmond I looked out of the window at the flashing lights reflecting upon the darkened fields.

Toby groaned and opened his eyes.

'Daddy,' said Stevie.

Relief swept through me. 'Are you in pain, my love?'

For a time he didn't respond, then slowly, he raised his hand and rested it on his crown. 'My head.' His voice was barely above a whisper.

'You had a seizure.'

'I don't remember,' he replied. 'How strange.'

With the roads clear, it seemed only minutes before we arrived at the hospital. Stevie clasped my hand as they wheeled

Toby into a treatment room - with strip lights on the ceiling, white and stark. We both stood aside as the paramedics transferred Toby onto a bed. An elderly doctor with slim face and spiked grey hair walked in. The paramedics updated him before leaving.

The doctor gave us a brief smile then focused his attention on Toby. 'I'm Dr Amin, Toby. I'll run some tests and see if we can find the problem.' He dispensed some wash into his palm and rubbed his hands together.

As the doctor hooked Toby to a monitor, we talked through the sequence of events and Toby described the symptoms he'd experienced, though he could barely remember them. He didn't mention Saul's involvement and I decided to follow, at least until we had some explanation for his seizure.

The doctor shone a light into Toby's eyes then fixed some ECG pads on to his chest and back.

Every flash and beep from the equipment set my heart pounding and I searched the doctor's expression for any hint of a diagnosis. Toby remained silent and still, and each time he closed his eyes I worried he was slipping back into unconsciousness.

As the doctor wrote up his notes I was desperate to ask questions.

He hooked the notes onto the end of the bed and slotted his pen into the pocket of his white coat. 'From my initial assessment, all appears normal with your heart and nerve responses,' Dr Amin said to Toby. 'If you'd suffered a heart attack that would be evident.'

The doctor raised the top end of the bed until Toby was sitting up.

'How is your vision and your head feeling?'

'Everything's clear. I feel tired but OK,' said Toby, and he moved his legs over the side of the bed.

'Wait, Toby.' I rushed over and hooked his arm. I turned to the doctor. 'Is he allowed to stand?'

'If he wants to. But slowly,' Dr Amin cautioned.

'You did say your head hurt,' I said.

'It's fine now,' he said. 'I'm tired and thirsty, that's all.' Toby stood up and his legs seemed steady.

'I'll ask a nurse to bring you some water while I arrange a brain MRI,' said Dr Amin. He paused. 'I understand from the paramedics there'd been an altercation between yourself, a neighbour and his son?'

Toby glanced at me before he spoke. 'Yes, but he didn't hurt me. Not from what I recall.'

'I could be wrong, but it didn't look like Saul was the cause of your collapse,' I said. 'I don't think we want to press charges.' I looked at Toby who nodded his agreement.

'Why is that?' said Dr Amin. 'You've suffered a significant seizure.'

'Because there was a misunderstanding,' I said. 'Neither of the men are to blame, and especially not Saul Vermaak's teenage son.'

'I'm afraid I lost my temper,' Toby said. 'And overreacted.'

The doctor's frown lines deepened but after a moment he nodded his agreement. 'After your scan, I'll look at the results before we make any decisions.'

Toby, Stevie and I waited, feeling shocked and exhausted, until a porter arrived to take Toby down for his MRI scan. I rang home and Rose wept tears of relief when I explained that her Dad was conscious and talking.

I hung up and dialled Saul.

'Thank God he's OK, Anya. I've been lying here waiting for your call. I've even opened the whisky.'

'You sound sober,' I said.

'Only one to soften the shock. I feel terrible about what happened. What I did.'

'I know you do, but for now, Toby's all right,' I said. 'I'll ring you when I know more.'

Stevie and I followed the MRI Unit signs down silent corridors until we took seats in the waiting area outside the scanning room. Stevie yawned and laid her head on my lap and after only a couple of minutes her breaths came evenly. I rested my head back against the wall and for a while I watched the clock opposite me as the second hand moved slowly and rhythmically round, resetting the pulse of blood in my veins to a more normal tempo. My eyes grew heavy and I must have dozed off for a time

190

before voices awoke me. When I opened my eyes a kindly faced nurse smiled down at me. Stevie jerked awake and sat up.

'I'm sorry I've kept you up,' said Toby, still seated in the wheelchair.

I looked into his eyes which were heavy with exhaustion. 'Please, don't apologise.'

'But I feel so foolish.' He placed his feet on the floor and got up out of the chair. 'I don't need this.' He turned to the nurse. 'Thank you.'

She nodded. 'If you can wait here, Dr Amin is on his way to discuss the results.'

The nurse left and I said, 'Did she mention anything about the scan?'

'I asked, but she said Dr Amin must see it first.'

'But you feel OK?'

'Other than feeling knackered because it's the middle of the night, then yes, I feel fine.'

Whatever the cause of the seizure, he appeared to have bounced back surprisingly well.

Toby sat between Stevie and I, and reached for our hands. 'Try not to worry.' He squeezed my hand. 'I'm not.'

'Let's see what the doctor has to say first.' And I wondered how he could remain so calm.

'I was so scared,' said Stevie.

'Of course you were and I'm sorry,' said Toby. 'This was my own foolish doing.'

I remained quiet. We'd await a professional opinion.

The corners of Dr Amin's mouth curled upwards briefly and he glanced down at his watch. 'As your scan has come back clear and because you're feeling much better, I'm happy to discharge you,' he said. 'I will have to make a note of the altercation with your neighbour, but we'll leave it at that, for the time being.' He paused. 'However, should further problems ensue from a physical perspective, I'll insist the police investigate the circumstances.'

Beside me, Toby released a breath and I too felt relieved that he'd been given the all clear, and Toby and Saul were off the hook.

'I want you to book an appointment with your GP for a full spectrum of blood tests, twenty-four hour blood pressure monitor and a follow up appointment.' The doctor looked from Toby to me. 'I'll write to your practice. I suspect your seizure was caused by extreme stress and possibly combined with a temporary restriction of blood flow to the brain as a result of the struggle, and yet we cannot discount you suffering another. You must not drive for a week and I'll print out some information for you both to read.'

As the taxi left Richmond and drove us towards home the streetlamps began to flicker off as the first pale streaks of dawn appeared above the trees. Toby dozed beside me and Stevie rested her head on my shoulder.

The taxi driver, a man who must have been nearing retirement, told me he preferred working nights because the roads were quieter and his passengers generally more relaxed. Then with a smile through the rearview mirror he told me that his wife preferred him working nights, too.

In contrast to the heat and dryness we'd experienced for days and weeks on end, a light drizzle began to fall and as we headed down Swallow Hill, Willows End appeared shrouded in mist. Our taxi driver pulled up beneath the Oak tree and the porch light, left on by Gemma, welcomed us home.

Chapter 26

Toby and I were finally getting ready for bed as Debra parked her Fiat in the bay by the yard. From our window I watched her gather her rucksack and tray of grooming brushes from the back seat of the car. Then she slung the bag over her shoulder and with a smile to herself she headed through the archway and into the stableyard.

With Toby sleeping soundly by my side, I slept until mid morning when I was awoken by sunlight creeping through the gaps in the blinds and warming my cheeks. As I slipped out of bed the sounds of laughter and the clatter of horses hooves on the cobbled yard travelled through the open windows. In the shower and as the water washed over me, I reflected on the events of the previous night. Could it be possible for stress to trigger a violent seizure? I'd never heard of that happening before. Toby had seemed satisfied with the Doctor's explanation, although we hadn't yet had a chance to talk it through thoroughly. We'd see how he felt over the coming days and perhaps the blood tests and blood pressure checks might shed more light on the problem, if there was one.

I sat at the dressing table to fasten my sandals and looked over at Toby, untroubled and still sleeping. He seemed vulnerable and feeling a sweep of affection, I wondered what I could do to smooth the rifts that had risen between us - the violence of our disagreement over the meadow sale, his argument with Saul, resulting in his collapse which then gave rise to a whole new perspective on everything.

As I headed downstairs I realised that the health and cohesion of our family must become the focus of my attention. Toby and Rose's health, the girls' exam results and Euan's anniversary. I made a cup of coffee and went into the garden, where the drizzle and clouds had been driven away by a breeze. The rose bushes swayed softly, casting their scent into the air. I sat and sipped my coffee then threw Freda's ball for her across the lawn. She was delighted with the game and when I returned back into the kitchen she continued to retrieve and drop the ball at my feet making little pleading growls. I threw it one more time into the garden and shut the door.

Nobody else was up yet and I spent the next couple of hours preparing lunch - roast lamb with garlic and sprigs of Rosemary, buttered new potatoes with fresh mint from the garden, steamed asparagus and peas and homemade yorkshire puddings. It was an attempt to get us to sit down as a family, to relax, talk and eat a proper dinner together.

The cooking aromas soon drew the girls and Toby from their beds and Toby seemed to be in a surprisingly chatty mood as we set the joint and dishes of vegetables on the table. Toby sharpened the carving knife then sliced the lamb as I served Yorkshire puddings and vegetables onto the plates.

'Only one pudding for me, Mum. And no meat,' Rose instructed.

'Have a little. You need some protein,' I said.

My mobile phone rang from the sideboard.

I passed the serving spoon to Stevie.

I felt a flutter of adrenaline when I saw the caller. 'Saul.' I glanced across at Toby. 'Everything OK?'

'I won't keep you. First of all, I'm so relieved Toby's OK.' His voice sounded thick with guilt.

'He's exhausted, naturally,' I said. 'And we'll have to see how he is over the next few days. Like I said, the doctor believes it was stress.'

'I'd like to apologise to Toby when he's up to talking.'

'I'm sure he'd appreciate that,' I said.

'I also wanted to talk about Dom. Could we meet tomorrow?'

'I've got a full day. Sorry,' I said. 'Can you say over the phone?'

He hesitated. 'Hold on a second.' For a moment the phone went silent.

I waited for him to continue.

'The reason Dom ran away was because he was afraid to tell me,' Saul exhaled, 'that he's gay. I hadn't a clue. Not an inkling. How bad is that? Anyway, he's told Rose. But I'm guessing she hasn't mentioned it to you.'

194

'No.' I glanced across at Rose who laughed with Stevie over something. 'She hasn't.'

'Dom tells me she's easy to talk to.' Saul paused. 'I know where she gets it from.'

I felt myself blush and turned to look out of the window. Toby had to be listening in and it felt awkward. 'I appreciate you telling me, Saul, but I must go. Please take care and be proud of Dom.' I hung up, powered off my phone and returned it to the sideboard. I poured myself a glass of water as my face cooled.

Toby stared into his dinner with his knife and fork poised over his plate.

'Take care?' He looked over at me with a scowl. 'What does he need to take care for?'

I sat back down. 'It's sensitive, but hopefully Saul and Dom won't mind my telling you. Dom has told Saul that he's gay. It's taken Saul by surprise and I imagine it'll take time to sink in. As it would if one of our girls told us the same thing.' I looked at Rose sitting opposite. 'Dom talked to Rose and she's been supporting him. That's why he came here when he ran away.'

Rose rested her cutlery on the side of her plate. 'I couldn't tell either of you. It's been difficult for him to tell anyone, let alone his Dad and he's already had to cope with losing his Mum.'

Toby's expression relaxed. 'It's OK, Rose. You're a good friend.' He shook his head. 'Poor Dom going through that and then I launch myself at him. I'm sorry you had to see that, Rose.' Toby reached for my hand across the table. 'I'm an oaf. Rushing in when I should have listened to you.'

Stevie jumped to his defence. 'You're not, Dad. I can understand why you reacted like that. You only wanted to protect her. Didn't he, Rose?'

'Yeah. Course,' Rose said, but she didn't sound convinced.

'Discovering a boy in your bedroom in the middle of the night must have come as quite a shock,' Stevie continued.

Rose's anger flared. 'Says you who invited Jake to sleep over the first night you introduced him to us as your boyfriend.' The colour rose in her cheeks.

'Hold on,' Stevie spluttered. 'I'd been seeing Jake since your accident.'

'That's OK then,' Rose said. 'I'm lying in hospital thinking I'll never walk again and you're shagging Jake behind my back.'

'Hardly behind your back,' said Stevie. 'We weren't sleeping together, then. You weren't ever seeing Jake. And you weren't even here.'

'How convenient for you,' Rose replied.

'Girls! Stop,' said Toby.

Rose's lips trembled. 'She started it by trying to blame me and Dom for your collapse.'

'I was not blaming you,' Stevie's voice rose. 'And you bloody well know it.'

'Yes, you bloody were.'

'OK,' I interjected. 'We're all tired and this isn't helping. No one is to blame. It was a situation no one could have anticipated.' I looked around the table. 'And I hope we'll all learn something from it.'

'Great,' said Rose. 'Another bloody learning experience. As if I haven't had enough of those lately.' She stared miserably into her dinner.

'Come on you lot. Let's eat before this gets cold and then I'll make us iced coffees for dessert,' I said, and hoped my woeful attempt at distraction might lessen the tension.

Over the following days, Toby appeared to return to his usual energetic self, although I was on constant alert for anything untoward in his behaviour or health. I returned my efforts to the fracking campaign, the sale of the meadow and Rose's ongoing rehabilitation. I knew I was neglecting the yard, but Gemma continued to remind me that I'd do the same for her. She was right, of course, and I loved her all the more for it.

Toby booked in at the doctors for a check up and blood tests and within a few days he received the results.

'The doctor rang to say all tests are normal. Isn't that a relief?' said Toby when he returned after his first full day back at work.

'How do you feel, physically?' I asked for possibly the hundredth time.

'Absolutely fine,' he said. 'Fit as a fiddle.' He patted my bottom, and reached for the kettle.

At least some things had improved.

Despite worrying about what the loss of our meadow could mean for the yard, long term, I conceded that it seemed sensible to provide some financial help for the girls' college years.

Gemma and I had always been meticulous in our finances, and ensured we made sufficient profit but without hiking up the livery fees unnecessarily. As one of the best value yards in the area we kept a waiting list for owners keen to bring their horses here. This gave us a real advantage. Our clients knew they received a good deal and were all the more appreciative because of it. Willows End was no charity, far from it, but at the same time, we didn't make as much money as I knew we could. Perhaps it was time for Gemma and I to review our longer term business strategy.

Finally, Rose's plaster had come off and with the aid of her crutches she seemed keen to visit the yard whenever possible. Stevie was often out, either riding the horses with Jake or socialising with friends. I sensed both girls growing tense about their upcoming exam results. When Stevie was home they bickered constantly over trivialities and, despite a few nerves myself, I stressed that it was out of their hands and they may as well try to relax.

'What if I don't get the points?' asked Stevie ignoring my advice. 'I'll have to go through clearing and who knows where I'll end up. I need a University close to Jake.'

'Let's not be too dramatic,' I said. 'After all, you worked incredibly hard.'

'That's not the point,' she said. 'My entire future's at stake.'

She was playing the star-crossed lover too well.

'Please, Stevie. Save the melodrama for results day.'

'That's not empathetic, Mum,' piped up Rose. 'Try seeing things from her perspective. That's what you're always telling us to do.'

'What would you like me to do? Get all het up so you can see how anxious I am.'

'No,' said Rose. 'Listen and nod sympathetically.'

Rose had recently announced she wanted to be a psychologist and had read so many research papers online that she kept citing her newfound knowledge at every opportunity. Apparently, hearing how Dom's mum had died at the hands of her patient wasn't any discouragement to her career aspirations.

'Nowadays, more young people need counselling,' she said. 'The experts blame social media and exam pressure. Online networking is a minefield and young people can't always handle it. I mean, I know I'm a teen but I realise how important it is to maintain a healthy distance. To live in the real world, not a virtual one.'

I listened, with a carrot in one hand and a knife in the other.

'People aren't all they appear to be online,' she continued. 'The filters - not only photographic ones, but the things they talk about. Half of the stuff people say isn't real. They make it up, or select the choicest cuts. They colour and glitter it to be something grander than their reality, so their lives will appear more important. It's what reveals modern man as so desperately insecure. We see beautiful people with their perfect lives and partners, children, holidays, top exam results, happy clappy achievements, and so on. We only see what makes the grade. Not the spots and scabs. Or the disappointments, bitterness and loneliness. The realities of life are rarely displayed in bright lights.'

I listened and kept my smile firmly in check, and thought, she'll make a brilliant psychologist. As long as she isn't too cynical, and allows her patients to do some of the talking.

'I can understand why people don't want to put bad news online,' I said. 'And think about this. What might people see looking in on our lives? You girls are bright, articulate, you live on this beautiful farm, with stables, woodland and a folly. And to top it all, you have horses.'

'Yes,' said Rose. 'But if we told the whole truth about our lives online. I don't mean Stevie's because hers is virtually perfect. But mine, for instance, people wouldn't be envious. In fact, they'd pity me. In the past two months, I've suffered a horrific accident which could have left me paraplegic, Pepper was murdered by a fracking intruder, and my dad collapsed and had a seizure.'

When Rose stopped speaking, Stevie got out of her chair, walked round and gave her sister a hug. 'My life isn't perfect, sis,' she said. 'He's my dad too. And I've been worried sick about you. Plus, all my friends are going to Ibiza, but we can't afford it.' She threw me a withering look. 'My love life could be about to sink and drown if I don't get the results.'

'But you'll still see each other during the holidays and at weekends, whatever your results,' said Rose.

'But it's all so uncertain,' said Stevie, and she cupped her brow and gazed out of the window.

'Maybe that's a positive,' I said. 'Too much predictability can allow us to take people for granted. To be apart might be a good test for you both.'

Stevie regarded me and shook her head. 'If only it were that simple. There are too many things that could interfere.'

'Look, we've only got two more sleeps,' I said. 'Then we'll know your results.'

'I've spoken to Gemma about Uncle Euan's anniversary,' said Stevie, thankfully changing the subject.

'It hadn't slipped my mind,' I said. 'Does she want to do this again? She may prefer to keep it low key.'

Stevie's face grew animated. 'Gemma loves my ideas. There's nothing she'd hate more than for us to pretend it never happened.'

'I wasn't suggesting that.' Although, I knew a part of me wanted to avoid the heartache that always accompanied Euan's anniversary. I'd far rather remember him privately.

'Me and Gemma think it'll be the perfect opportunity for us to come together after our troubled summer. She also thought it would be good for you and Dad. You know, after things got awkward with Saul.'

My heart began to pound. So Gemma did suspect something had gone on between me and Saul, and that was the reason Toby had overreacted.

I should be more careful with what I shared with Gemma. And I felt annoyed that she'd been discussing all of this with Stevie, her niece and my daughter. Stevie might be eighteen but it seemed inappropriate.

'Are you going to share your plans with us?' asked Rose. 'Or is it a puzzle for us to solve?'

'Happy to.' Stevie sat up on the edge of the dining table and swung her legs back and forth. 'It'll be another garden party, of course, and we'll invite the usual friends. And you know how much Euan loved classical music? We're going to have a virtual orchestra,' she announced, proudly.

'How?' asked Rose.

'A big outdoor screen that links to YouTube. Jake's dad's got a data projector we can borrow. We'll select the pieces. And we'll have strings of coloured lights and sparkling wine, fruit salads and iced cupcakes, bright picnic blankets and lots of cushions so we can all sit around on the lawn.'

'Sounds gorgeous,' I said. 'Thoughtful and magical.'

'And, here's the best bit,' she continued. 'We all dress up in classical style dress. Any period we like. I was thinking about Elizabeth Bennett and Mr Darcy, for me and Jake.'

'Lol,' said Rose. 'Does Jake know?'

'Not yet. But he'll like the idea.'

Rose sniggered.

'It's marvellous,' I said. 'I'll give my character some thought.'

'You'd make a perfect Nicole Kidman in Portrait of a Lady,' said Stevie.

'You mean Lady Isabel Archer.' Rose corrected.

'Of course,' said Stevie, and she swept the hair off her face.

'What about costumes?' asked Rose. 'I haven't got any dresses below the knee.'

'I've found a fantastic costume shop in York. Hire or buy. I'm going over to try on after my results.'

'Can you pick a dress for me?' Rose asked her. 'I'm only an inch taller.'

'Course, and I'll make sure it's pretty, too,' she said, and clapped her hands excitedly. 'I've designed the invitations.'

'Euan would love your ideas,' I said, and I suddenly felt proud and emotional. 'And yes, invite the usual suspects.'

'You mean guests, Mum.' Rose corrected me, but laughed.

'Do you know how I came up with the classical idea?' said Stevie.

'Tell me,' I said.

'The other morning you were listening to a beautiful tune. It was one of Uncle Euan's favourites.'

'Oh. I wonder which piece it was,' I said.

'I don't know the name, but you were dancing as you cooked. You looked happy and carefree.'

'I didn't see you,' I said, feeling self-conscious. Although I remembered the precise piece she meant. 'I'll come too and we can try dresses together.'

'Brilliant. You can help me choose for Rose.'

'Nothing too voluminous with my gammy leg,' said Rose.

Chapter 27

I didn't respond to Saul's confessional message, despite phrasing and rephrasing my reply several times each day. I deleted his message, although I'd replayed it in my mind over and over. I couldn't decide what I should say to him to make him accept the way things had to be. It had been a mistake to go into his bedroom. Ripping off his clothes was lunacy. I never should have allowed myself to get into that situation. It wasn't even as if I could blame alcohol. No, taking a lover was something I could never do, not to Toby, even if the idea of it was occasionally tempting.

I'd spoken to Saul and exchanged emails about Toby's health, Dom's 'coming out' and the fracking, in a strictly platonic way, but he'd replied with a kiss or two at the end of each message. And yet I should deal with it and to have kept him hanging was unfair. But I also knew why I'd avoided it.

The next morning I checked my emails and as usual I'd received one from Saul. However, this particular one sounded alarm bells. 'I have dire news on the fracking. We must meet.'

I rang him and he picked up straightaway.

'Any chance you can come over?' he said.

'We'll have to talk on the phone. My car's in the garage.'

'I'll pop over,' he said.

'I'm really busy, Saul,' I said, desperate not to have to meet up and face talking about other things.

'This is too important,' he insisted. There was an urgency in his tone that left no room for manoeuvre.

Toby had driven Rose into Richmond to buy a pair of trainers and as Stevie had stayed over at Jake's, the house remained quiet. 'Fine. I'll see you soon.'

I jogged upstairs, changed into fresh clothes and brushed my hair.

When I answered the door, Saul raised an eyebrow. 'I thought your car was in the garage?' He glanced over his shoulder at my Volvo.

'Sorry,' I said, without further explanation.

'Is Toby in?' Saul asked, and looked past me into the hallway.

'Thankfully, no.' I stood aside. 'Come in.'

The day was hot and the air already felt still and muggy. I led Saul through to the garden where we sat beneath the gazebo. Pale pink Rosa Eden coiled around the slatted roof and the air was perfumed with their scent - delicate and fresh.

Saul eased himself closer to me.

'Would you like a cold drink?' I said, and shuffled a few inches away.

'A whisky would suit right now.' He looked directly at me and his eyes darkened.

'You've got me worried.'

'Do you know if Toby has signed over some land to Maria Walker?'

'How do you know about that?'

'Have they signed on it?'

'The contract is drawn but Toby and I both have to sign it. Gemma too, and I haven't seen it yet.' I paused. 'Why?'

'Because Maria Walker is subletting your land to Quadrillum.'

'No! She wouldn't.'

'Apparently she would. Nicola's told me.'

I'd emailed Nicola only yesterday and she'd promptly replied.

'But Nicola hasn't mentioned anything to me.'

'Because,' he hesitated, 'she thinks you may already know.'

'What?'

His voice softened. 'She doesn't know you like I do.'

My mind had been so preoccupied, that the possibility of this scenario hadn't entered my head. And again, I regretted not having tackled Toby further over the sale. But I knew why I hadn't. After his seizure I was nervous about upsetting him or causing any undue stress.

I raked a hand through my hair. 'Toby will have no idea what Maria has in mind. I'll talk to him.'

Saul shook his head lightly and touched my arm. 'Don't assume anything.'

'But if that land's already sold…' A vision of a fracking plant visible from my bedroom window filled my mind and my eyes stung with tears. 'Why's he doing this, Saul? Toby must have known what Maria wanted it for.'

Saul put his arm around me. 'I'm sure he knew. But perhaps give him the benefit of the doubt until you find out if it's still pre-sale, because you may still be able to prevent the sale.'

'What if it's a done deal?'

'Like you say, you haven't signed yet.' Saul drew me close. 'We'll face that together. When and if.'

I felt his palm upon my cheek and he leaned his head towards mine. His pupils widened and for a moment I watched my reflection in them.

'Whatever happens,' he said. 'I want you to know I won't let you come to any harm.'

I leaned into him and felt the firmness and warmth of his skin through his shirt. 'I thought things were finally working out.'

He gave me a squeeze and stroked my hair. 'They will. I promise.'

'Anya?'

We hadn't heard or seen Gemma come into the garden.

Instinctively, I jerked away from Saul but he reached and took my hand.

Gemma approached and stood before us. Her eyes sharpened. 'What's going on?'

I slipped my hand from Saul's.

'You know Toby is selling the meadow to Maria?' I said.

'Yes,' she said. 'We've discussed it.'

I stood up. 'I'm not sure we have fully. And we definitely didn't know she'd be subletting the land for fracking.'

Gemma shook her head vehemently. 'She wouldn't dare. Besides which, I understand that any fracking activity must be a minimum of 500m from any homes.'

'Not any more,' Saul said. 'England's fracking body have recently challenged that ruling, and won, reducing the distance to 250m. This was last week, which puts both of your homes at a 'safe' distance.'

'No chance. I'm ringing Toby.' Gemma pulled her phone from her pocket.

I stood up. 'Wait, Gemma. At least until he comes home. He's with Rose and I don't want her stressing.' I didn't want Toby wound up either, but we couldn't let this go.

'Fine,' she said, and looking like she had no intention of leaving, she folded her arms.

It was clear from her expression that the protection of the meadow wasn't the only thing she had in mind.

Saul stood up. 'I'll get back.'

'I'll see you out,' I said. I glanced at Gemma who pursed her lips in disapproval.

As we entered the hallway I heard the rumble of an engine on the drive. 'That might be Toby back.'

'What do you want me to do?' Saul said, and his face grew alarmed.

'Leave quickly and I'll ring you.'

Saul gave a small nod and walked swiftly out of the front door.

From the doorstep I watched Toby as he clocked Saul leaving. His expression was full of hostility as he yanked on the handbrake.

I jogged over and opened Rose's door as Saul made a beeline for his car.

Rose beamed out at me. 'Hey, Mum.'

I lifted the bag from the footwell and took her hand.

'They're the exact pair I wanted,' she said. 'Perfect colour, and in the sale.'

I avoided Toby's eyes as I hooked her arm. 'What colour did you pick in the end?'

'Peach with white stripes. I shan't wear them in the yard.'

'Not for at least a week, anyway,' I said and pulled her to standing.

Toby got out and glared after Saul's pickup van, now driving away. He kicked the ground and pebbles scattered.

In bright mood and oblivious to Toby's reaction, Rose set off into the house to try on her trainers. When she was safely inside, I turned and followed her in. My anxiety spiralled.

The moment that Toby snatched my wrist, Gemma walked into the hallway. She stopped and watched as he lead me forcibly towards the office. I caught Gemma's eye and she raised her palm to her mouth. In the doorway I struck my ankle against the frame but suppressed a cry.

Toby slammed the door shut behind us. 'What did that arsehole want?'

I wrenched my arm from his. 'For starters, stop dragging me around like you're some kind of neanderthal. Secondly, I'm grateful to Saul for letting me know what the meadow will be used for once Maria has it in her claws.'

'And how did you show him?'

'Sorry?'

'How grateful you were.'

I ignored his pathetic jibe. 'Be honest with me, Toby. Did you know that Maria wanted to lease the meadow for drilling?'

'Don't be ridiculous. She needs the grazing.'

'And don't you be so naive,' I said. 'I've always disliked Maria. She's rude and obnoxious. Give me that contract, Toby. I forbid this sale.'

'You're wrong. Maria and I have discussed it and it's because she's struggling for land that we came up with the idea for the meadow. Which we barely use, unless it's to ride through. Oh, and to have sex in.'

'This is serious,' I said, my frustration building. 'Saul says fracking proximity laws have been reduced to 250m and our home is only just over 300m away. Gemma's, too. We'll be powerless to prevent it.'

Slowly and deliberately, Toby rubbed his jawline. 'Too late, I'm afraid. Our solicitor emailed it across to Maria yesterday.'

'But even if Maria's signed it, we haven't.'

'But I have and they only needed my signature,' he replied, matter of fact.

'No, Toby!' My voice rose in panic. 'Any land here is in yours, mine and Gemma's names. All signatures are required.'

'Not according to our solicitor.'

'This is bullshit.' My anger erupted. 'If Maria's already signed you have to retract it.'

Toby looked at me with a blank expression that masked his thoughts.

'Please,' I begged. 'By whatever means. I'll move out if they frack here. So have a good think about that.'

'Where could you go?' he said. 'And these health issues are blown out of all proportion and unproven.'

'You haven't bothered to research this, have you, or listened to a word I've said?' I was infuriated by his patronising attitude. His disregard for what was important to me, to our whole way of life, seemed to be ignored. 'If you can't sort this out with Maria, I'm leaving you. And I'll take the girls.'

I marched from the office and found Rose with Gemma in the hall, admiring the new trainers.

They looked up and caught my expression.

'Can you talk some sense into your dad?' I said to Rose. 'He's sold our meadow to Maria who's leasing it to the frackers.'

'He can't.' Rose's face paled. 'Is Dad in there?'

I nodded and with her jaw set firm, Rose hobbled off to tackle him.

Gemma took my hand and I could see she was close to tears herself. 'Are you OK?'

'No. Though I should be used to him manhandling me by now.'

'Don't put up with this, Anya. I'll tackle him too.'

I led Gemma into the kitchen so we could talk out of earshot.

'I think Toby's mad with jealousy over Saul,' she said. 'That's why he's being so difficult.' Gemma looked directly at me. 'Has he got any reason to be?'

I shook my head quickly. 'Of course he hasn't. He's being irrational. Though his jealousy is out of character.'

'Be honest, Anya,' she lowered her voice. 'From where I'm standing it looks like there's something going on between you and Saul.'

'You're wrong, Gemma,' I said. 'I'm keeping my distance.'

'It didn't look that way sitting all cosy out there.'

'I'm not interested in Saul. I love Toby. Though God only knows why he deserves my loyalty right now.'

'Saul's after you, so you've got to be up front with him.'

'I know. And I will.'

'Then do him a favour and put a stop to this pointless pursuit of his.' She looked me up and down. 'You don't normally wear a skirt and pretty sandals.' She raised a brow.

I turned round and shut the kitchen door. 'I'm not falling for him. I need friendship. I need support. Which is more than my husband's offering.'

Gemma walked over to the dresser, picked up the bottle of Jack Daniels, along with two tumblers. She poured two generous measures.

'Here.' She placed one in my hand. 'It'll calm you down. But sip it.'

I raised it to my lips. 'I don't know Toby anymore. He agreed to sell our meadow without discussing it with either you or I first.'

'And you don't think it's money that's blinding his vision?' she replied.

'The money would help, but we're not that desperate.'

Gemma slugged back her drink. 'OK.' She set her glass on the worktop. 'Here's what we're gonna do. We're going to visit Maria. And we're going to reason with her.'

'You said to sip.' I followed her example, raised my glass and took a gulp. 'You do know Maria won't listen to reason.'

'If she won't listen,' Gemma continued. 'We'll blackmail her.'

'With what exactly?'

'You'll have to trust me on this.'

'Tell me,' I insisted.

'I will, but not yet.'

'OK.' I knocked back my whisky and banged the glass onto the tabletop. 'Let's go.'

'We'll go on horseback,' she said. 'But first, I'll have a drop more Dutch courage,' she said, and poured another shot. 'Need one?'

'Damn right I do.'

We raised and chinked our glasses.

'Don't you want to change first?' she said, and regarded me with suspicion.

I looked down at my skirt and sandals. 'These will do just fine.'

We downed our second shots and I dropped my glass into the sink of water.

'Let's go, sister,' I said.

Chapter 28

I felt tipsy as I mounted Ebony and adjusted my skirt. Of course, Gemma had been right about the sandals but we needed to tackle the problem before it was too late.

Gemma pulled Maya back to ride alongside me. 'Do you think Maria will be in?'

'If she isn't we'll break in and steal her computer and printer.'

'Remember there's Frankie,' said Gemma.

'We could do without him being there.'

'How old is he now?' asked Gemma.

'Mid thirties-ish. But mumsie still makes all the decisions.'

'He's the Rottweiler.'

'Hardly,' I said. 'More the skulking cat beaten into submission by its overbearing mistress.'

'If Frankie's there, I'll distract him while you work on her,' said Gemma.

'We do whatever it takes. I'm not leaving without that contract and this resolved.' I felt driven and determined - lightheaded with the thought of what we must do.

As we rode over the brow of the hill, past the folly and down to the lane, our voices echoed amongst the trees.

'Stay close. You're the one with the 'information'.' I gestured.

Her expression grew serious. 'Should it be necessary.'

Despite my curiosity I knew Gemma well enough to know that she'd have her reasons for not sharing what she knew.

'I've no idea what's really been said between her and Toby,' I said. 'So we'll have to wing it. But with caution. Look at me if you're unsure and I'll do likewise.'

At the bottom of the hill Gemma dismounted. She heaved and lifted the gate off its latch. 'We must get this fixed.'

'The gate and the damn contract,' I said.

We rode the horses down the track towards Shadow Blithe Farm and despite the alcohol in my blood, my mood darkened.

In my mind I rehearsed what I'd say. If all else failed, I'd get down on my knees and beg.

I heard voices ahead and glanced across at Gemma. A man and a woman, raised voices, but too muffled to distinguish their words.

When we rounded the bend I saw Maria and Frankie standing on the grass verge. Frankie wielded a sledgehammer and brought it down onto a wooden post with a thud that rang through the woods. Startled by the noise, Ebony stopped short.

Maria looked our way and Frankie rested his hammer on the ground.

'Greetings, ladies,' said Maria resting her hands on her hips and all smiles.

We drew nearer and I smiled as warmly as I could muster. 'Do you have five minutes, Maria?'

'Not usually. But as it's you,' she kindly offered.

'Can we talk inside?'

A frown dug into her weathered brow and she turned to Frankie. 'You finish off here, son.'

As Gemma and I followed Maria down to the farmhouse her left side stooped with each step. An arthritic hip perhaps. She had to be approaching seventy.

Shadow Blithe sat in the deepest part of the valley, hidden away and nestled amongst an ancient copse with hillsides to either side of the small farmhouse. And yet it remained a strangely enchanting spot. A stream flowed beside the lane and on down the length of the valley where it eventually joined the river Swale. Sunlight trickled through the trees onto the track causing the flintstones to glimmer like marbles. Toby and Gemma had always referred to Shadow Blithe as, The Coven, which didn't seem unreasonable given Maria's personality, her wild black hair and her penchant for floaty dresses, in predominantly witchy colours. Concealed beneath her haggard features there was still some prettiness from her younger years and despite her manner, I had a degree of admiration for her workwear. She was a rebel; an individual in her own eccentric way. Regrettably for us she was a rebel who cared less for the environment and more about the weight of her purse.

As I watched her now, I was taken back to the first time I'd visited the Walkers to introduce myself, soon after I'd moved in with Toby. It had been an awkward and counterproductive encounter. I never should have visited on my own and I certainly shouldn't have gone inside. Norris, Maria's now deceased husband had opened the door, wearing only his shorts. His bare chest was thick with curly red hair. He'd leered at me from the doorway and swayed unsteadily on his feet as I'd introduced myself.

'Come in, my lovely,' he'd slurred, then staggered aside.

Instead of making an excuse to leave, I foolishly followed him into the sitting room, where the curtains were half drawn and with only one dimly lit lamp in the corner.

'Take a seat.' He'd patted the sofa. 'Can I tempt you with a taste of parsnip wine?'

Without waiting for my reply he retrieved a bottle from the minibar fridge and filled a glass to the brim. As he handed it to me the wine splashed onto my chest and legs.

'Oops!' he said, spilling some more.

'It's fine.' I took the glass and patted myself dry.

He lumbered back to the bar and grabbed a bar towel. 'Here, let me.'

Before I could protest he toweled my chest. Instinctively, I recoiled, whereupon, Norris lost his balance and fell on top of me. Fortunately, or unfortunately, depending on how you viewed it, Maria chose that moment to walk into the room.

'What on earth are you doing?' she barked.

Norris propped his arms against the back of the sofa and gave me a cheeky wink before pushing himself to standing.

Maria grabbed the back of his shorts, dragged him to the door and shoved him out with a slap on the back of his head. 'Get out, you drunken fool.'

She looked me up and down with her lips in a snarl. 'I won't apologise for my husband's behaviour.'

'Really, there's no need,' I said, getting up and extending my hand. 'I'm Anya...'

'I know precisely who you are,' she interrupted. 'I've heard plenty about you.'

'Oh?' I said, curious.

'Yes, and none of it flattering.'

'Sorry?' I'd said.

'Well, I can see how you managed to wriggle your way into becoming lady of the manor.'

I stood up. 'I'm not sure what you're getting at. It seems I've made an error in judgement. Your husband may have had a drink or two, but at least he made me welcome.'

'My husband is a stupid man. He'd invite a sheep in for a shag if he got half the chance.'

I'd heard enough and I drank back my wine. 'Delicious!' I said, and went to place the glass back on the bar. 'Please thank your husband for his hospitality.' And I headed out to the front door without a backward glance.

'You stay well clear of my husband,' she called. 'Do you hear me?'

I didn't bother to reply and shut the door behind me.

My difficult relationship with the Walker family continued in the same vein from that initial and farcical encounter. When Norris died, from alcoholism, and we were invited to his funeral, I'd felt it prudent to decline. Toby, Gemma and Alan had attended, without an ounce of enthusiasm between them.

'He's probably better off up there,' Alan said, casting a cursory nod skywards.

None of us had contradicted him.

Maria led Gemma and I through the drab entrance and into the drearier living room. It smelt strongly of animals.

'I assume your visit is related to the meadow?' said Maria without a hint of a smile on her long, bony face. 'Given that I haven't had the pleasure of your company since that wild beast of yours escaped.'

'Indeed, the meadow,' I said.

The wild beast she referred to was Pepper when he'd escaped into a field of heavily pregnant ewes. After I'd received Maria's emergency call and dashed over to catch him, I'd found him grazing peacefully amongst the flock who had appeared unphased by his presence. Maria had threatened to prosecute us if any of the ewes aborted, and she had been adamant they would do. By some strange miracle we never heard back from her.

'I assume you heard about Pepper?' I said, suppressing a more honest response to her insensitivity.

'Yes, I heard you attempted to jump a fallen tree but hadn't bothered to check the landing.'

She knew precisely how to wind me up, but I remained outwardly impassive.

'Such a waste of a fine beast. Still, accidents happen.' She waved her hand in a dismissive manner and sniffed. 'At least you weren't hurt.' Her expression didn't disguise her insincerity.

Now wasn't the time to tell my version. Tact and diplomacy, I repeated to myself.

'I'd offer you a drink, but I've only got cider,' she said, and turned on the standing lamp. She left the curtains closed.

'Cider would be lovely,' said Gemma.

'And madam?' she asked me.

'Thank you,' I said.

Maria disappeared and shortly returned with a tray of glasses. And, I noted, surely too quickly for her to have popped anything nasty into mine. She handed me a glass, chipped and half-full, and nodded for me to take a seat. I drank a mouthful then sank into the sofa which creaked beneath me. As I looked around the room, I wondered how she could afford to buy our meadow. There were no pictures, ornaments, books or soft furnishings. The carpet was sticky with filth and there were rubber plants on the window sills, their leaves ragged and dry.

I sipped the chilled cider. It tasted delicious. 'Did you brew this, Maria?' I asked.

'Do you like it?' She slugged a mouthful and wiped the back of her hand across her mouth. 'It's a new recipe. A few extras to give it a kick.'

'It's tasty,' agreed Gemma. 'You must share the recipe with us.'

Nice one, Gemma, I thought. Butter her up.

'Not possible, I'm afraid. I'm going to patent and market it, once I've fine tuned it.'

'It's perfect already,' I said.

'Enough of your flattery,' she said, with a steely glare. 'Shall we discuss my purchase?'

'The thing is,' I said. 'Toby told me our solicitor emailed over the contract for your signature.'

She nodded. 'Took them long enough, but yes.'

I took a deep breath. 'I'm really sorry,' I said. 'But there's a mistake that makes it invalid.'

She shrugged. 'I've read it word for word and it's as Toby and I discussed'

'And have you printed and signed it?' I asked.

'Of course. It's in the envelope, ready to post this afternoon.'

'Would you mind holding off?' I asked. 'In fact, better still, rip it up. It's void.'

I looked across to Gemma for some inspiration, when an idea sprang to mind. 'You see, Maria, the price on the contract is incorrect.' I paused. 'There's an extra zero. Which means you'll be paying £500K instead of £50K.'

If Maria could have dispatched me with a scowl, I'm certain she would have succeeded. Instead, she stood up, knocked back the remainder of her cider and marched out.

Gemma nodded and mouthed, 'Good one.'

'Heck,' I said. 'Do you think she'll open it?'

'Course she will. Hopefully, in here.'

I heard the front door slam and Frankie walked in.

'Hello.' He stood, slightly hunched with his hands hanging awkwardly at his sides. 'Where's Mum?'

'She'll be back in a minute.' Gemma gazed fondly at him and patted the sofa.

Frankie went to sit next to her. For a moment we sat in silence.

'Nice day for it,' said Frankie, looking quickly aside to Gemma.

'It's so warm out,' Gemma said, and fanned her face with her hand. 'Thirsty work fixing that fence, I imagine.'

Frankie, nodded. 'Right enough, but I'm a fast worker.'

'I can imagine,' replied Gemma, and with a smile she flipped her hair.

Frankie blushed and looked at his feet like a shy teenager.

When Maria returned she frowned at Frankie, and plonked herself down on the armchair. She tore open the envelope, straightened out the papers on her lap and read them closely.

'But this says £50K.' She looked to me and then Gemma.

'Really? Our solicitor told Toby she'd got it wrong,' I said, and turned to Gemma who nodded with a serious expression.

'What a relief.' I paused. 'The other problem…,' I paused again, still thinking, 'is that we've actually had a change of mind about selling. So, if you can pass me that contract I'd appreciate it.'

Maria laughed. 'Not a chance. Toby sold it in good faith.' She flapped the contract above her head. 'And the contract is signed.'

Gemma stood up.

Maria, Frankie and myself turned to face Gemma as she took a long and leisurely drink of her cider.

'Then, Maria, if you're not prepared to hand back the contract I'm afraid I have no choice but to share some information.' She looked down pointedly at Frankie. 'With your son.'

Maria opened her mouth to speak, but instead glowered back at Gemma through pincer black eyes.

'Shall I share what I know?' Gemma asked and gave Maria a brief, unfeeling smile.

I saw confusion and alarm wash over Maria's face. I could smell her fear.

Maria swallowed. 'I'm not sure what you mean, but perhaps we can talk in private?'

'Oh, that won't be necessary,' replied Gemma. 'Frankie has every right to be here. The farm, including our meadow, will be his one day.'

I recalled that Frankie had attended the fracking community meeting. But Maria hadn't.

'What's she talking about?' Frankie asked, as suspicion swept across his face.

'Nothing of any consequence.' Maria turned to me. 'And what does Toby want to do with the land?'

'I'll tell you what he categorically does not want. He doesn't want it to be used to frack on. Did you tell him that was your intention?'

Frankie jumped up. 'We're not having those dickheads on our land.'

Maria disregarded Frankie's protests. 'And who told you that was my plan?' She fired at me.

'Is it true?' I asked.

'Irrelevant. Given the land is mine I'm free to use it how I wish. It's nonsense that a hole in the ground can do any harm. Liberals and tree huggers live in a dream world.'

'But I've looked into this, Mum,' said Frankie. 'Water supplies are contaminated with chemicals, it causes earth tremors, gas leaks trigger explosions.'

'I've told you, son. Don't believe everything you read online. Most of it's fake news spread by socialists and communists.'

'So, are you saying you won't tear up that contract?' Frankie asked her.

Maria rubbed her chin. 'That's precisely what I'm saying, son.'

'Dad would never have allowed this,' he said.

'Your Dad isn't here and I decide what's best long-term. They'll drill for six months and we'll be well paid. You can even get a job with them. They'll move on and we can return it to its natural...'

'I really didn't want to have to bring this up,' Gemma interrupted. 'But you leave me with no choice.'

Maria stepped up to Gemma with her fists clenched and her mouth set in a hard line. 'If you dare to speak what I believe you're threatening.'

Gemma stood her ground, unblinking, and seemed to grow another two inches. 'Trust me,' she said. 'I do dare.'

And in the long and uncertain silence that followed I watched Maria's cheeks turn from blood red to pasty yellow until finally she turned away and slumped back down into the armchair, defeated.

Her eyes blazed as she looked from Gemma to me. 'This is blackmail,' she said, and her upper lip twitched as though she might either burst into tears or at the other extreme, lunge at us.

'And yet,' I reminded her. 'You deliberately misled Toby over what you planned to do with the land.'

'He didn't ask questions,' said Maria. 'On the contrary, he was only interested in how much he'd get for it.'

'Toby isn't here,' I said. 'But Gemma and I are interested and we co-own the land.'

Gemma held out her hand. 'Will you give me the contract?'

Reluctant and slow, Maria lifted her hand. Calmly, Gemma took it from her.

'That meadow was as good as mine, so let me assure you both, I'll return the favour, tenfold.'

'You've got nothing on us, Maria.' I felt tired of her anger and bitterness. 'But we do have something on you, remember? Accept that you were in the wrong, and we'll forget how underhand you've been.'

'Our solicitor will be retracting the deal within the hour,' Gemma added.

I walked to the door and turned round. 'Don't bother getting up. We'll see ourselves out. Goodbye, Frankie.

As I approached Ebony, he whickered his greeting.

I untethered him, drew the reins over his head and stroked his muzzle. 'Such a patient boy.'

The moment I decided we were out of earshot, I turned to Gemma. 'What were you threatening to reveal?'

Gemma drew Maya alongside, as though to conspire. 'I didn't want to tell you, but given what went on in there, it's only fair that I do. But you must swear never to breathe a word. Not to Toby or anyone.'

I felt a jab of nerves but nodded.

'And I mean never,' she repeated.

'If I had more patience I'd try and guess, but I'm at a complete loss.'

The thought of keeping something important from Toby didn't sit well, but perhaps sometimes, secrets were a justifiable and necessary evil.

'I won't tell Toby because I hate to upset him. And clearly whatever it is you're going to tell me, is going to do that and more.

'This will come as a shock.' She took in a sharp breath. 'You remember how after Euan died, Dad would sit and talk with me?'

'He was worried about you. We all were.'

'Toby never seemed to be,' said Gemma.

'Toby was too wrapped up in his own grief,' I said.

She nodded. 'Perhaps. Anyway, Dad and I grew closer and I discovered things. How he and Mum had met. What they argued about.' She paused. 'I even found out that Mum had an affair.'

'Really?'

'You know I was only nine when she died?'

'Too young. For you and Toby, and for her.'

'Losing her almost broke us. And then Euan...'

Gemma's words evaporated and his name floated in front of me before being ripped away. I was desperate for her to continue.

'Your mum was a beauty,' I said, recalling the photographs of her that still adorned the walls of Willows End.

'She was. And not only was she pretty, she was vivacious.'

'You mean a bit of a flirt?'

'I guess. She was like it with women, too. She loved people. So Dad said.'

'Now I know where you and Toby get it,' I said.

'I call it being friendly,' said Gemma, with a slight laugh.

'Go on,' I urged.

'Dad hired in help each summer for the harvest. Young, bronzed and muscular men, working barechested in the fields.'

'I can picture that,' I said.

'Mum had a summer long affair with one. Thomas. A real Adonis by all accounts. And not only did she tell Dad, she also threatened to leave him if he didn't allow their affair to continue.'

'Bloody hell! That must have hurt.'

'Poor Dad. The pain of it dwelt on his mind all those years.'

'And you must have been shocked, too.'

'At first. But not when I thought about how Mum was.'

'What's it got to do with Maria?'

'That was Dad's next confession. One night we got hopelessly drunk and in amongst our ramblings, he told me he'd had an affair with Maria. He was devastated by Mum's love affair and so he sought revenge, or at least didn't resist temptation. Turns out Maria was perfectly willing, despite being married.'

'I can't see Maria and Alan together at all,' I said. 'Your dad was a looker and she's mealy mouthed.'

'I know. But Maria was young and pretty then and Dad's head must have been all over the place. So I can understand it.'

'How long did the affair go on for?'

'Not long. Seems Maria had always been desperate for children and had never conceived with Norris. With Dad's...help, she soon fell pregnant and that ended the affair.'

'Bloody hell, Gemma,' I said, trying to digest her revelations. 'And your Mum never knew anything about Alan's affair, or Frankie?'

'Dad said not. He never confessed, wisely, and Maria wanted her husband to think Frankie was his. So everybody was happy.'

'I can't believe you've kept this to yourself all these years.'

'What choice did I have? Telling Toby would have only been selfish. Plus, making it known would have genuine repercussions for Willows End and inheritance.'

'Of course,' I said. 'What if Maria ever decides to tell Frankie?'

'You mean destroy her only child's life by admitting his Dad was never his father? I might not be a mother but I don't think she could do that to him.'

'Rest assured, Toby will never hear it from me,' I said. The enormity of doing so wasn't something I wanted to contemplate.

These were scandalous revelations. In all my years with the Kubiks and living as part of the family, such deceit and lies had never entered my sphere of thought. From the outside, and even on the inside, the Kubik family and business appeared normal, successful and respectable. But in reality, things beneath the surface were about as far from 'normal' as you could imagine.

Gemma leaned across the gap between the horses and touched my arm. 'I know you won't.'

'No wonder Maria relinquished the contract. You're brilliant. I could bloody kiss you.'

As we rode home through the woods, I reflected on Gemma's words and wondered how I hadn't noticed the resemblance between Frankie and Toby before. Frankie was a younger version of Toby. Tall, strong, handsome with dark curly hair. Frankie seemed quieter and lacking in confidence, but he'd grown up with different parents. Shocking disclosures all round.

Toby listened in contemplative silence as I replayed our visit to Maria, while I omitted any mention of illegitimate offspring. I knew I was deceiving Toby just as his parents had deceived one another, but because I was still fuming over his part in all of this it somehow made it easier.

Toby got up and began to pace the kitchen floor. 'I'll check with Fiona if we can still sell it but after adding a clause to prevent any subletting.'

'No you won't,' I said.

'We can't risk it,' Gemma added.

'Once Maria owned the meadow, she'd do whatever it took to get her own way,' I said. 'She's manipulative and calculating.' I paused. 'And what's more, she seems to have a grudge against us.'

I turned to Gemma. 'I'm not imagining it, am I?'

'No. She's bloody difficult and deliberately so. It's obvious she hates us. She always has,' said Gemma.

Toby considered this for a moment. 'Mmmm. You might be right.'

'It's settled then,' I said, decisively.

I felt relieved that we'd averted disaster and although I knew fracking would be an ongoing problem, at least I wouldn't have to face seeing it from our front door.

As for my relationship with Toby, I was prepared to do whatever was necessary to get our relationship back to some sense of normality. However, I was not prepared to tolerate any more of his aggressive or controlling behaviour, whether it be emotional or physical.

Chapter 29

I looked at my reflection in the dressing room mirror and caught Stevie's eye as she stepped into a pale silk dress. 'Are you sure this one suits me?' I asked her. 'You don't think it's too revealing?' I pulled up the scoop neckline to cover more cleavage. 'It's supposed to be a celebration, not a wake,' she said. 'You're right. I like it.' I lifted the skirts and looked sideways on. The criss cross ribbons on the bodice tied into a bow at my bust and it felt snug, if a little low cut.

Stevie twirled and her skirt swished in a swirl of netting and silk. 'So girly,' she said. 'But I love it.'

'It suits you,' I said. 'I've never seen you as a princess, but you do remind me of a certain character with a ball to attend.'

'I'm sure I can make believe for a few hours,' she said. 'It'll be fun. More importantly, it's an opportunity for us to lighten up what could otherwise be another sad day for us all, especially Gemma.'

'You're right, Stevie. It'll help her to get through it. Not sure about this dress though. Do I look like I'm trying too hard?' I asked.

'Get away, Mum. You're still young and beautiful. You'll take Dad back to your wedding day.'

'Not sure about that,' I said with a laugh.

The following morning I took Stevie to collect her A-Level results. They weren't as good as any of us had expected and once we returned home she grew hysterical, hid herself in her bedroom and refused to talk to me. The only person she allowed to console her had been Rose, who used her newfound counselling skills to listen patiently and nod at appropriate moments. I popped my head through the door at one point with two cups of tea.

'Tea? The only real remedy for shock.'

With a hand clasped to her forehead, she nodded. 'I'll try.'

Rose hooked Stevie's arm and helped her to sit up.

'It's literally my worst nightmare,' she said.

'Come on, love,' I said, and set the cups on her bedside cabinet. 'You were only a couple of points below, so you may still get accepted.'

'I won't. Do you know how tough it is to get into Leeds?' she replied. 'I'm trying to be realistic.'

That's one way of putting it, I thought, and I caught Rose's eye who pursed her lips in solidarity.

'Keep trying to get through and see what they say,' I suggested.

'Someone's supposed to be calling back.' Stevie gave a heavy sigh. 'That was over an hour ago.'

'They will. It'll get sorted,' I said, and sat on the end of her bed. 'The thing is, sometimes, what appear to be obstacles, become the stepping stones that will lead us to unexpected and better opportunities.'

Stevie nodded sagely.

'I know you did your best, but we can't control all that happens in our lives - exams included. We can, however, decide how we react to situations,' I said, but beginning to annoy myself with my advice.

'You're right, Mum. I'll think about that,' said Stevie.

I decided it would be unwise to interfere further for now and I gave her a hug and left them talking.

Thank heavens for Rose - so thoughtful, patient and wise.

By dinnertime, Stevie had emerged from her room, freshly showered and dressed and with an altogether brighter expression and demeanor.

'Jake's on his way over. He's promised this won't stop us from seeing one another.'

'Of course it won't,' I said. 'But pick the right University course for you and try not to base it around seeing Jake.'

'But equally, we don't want to spend too much time travelling. Manchester or Newcastle run a similar course so I'm trying them.'

'Excellent. Both highly reputable.'

'Anyway, I can't mope around,' Stevie said. 'I've got to finalise the plans for Euan's party. Buy the food, sort out decorations etc.' She paused. 'I think I might enjoy a career in event planning.'

'You'd be brilliant,' I said. 'Persuasive, organised and you speak so eloquently. That's quite a tall order for an eighteen year old.'

Stevie ran over and hugged me. 'Thanks for the vote of confidence, Mum.'

I squeezed her tight. 'But keep an open mind. For now, at least.'

Toby arrived home and brandished a huge bouquet of flowers. I wondered what he'd done for me to deserve them.

'These are for my diligent and intelligent daughter, who may not have got the precise grades she wanted, but whom we are proud of nonetheless.'

'Oh, Dad.' Stevie wrapped her arms around his neck. 'I love you.'

Toby looked my way and I mouthed, 'Thank you.'

I admired Stevie's resilience and ability to bounce back from disappointment. That would hold her in good stead, whatever the future held.

Chapter 30

I placed the tray laden with plates and cutlery onto the trestle table on the edge of the lawn then called across to Stevie and Rose.

'One hour, girls.'

'But we're nowhere near ready,' cried Stevie, who stood on a garden chair to hang a string of lights between two branches.

'The table looks beautiful,' I said.

The girls had dressed it with a pastel blue tablecloth, bowls of fruit and vases filled with roses, African lilies, coneflowers and forsythia, picked fresh from the garden.

'Don't panic,' I said. 'What we don't get done we'll ask our guests to help with.'

'We can't do that,' Stevie said.

'OK,' I said, decisive. 'You two get ready. Gemma and I will take over.'

Rose grinned and called, 'We'll be quick.'

She chatted with Stevie, her voice full of excitement, as they headed back inside.

'Where's the ice bucket, Gem?'

'Too soon for ice,' she said. 'It'll melt.'

'What I actually meant was, where's the chilled wine?'

'Utility fridge.'

I walked back inside, poured two glasses and returned to set up the data projector. On my laptop I found an upbeat piece, where the violinist swirled and danced as she played.

'How does she do that?' I asked.

'She is a woman,' said Gemma. 'And we all know women are better at multitasking than men.'

'I've never been able to do two things well at once,' I said, and handed Gemma a glass of wine.

'Mmm, you are one exception,' she said, and paused at the table. 'You focus entirely on anything you're doing and it can be impossible to hold a conversation with you.'

'Do you mean I ignore you?'

'Exactly. It might seem rude, if I didn't know you better.' She sipped her wine. 'Whereas I can do many important things at once.'

'Oh?'

'I can read a book even while compiling a mental list of things to do.'

'Impressive. If my mind wanders when I'm reading, I lose the thread and have to go back,' I said.

'Actually, I was being unfair by saying all men can't multitask.'

'Why's that?'

'For instance, the other night, Nick was kissing me...all over and he still managed to talk.'

'Wasn't that distracting?' I said with a snigger.

'Not in the least. In fact, it enhanced the experience.'

'Thanks for the sex tip, Dr Ruth. We'll try it.'

Once again, Gemma surprised me. Her resilience seemed extraordinary, given her recent and hellish experience with Rob. But I knew well that beneath her buoyant exterior she was still fragile. Her survival defence had long been to keep that side of her well hidden.

'You're welcome. But please don't share your success, or otherwise, with me.'

I giggled. 'You're funny when I mention anything intimate about your brother.'

She shuddered. 'Can you blame me?'

'And yet you share so much about your sex life.'

'I thought you liked me to,' replied Gemma.

'Oh, I do.' I nodded agreement. 'How many are coming today, by the way? I couldn't get a definitive answer from Stevie.'

'Twenty two - if they all turn up.'

'And how are you feeling about it all?' I looked at her.

'I'm OK, I think. I even thought about inviting Nick, but then decided I might put him off me if I felt maudlin and wanted to reminisce.'

'True.'

'Rose says she's glad Dom and Alex decided to come after declining initially,' Gemma said with a playful smile.

'The Vermaaks are coming?' I said, surprised. And I felt an unwelcome jolt of nerves.

'I'm sure we told you.'

'If you had I'd have remembered,' I said. 'And they didn't even know Euan.' I paused. 'You know how tense things have been between Saul and Toby.'

'Yes, but you said you'd sorted all that out and you and Toby were getting on much better.'

Gemma was normally more intuitive and tactful. Perhaps the Vermaak's coming was more the girls' idea.

'I know we have, but...' I didn't know what to say. If I protested too much she'd become more suspicious. I'd been demonstrably more affectionate towards Toby both when we were alone and in front of Gemma and the girls to try to alleviate any concerns they might have over my friendship with Saul.

'I'm happy they're coming,' she said. 'I really like Saul and they'll make it into a proper party. Which is the whole idea.'

I went lightheaded. 'They won't understand all of this.'

Gemma walked over to me, glass in hand. 'If I'm OK and Toby and you are getting on fine, why are you so bothered?'

What other grounds could I have to object? I sighed. 'What if Dom feels scared of Toby?'

Gemma replied quickly. 'Rose assures me Dom's not worried and Toby even rang him to apologise.'

'I didn't know.' Something else Toby had failed to mention. 'Sorry, Gemma. You surprised me, that's all.'

I wondered if Toby knew Saul and the boys were coming. Maybe he did.

Gemma regarded me with a quizzical expression. 'The Vermaaks will help distract me and the girls,' she said. 'And I really could do without wallowing in memories.'

'But the memories are still important,' I said, feeling another wave of sadness.

'You know I never stop remembering.' Gemma looked at me seriously for a moment. 'But I am trying to move on.'

'I know you are.' I touched her shoulder. 'And you're doing brilliantly.' I looked at my watch. 'We should dress,' I said, changing the subject.

'How are you doing your hair?' she asked.

'Simple. Loose and a jewelled clip.'

'I'm piling mine on top.' She gathered up her hair. 'What do you think?'

'Elegant and beautiful.'

'That's the idea,' she said. 'A new me.'

I kissed her on the cheek. 'You're beautiful however you dress or do your hair.'

Dressed in his dinner suit and with slicked back curls, Toby adjusted his cravat in front of the bedroom mirror. 'Do I look OK?'

I set my glass on the dressing table and walked behind him.

I cupped his buttocks with my hands. 'Incredibly sexy. If you must know.'

He turned around and pulled me close. 'I meant my cravat.'

'Looks good to me. Though I haven't a clue how to tie one,' I said.

'I can't wait to see you in that.' He gestured to my red silk dress hanging on the wardrobe door. 'Shall I help you undress first?' He cocked an eyebrow.

'I'm tempted, but I think I'd rather surprise you.'

'Ahh. You mean you want to make an entrance?'

'Not at all.' I nudged him.

'Who's coming today?'

So he didn't know. 'It's a surprise. For me, too.'

'And how's Gemma?' he asked.

'She says she's fine,' I said. 'But a party seems to re-energise the heartache each time.'

'I wish we could let it go, too,' he said.

I nodded in understanding. Toby leaned close and as we held and kissed one another I felt that we were finally coming through our difficult period. Euan's party, with Saul and the boys coming, might show us all how things could and should be, both now and for the future. Toby and I, close and very much together, and the Vermaaks, our new family friends.

226

It was these moments of closeness that reminded me why Toby and I were still together. The tone of his voice and the things he said to me. The way he made me feel loved and special. At least, most of the time. And more than anything, how he touched me, never failing to ignite my desire so that I never stopped wanting him. He was the drug I'd grown dependent on. I'd never outgrown him like some couples seemed to. Maybe this was in part because of his elusiveness and the veiled intricacies of his mind that made me want more - keen to know his thoughts on things and to reach into the depths of his mind.

When we drew apart, I looked at him and his eyes glistened. 'I'll never stop loving you, Anya. You're mine, you know. Nobody else's. Don't ever forget that.'

I brushed away a tear that rolled down his cheek and my voice trembled. 'I'll always want and love you, too.'

'Will you though?' he said.

'If I can say that after what we've been through, then yes. Sometimes you drive me insane.' I cupped his neck with my hand. 'But you do something to me, Toby. Something that I need. And I don't ever want to lose that.'

'We should talk more,' he said. 'I mean like this, properly.'

'Hey, Mum, Dad.'

Still holding one another we turned to the doorway.

'Sorry to interrupt,' said Stevie with a sheepish smile. 'What do you think?'

'Exquisite.' I squeezed Toby's hand. 'And beautiful.'

'Not like a princess, I hope?' she said.

'More like a powerful queen,' I replied.

She raised the book in her hand. 'Then I'll quote from this so people will know who I really am.'

Toby laughed loudly. 'Or you could tell them?'

'That wouldn't be so much fun,' I said.

Stevie opened her copy of Pride and Prejudice and held it up. 'There is a stubbornness about me that never can bear to be frightened at the will of others. My courage always rises at every attempt to intimidate me.'

I clapped my hands as she finished. 'Bravo, Stevie! Perfect for you.'

'Thank you.' She curtseyed and smiled.

I glimpsed the clock. 'I must dress.' I kicked off my sandals and unzipped my shorts.

'Come on, Dad. You can help me in the kitchen. It looks like Armageddon.'

'Great.' Toby pecked me on the lips, and with reluctance, followed Stevie out.

I liked the idea of Anna Karenina and my rose-red dress looked opulent enough for a woman of her literary standing. And perhaps the anonymity of disguise might help make the next few hours more bearable. Amongst Stevie's accessories I'd found a peacock feather and jewelled clip for my hair along with a black velvet choker. I completed the look with a ruby lipstick and black eyeliner. I thought the overall effect looked dramatic, but pleasing.

The weather remained glorious, despite an occasional wispy cloud that drifted across the endless blue sky.

When I returned to the garden, I was surprised to see many of the guests had already arrived. The girls and women wore an array of long dresses, in pearl, honey, plum, sapphire, and seafoam, with ribbons in their hair, while most of the men and boys wore white shirts and suits.

Music and laughter filled the garden which was awash with flowers and sunlight.

Toby spotted me, and marched across the lawn.

He encircled my waist with his arm. 'You look incredible, Mrs Karenina.'

'Thank you.' I lifted my face and kissed him on the lips.

'A drink?'

I raised my empty glass.

'Come.' He took my hand and led me to where Gemma stood surrounded by chattering girls. She looked stunning in a full length jewelled gown that clung to her goddess-like figure.

Suzie, one of the younger girls, tried to persuade Gemma to play Ariana Grande.

'Hold your horses,' said Gemma. 'I'll have everyone dancing with the next one.'

'Which one?' Suzie asked and gazed adoringly up at Gemma.

As Toby refilled my glass I watched Rose walk cautiously across the lawn, her face bathed in light. Her shiny blonde hair hung loosely to the side and her pastel pink dress fell like silken petals. Even in her trainers she looked as tall and slim as a stem and the fit of her dress revealed her blossoming womanhood. My eyes stung and I wondered if she was aware of how beautiful she was; not only physically, but in her gentle way with everyone.

I gave her a wave and went to greet her. 'Oh, my darling.'

'Why did women ever put up with these dresses?' she said, and pulled at her skirt with disdain.

'I imagine they didn't know what they were missing with mini skirts and shorts. Trousers and jodhpurs, for that matter.'

Gemma's asked if I can take photos. It's a bit awkward but I'll try.

'I'll help you. But let's ask guests' permission if we want to use them.'

'Course...' She stopped and peered over my shoulder.

I swung round and followed her gaze as Saul, Alex and Dom walked beneath the rose laden gazebo. In breeches, shirt and long leather boots, Saul looked like an action hero from a movie. He carried a whip in one hand and a bottle in the other. Dom and Alex wore slim trousers with loose fitting shirts. The three of them proved an arresting sight. The talk hushed as our guests turned to watch them.

Toby, who'd been chatting with Stevie and Jake at the drinks table, shot me a look of warning before walking directly up to Saul.

My legs turned weak as Toby exchanged words with Saul. Toby's back was to me and I couldn't see his expression. But when Saul put a hand on Toby's arm and broke into a smile I released my breath.

Rose stared.

'I guess they know this is for Euan, who they've never met,' I said.

'That doesn't matter,' she said. 'Gemma's OK. She doesn't cry so much now.'

'I imagine in private...'

A familiar movie track began to play and I turned to the screen. Some of the younger girls ran up and as they danced, their skirts swirled round them like shining catherine wheels.

'How adorable,' said Rose.

'I remember you and Stevie like that.'

'I would now if my legs allowed,' she said.

'Be patient and you'll dance again.'

Rose left to join the dancers. She leaned on her crutches and clapped her hands to the music.

I walked to the table to collect my drink. As I stood there sipping from my glass and listening to the music I sensed somebody approach from behind. Something brushed against my dress.

'I hope this isn't awkward for you.'

I turned around to face Saul. 'Of course not.' I waved away his concern. 'It's good to see you all here.'

He reached for the Prosecco and tilting his glass, poured slowly so that the bubbles didn't overflow. 'We don't need to pretend.'

'I think we do,' I said, and felt my cheeks burn.

'Fine,' he said, in a tone that suggested it wasn't. 'I only wanted to say well done for getting that contract off Maria. How did you?'

'My smart sister-in-law threatened to spill some family secrets,' I said, then added. 'But please keep that to yourself.'

He leaned closer and whispered. 'Maybe you'll tell me sometime?'

'I'm sorry, I must speak to Toby.' I turned abruptly and walked away, feeling awkward and rude.

I found Toby sitting beneath the gazebo and staring into his pint. He didn't look up. Droplets of condensation dripped down the side of the glass as his other hand thrummed his leg.

I gathered my skirts and sat beside him. 'Are you all right?' I tried to meet his eyes but they remained distant.

There came the drone of a wasp as it flew past my face and I watched it land on Toby's knee.

He appeared unconcerned and watched it crawl. 'Why shouldn't I be OK?'

'Because Saul's here.'

He looked sharply at me. 'I'm sorry Anya, I tried, but it upsets me to see you with him.' He swiped at the wasp which landed at my feet. Toby raised his foot and stamped on it.

'I can hardly ignore him,' I said quietly. I noticed Jake and Alex chatting close by. 'And it was Saul who came to speak to me, not the other way around.'

'Try harder,' his voice grew louder. 'I will.'

'Forget about Saul. I have.' I looked across the lawn. 'We should think of Gemma and all the effort Stevie's gone to.'

He lifted his glass and took a long drink. 'You go and enjoy yourself.'

'Only minutes ago we were happy and close again.' I reached for his hand but he slid it away.

Feeling close to tears, I stood up. 'If that's how you want it.'

I brushed past Jake and as I did, he gave me a look of concern. I imagined he'd overheard mine and Toby's exchange.

Stevie, Gemma and the smaller girls were dancing, while Rose - albeit stiffly - swayed in an effort to join in. Despite all that Rose had been through, she'd grown stronger and had started to breathe in life again. Why couldn't I be more resilient like her? I wiped away a tear and realised the only person stopping me was myself. I ran across the lawn and joined the dancers and when Gemma saw me, she tipped her head back and laughed. I spun and danced in circles and felt dizzy with a sudden and unexpected joy. When I spotted Saul watching me from beneath the tree, he raised his glass, but I turned away.

Chapter 31

As I danced, I felt unbound by time and my mind emptied of all but the melody, movement and rhythm of the music and the brightness of the sun overhead. As Vivaldi's, 'Storm' ended I felt breathless and euphoric and although I wanted to stay this way I didn't want to leave Stevie to cope with the catering alone.

'I must serve the food,' I called over to Gemma.

'Drink more.' Gemma laughed and her face glowed in a way that I hadn't seen for far too long.

'Oh, I'll do that, too.'

As I walked across the lawn, I scanned the clusters of guests for Toby. On the bench beneath the gazebo, I noticed his near empty pint glass with wasps humming and drinking greedily.

In the kitchen, Stevie removed a tray of sausages from the oven.

'Have you seen Dad?' I asked.

'He came through a while ago.' She slid the sausages onto a serving plate. 'Can you help, Mum?'

But something seemed amiss and I felt uneasy. 'Give me a minute,' I replied.

I went into each room, downstairs and up, calling Toby's name as I went. At the front of the house, the air seemed still save for the murmur of music, chatter and laughter that travelled from the back garden. As I made my way down the slope of the lawn towards the river, Freda, who thought it was time for a walk, yapped at my feet. I kicked off my heels and left them lying in the grass, and my skirts swished against my ankles. Up ahead a wind moaned amongst the trees and it seemed as though I'd never heard it before as its lilted tone carried me forwards. Beneath the weeping willows the air felt fresh on my face and a glassy whisper blew in from the river where currents bubbled and prattled over rocks and pebbles as the water flowed shallow and crystalline.

Freda trotted on ahead.

The grass cushioned my feet as I walked on and with the wine swimming through me I felt as though I were floating somewhere between the ground and sky - like a bird overhead that looked down upon the earth. All around me everything appeared clearer and sharper, as if the dust and heat had been washed away.

I stood still. The air seemed charged with an unearthly silence and a sense of dread grew inside of me. The birds had ceased their song and the breeze dropped to an awful hush amongst the branches and murmuring leaves. Even the water seemed to flow soundless and distant. Separate. Sun particles, if there was such a thing, seemed suspended in the air and coated the trees and the dust laden path. Even the surface of the water - flowing silver and smooth on its journey to the sea. I lifted my face and the leaves dipped and brushed my skin like feather tips.

Further ahead, I heard Freda whine and a familiar voice.

I ran onwards and around a bend in the path, dodging and jumping over roots and raised stones as I went. Up ahead I saw Toby sitting beside Euan's memorial stone only a few yards from the water's edge. He gazed down as though mesmerised by the gentle swell of the water. Freda lay at his side and looked up at me as I neared.

'Toby?'

He continued to stare, unblinking and with his mouth slightly open.

I knelt down and put my arm around him. His shirt was damp with sweat. Freda whimpered and jumped onto my lap.

Toby turned to me with eyes wet and bloodshot.

I lifted my palm to his cheek. 'Oh, my darling.'

He nodded slowly. 'You heard it, too?'

'Heard what?'

'That sound. It shook the ground.'

'When was this?' I said.

'Moments ago.'

I searched his eyes. 'Did you fall? Do you feel ill?'

He gave my hand a squeeze. 'I'm pleased you've come. I've missed you.'

'But I'm always here.'

'I'm sorry,' he said.

So, he felt guilty. I'd wanted him to say sorry for so many weeks. But somehow it seemed all wrong. 'Why are you sorry?'

'For leaving you.'

'I don't understand.' My voice cracked. 'We're here now, aren't we?'

I heard someone approach and I turned. Gemma and Saul stopped a few feet away.

'Is Toby all right?' asked Gemma. 'We saw you'd both disappeared.'

'No, Gemma, there's something terribly wrong,' I said.

Gemma sat at his other side and I watched Saul turn and walk discreetly beneath the tree.

'Look at me, Toby,' said Gemma, as she touched his chin.

Toby flung out his arms, knocking me aside.

He scrambled up. 'I'm sorry.'

'But what for?' asked Gemma.

I jumped up too.

Toby turned to me and clasped my shoulders. 'He said you were too good for me.' His eyes looked feverish and beads of perspiration dotted his face. 'That I'd destroyed you. Which was why you no longer wanted me.'

And all at once I knew. I knew who Toby referred to.

'Euan was wrong. I forgave you.'

'He said you were leaving me. That I deserved it.'

I swallowed hard. 'I never would have left you. We talked it all through.'

'He punched me. But I didn't hit back...'

'Was Euan drunk?' I asked. 'You were right not to retaliate.'

'He told me something.' Toby shook his head vehemently. 'But I didn't believe it. I've never believed it. He only wanted me to hit him.'

I looked away, suddenly unable to listen. 'I'm going back to the party, Toby. We'll talk when you're making sense.'

'What did he tell you?' Gemma shot me a warning look and held Toby's hand, protective.

Without a pause, he said, 'That he slept with Anya.'

I felt the blood rush to the surface of my skin and I burned with shame.

I spun around. 'No. Euan had drunk too much. He was baiting you.'

Gemma glared at me and then put her arm around Toby. 'Then what happened?'

Toby's head jerked backwards and he clutched at his scalp and tugged frantically at his hair. His eyes darted wildly and his words became slurred. 'I pushed...him...'

'Euan?' Gemma's voice rose and trembled.

Toby's eyes began to roll exactly as they had done that night in Rose's room. He gave an agonising moan.

Gemma gripped him tighter - clinging to keep him close.

Toby's features contorted. The veins stood out on his temples and neck as a pressure seemed to build inside of him. He released an animalistic howl that shattered the silence and reverberated all around us. He lost his balance and seemed to fold in two. Gemma could no longer hold his weight and he plunged to the ground.

Toby lay crumpled and limp and with eyes barely open. I tapped his cheek. 'Wake up, Toby,' I cried.

But I felt him drifting away from me and I wanted only to follow him.

Panic rose within me - suffocating me and tearing through my gut. I pressed two fingers to his neck. Nothing. I moved my fingers and pressed again. I lowered my palm to his darkening lips. Breathless and still.

My mind switched from incomprehension one moment to the realisation that it had happened. I wanted someone or something to suck the breath from me too - to take me away from here, so that I wouldn't have to exist without him.

I looked up to find Gemma rocking on her haunches with her palm clasped to her mouth.

This wasn't how life was meant to be. This was happening somewhere else - to someone else.

'He's gone,' Gemma said, and her tears became an unbroken stream as she dropped to her hands and knees.

'No, Gemma.' My tongue and lips felt thick and bruised. I began to compress Toby's chest. I tried to control my own breaths and exhaled a shudder of air into his mouth. And another breath.

I felt a hand on my shoulder. 'Stop...'

I followed Gemma's gaze. A trickle of blood oozed from Toby's ear and dripped to the grass beneath. A thick and deathly red, slowing as it reached the earth, merging with the soil.

'He cracked his head when he fell,' I said.

I ran my fingers over his scalp and neck but found no marks. His skin seemed to turn to ash in front of me. He had already slipped through my fingers as he fell into a dreamless and endless sleep.

Gemma clasped her arms around herself. 'It's a hemorrhage.' And her body began to shake at the violence of her realisation.

Saul hunched down beside me. 'I've called for help...' But his words trailed away.

'He's already gone.' Gemma cradled Toby's head in her lap. 'It's too late.'

'Stop it, Gemma.' I thumped his chest in a final attempt to deny what was now too clear. 'Help me wake him.'

Gemma spoke through her tears. 'A weakness in the vessels killed Mum, too.'

And in that instant, the significance of her words hit me. Everything before me swayed with uncertainty. 'My girls.' Drunk and dizzy, I sank to the ground and retched.

And as I wept, my tears fell upon Toby's skin; cool, vacant and grey.

Whenever I look back on that day, I cannot recall there being a time, prior to or since, that I felt so alone or had such a bleak view of the future. Without any doubt, something inside of me, a jewel of energy, dissolved the day we lost Toby.

Chapter 32

Six months later

Gemma and I rode the horses side by side up the track to Orben Moor. And as we progressed higher, a burly wind from the north fired the horses blood and their paces quickened in readiness for speed. I looked around at the rocky outcrops and undulating mounds in all directions and I realised how much I'd missed this view.

Since Toby had passed, this was the first time I'd relented to Gemma's pleas to ride out with her. Despite the terrible revelations on that day, she'd remained with me, had cared for me and encouraged me to talk, to grieve with her and to share our grief.

In my darkest moments I swung between feeling desperate to hear him talk to me one last time in that deep and self-assured voice of his, and then falling back into tearful self-pity.

The feelings of guilt and betrayal I'd experienced had, for a while, overwhelmed me; the weight of responsibility for Euan's death, for betraying my husband, as well as my sister-in-law and best friend, Gemma, and for Toby's jealousy and the stress it must have caused him. On top of everything, I believed that the combination of all those factors had triggered the bleed on his brain and sudden death. The doctors told me the weakness had always been there and the eventual rupture inevitable. They even suggested it could have given way decades earlier. But that would never offer consolation. Furthermore, I saw my guilt as an indulgence and that rather than wallow in misery I should work out how to make our children's and Gemma's lives better, or at least bearable.

Each time I saw Gemma with Saul I found that their blossoming friendship alleviated my conscience, by some small degree.

For the first twenty minutes we rode in silence - my mind full with thoughts of Toby. As the wind intensified, clouds billowed and raced across empty pockets of blue sky. And as we passed beneath a cluster of Elm trees the wind shook their branches sending a shower of cold water down upon us.

Gemma turned to me. 'Are you glad you came?'

And the wind coiled around us, and made our hair and coats billow.

'It's beautiful up here. Always. Maybe more so because I haven't seen it in so many months.' I gazed up into the branches. 'And look how the leaves are already beginning to bud. New life will burst free soon.'

Gemma nodded. 'It's Spring. New beginnings. Soon, we can open our doors again. Let air in through the windows.'

'Yes. I've hibernated all winter. But I can't hide forever. It isn't fair on the girls. And it isn't fair on you.'

'Sorry I'm always checking on you,' she said.

'I remember doing the same to you.'

The track steepened and the sound of birds amongst the hedgerows underlined the silence that followed between us.

'Anya?'

I turned to her. 'Yes?'

'I need to know something.' The horses continued walking side by side and she held my gaze. 'Did you love him?'

'Of course. I'll never stop loving him.'

She shook her head lightly and her green eyes pierced mine. 'I don't mean Toby.'

Her words rippled through me and I couldn't reply. All these months she hadn't once challenged me over my betrayal but I knew it would come, when she was ready - when we were ready.

'Please, Anya. Be honest with me.'

My heart pounded as I spoke the words I never believed I could. 'It was once only, Gemma. A stupid drunken one night stand. The minute it was over I regretted it. We both regretted it.'

But I knew it was guilt that held my regret.

'If Euan was so drunk, he couldn't have made love to you.'

We reached the brow of the track and I reined in Ebony. 'Euan loved you!' I said. 'He loved you, Gemma. So, so much. And that was the end of it. For him and for me.'

'Did you love him?' she asked again, her voice barely above a whisper.

'More like a brother.'

'We don't sleep with our brothers.'

'We were foolish and drunk,' I said. 'I felt wretched and confused after Toby's affair. But it only happened once. Once was enough for us both to know how wrong it was.' I had said it. My breath shuddered with my confession.

'I know you loved Euan.' Gemma nodded, almost to herself. 'I've always known.'

'You can't know.' I hesitated. 'How could you know?'

And I could see in her expression that she'd already come to terms with this unforgivable deceit.

'Because when Euan died, your grief felt and looked like mine. You could no more hide it than I could. At first I must have been oblivious, but weeks later as I tried to understand what had happened to Euan, I'd lie in bed at night, turning everything over and over in my mind. And something clicked. I didn't know about your sleeping together. Though I've often suspected you may have. Euan never gave that away. I had noticed a growing closeness between you. I've never been a jealous woman. Never of you, Anya. Strangely, not even now. But I am observant.'

My throat tightened. 'I did love him, Gemma.' With a convulsive sob, I said, 'And I'm so, so sorry. I've hated myself for so long because of what I did to you.'

Gemma nodded and she too began to cry, quietly and instinctually.

'But Gemma, I love you more. I need you to know that.' And the wind rushed past and whipped the words from my mouth.

I felt a rush of blood to my head and I saw a clearer view of what lay ahead. Even a feeling of hope that I'd suppressed for many months. My lungs filled with air.

'I love you too,' said Gemma and as she looked at me, I knew that she still meant it.

I'd long known Gemma to be one of those rare people with a depth and capacity for forgiveness and goodness and I recognised how fortunate myself and the girls were to have her in our lives.

'We must try to live again,' I called to her. 'Let them move on.' The wind snatched my words.

The moorland before me, the vastness, the colours, the open sky, seemed to rush towards me and I breathed it all in.

When I released the reins, Ebony leapt forward. At my side, Gemma on Maya mirrored our movements. I bent over the arch of Ebony's neck as the wind slashed his mane against my hands. And as the horses hooves pounded the earth beneath, I felt my heart and mind open, finally, to release the pain that had twisted inside of me for so long.

Sometimes in our lives, things happen that will change us irrevocably and forever. And with the strongest will, there is nothing we can do to either anticipate or alter these events. We're given no choice but to accept the inevitability of them; as certain as the turning of time and the passing of our years here.

Some things bring joy; falling in love, the birth of our children, the scent of a rose in bloom or waking at dawn to watch the sunrise. But, it seems to me the things that change us the most are the ones that bring with them sadness. They force us to see life for the fragile state that it is and in doing so, we must learn to embrace each new day and squeeze every ounce of life, experience and happiness from it.

The End

'For life and death are one,
even as the river and the sea are one.'
~ Khalil Gibran

'The life of the dead is placed in the memory of the living.'
~ Marcus Tillius Cicero

Only For You

If I were a bird in a nest up high
I'd awaken at dawn
and sing my song to you alone
I'd fly down and circle your home
And when you noticed
You'd lift your hand
Invite me to land
Softly, alighting there
Your finger upon my feathered wing.

If I were the moon I'd shine only on you
My light reflected in your eyes
As twinned silvery orbs
I'd shine into the very depths of you
And dance through and between
the air you breathe
and the words you speak
...only for you.

By Anya Kubik
Dedicated to Toby Kubik

About the Author

Olivia Rytwinski grew up in Worcestershire, England. She studied English & Drama at Worcester University and has a Postgraduate Diploma in Marketing from Leeds University. Today, she lives in North Yorkshire with her husband, two children and their dog, Pip.

Dear Reader,

Thank you so much for reading, 'I Never Knew You', and for taking this journey with me. I hope you have enjoyed and gained something from the experience. If you have, please consider leaving a book review on Amazon, Barnes & Noble, Lulu or Goodreads.

With much appreciation and thanks,
Olivia Rytwinski

Printed in Great Britain
by Amazon

63167945R00142